I0676602

SHERLOCK HOLMES

CONSULTING DETECTIVE

AIRSHIP 27 PRODUCTIONS

Sherlock Holmes: Consulting Detective Volume Two
Airship 27 Productions
airship27.com
airship27hangar.com

"The Affair of the Wretched Flesh" © 2010 Joshua Reynolds
"The Problem of the Western Mail" and "The Last Deposit" © 2010 I. A. Watson
"The Case of the Missing Engine" © 2010 Bernadette Johnson
"The Adventure of the Phantom Raiders" © 2010 Andrew Salmon

Editor: Ron Fortier
Associate Editor: Charles Saunders
Production and design: Rob Davis
Illustrations ©2010 Rob Davis
Cover © 2010 Ingrid Hardy

All rights reserved under International and Pan-American Copyright
Conventions. No part of this book may be reproduced in any manner without
permission in writing from the copyright holder, except by a reviewer, who
may quote brief passages in a review.

ISBN-13: 978-0615973036
ISBN-10: 0615973035

Printed in the United States of America

10 9 8 7 6 5 4 3 2

Sherlock Holmes
Consulting Detective
Volume Two
Contents

"The Affair of the Wretched Flesh"
Joshua Reynolds...4

"The Problem of the Western Mail"
I. A. Watson..47

"The Case of the Missing Engine"
Bernadette Johnson...69

"The Last Deposit"
I.A. Watson..113

"The Adventure of the Phantom Raiders"
Andrew Salmon..136

Afterword
Ron Fortier..181

Sherlock Holmes
Consulting Detective

"The Affair of the Wretched Flesh"

by
Joshua Reynolds

The sound of a Stradivarius in the night inevitably fills me with a sense of creeping dread. It was by the manic, mournful echo of that bow across those strings that I knew when my friend, Sherlock Holmes, had fallen afoul of the mundane.

Such was the case on the night of January 3rd, when the slithering strains of sound rose from the armchair near the window, Holmes hunched forward like some melancholy bird of prey. Pipe smoke wreathed his head like an off-kilter halo. It was a blustery, unpleasant night, and there was nowhere within the confines of 221B Baker Street that I could secret myself from the haunting melody.

Thus, with a sigh, I set aside my paper and rose to bait the dragon in its den.

"Holmes," I said.

The music soared. Somewhere below us, I knew that Mrs. Hudson would be glaring upwards in disapproval.

"Holmes," I said again, slightly louder.

The bow screeched across the strings with an evil hiss and Holmes sat back in his chair.

"Watson," he said. "I grow weary."

"Have you eaten?"

"Bread and water. No more sustenance was required."

"Then I am not surprised that you are feeling faint, my friend."

"It is not the pangs of the stomach which gnaw at me, Watson, but rather something infinitely more ethereal." Holmes twisted his head, looking up at me. "How long has it been?"

"Since?"

"A case, Watson, a case!" Holmes barked, stabbing the air with his bow. "My mind reels beneath the weight of boredom. It sinks into a morass of despair-"

It was by the manic, mournful echo of that bow across those strings that I knew when my friend, Sherlock Holmes, had fallen afoul of the mundane.

"A trifle melodramatic, perhaps?"

Holmes sniffed, and turned back to the window, his reflection glaring sullenly at me.

"I have not had a case in weeks," he said, finally.

"A week and four days, to be exact."

"Precision does not suit you, Watson. You are singularly ill-equipped for it."

Stung, I said nothing. Arguing with Holmes was rather like arguing with a badger. Right or wrong, you were guaranteed to get bitten.

Holmes must have seen my expression reflected in the window, for he gave one of his characteristic short, sharp barks.

"Don't frown on my account, Watson."

"I wasn't-"

"Tut-tut, say no more! Say no more!" Holmes rose, face alight. "Things are always darkest before the dawn, Watson."

"Holmes, I must say that this outburst of good cheer is uncharacteristic to say the least-"

"Uncharacteristic? Perhaps. But not undeserved. Hark, I hear a most queenly tread…" Holmes pointed at the door with his violin bow, extending it like a fencer's foil.

The sound of knuckles rapping against the door caused me to start slightly.

"Come in, Mrs. Hudson! Come in!" Holmes said loudly.

"Mr. Holmes, Inspector Lestrade is-" our landlady said, as she opened the door and stepped aside.

"–here to see me, yes, yes, I am aware," Holmes said, tucking his bow beneath his arm and reaching for his pipe and a box of matches.

"Oh, were you?" Lestrade said, sourly. A sallow, ferret-faced, dark-eyed fellow, Lestrade looked more akin to a criminal than one of Scotland Yard's finest.

"Quite," Holmes said, without elaborating further. He lit his pipe and puffed contentedly when it caught. He cocked an eye at Lestrade. "Well?"

"You're not going to tell me, are you?" Lestrade said.

"I am not a mind reader, Lestrade," Holmes said, lips quirking in a quick smile. His eyes flickered the length and breadth of the hapless inspector and Lestrade shifted uncomfortably.

It was warranted, that discomfort. Lestrade was ever uncomfortable with my friend and his keen intellect. Something about Holmes–dare I say, his personality?–simply rubbed the Inspector the wrong way in all ways and Holmes took every opportunity to reinforce that feeling by playing with Lestrade mercilessly, the way a cat will with a mouse.

I disapproved, of course, but despite my intentions–and actions, at times–I was not Holmes' keeper, merely his chronicler. And, to hear him tell it, a poor one at that.

"Well, the reason I'm calling is–"

"A theft?" Holmes said, idly.

Lestrade frowned. I was unable to stop myself from giving a snort, and the Inspector's glare shifted from Holmes to me. I held up my hands, indicating that I had had nothing to do with Holmes' question.

"It was a theft, was it not?" Holmes said, pipe smoke wreathing his features. He took his pipe from his mouth and gestured with the end. "Animals, if I'm not mistaken."

Lestrade took off his hat and sucked on his teeth. He sighed. "No getting around it. Yes, blast you, there was a theft–"

"Of animals?"

"Yes! Yes, animals," Lestrade ground out. I took pity on the Inspector and said, "Do take a seat, Lestrade. Would you like some tea?" I gestured to the still warm pot Mrs.Hudson had brought up earlier. "It's a cold night out, and I'm sure you could use something warm in your system."

"No thank you, Doctor. I'll say my bit and be off, I think," Lestrade said stiffly. Holmes made a sound half-way between a chuckle and a grunt. He turned his chair from the window and plopped down, legs extended, posture abominable. He fluttered a hand.

"Speak," he said.

And Lestrade did, in clipped tones. "A ship bound from Capetown came into Royal Albert Dock last night. Carrying a cargo of exotic animals for the Royal Zoo. Breeding stock, I gather, though I don't know much about such things–"

Holmes made another sound, but composed himself quickly, before Lestrade could do much more than furrow his brow. "Go on, go on," Holmes said.

"It seems that at some point between the unloading and the delivery, several of the creatures disappeared, cages and all."

"Ah," Holmes said, sucking on his pipe. His eyes closed. "And?"

"And? They disappeared!" Lestrade said. "That's it!"

"Yes, Lestrade, but why come to me?" Holmes said, eyes still closed. Lestrade's face went tight and his nostrils flared. I could tell that he was dangerously close to exploding. There were times when I admired the Inspector's iron control of his emotions, especially when it came to Holmes. He had yet to resort to physical violence, though Holmes prodded him mercilessly. "I'm sure even a blind child could see why the beasts were stolen."

I could, at least. Exotic pets were a fashionable accessory from the lowest stratum of society to the highest. The more exotic, the better. I myself had debated the peculiarities of purchasing an ill looking monkey in the East End only a few days before, if only to get it the proper treatment.

"Of course," Lestrade said. "We did check, you know. We have had experience with this sort of thing, you know." Lestrade let out a breath. "We've checked the usual spots where that sort of trade one might find. Nothing. No one has heard nothing about these beasts…"

After a moment of silence, Holmes cracked one eyelid. "Ah."

"No sign of them. Except the cages."

"The cages?" I said. Holmes smirked. Lestrade nodded.

"We found them all asunder not a few alleys away from the docks. Just ripped apart…" he said, trailing off. "Not dismantled, you understand, but completely destroyed."

Holmes eyes were closed again. "No sign of the animals, I assume? No sightings of a lion in Piccadilly?"

"How did you know one of them was a lion?" Lestrade said. Holmes snorted.

"As with anything, the thieves obviously stole the most important items. The shipment, if I recall correctly, consisted of a pair of young male lions, the same again of leopards, a female elephant, a bevy of wild dogs, and an eight strong troop of baboons. The lions, one can assume, would have been the first cage stolen. Plenty of buyers there, in the lofty reaches of the aristocracy–" Holmes stopped. He took out his pipe and pointed at Lestrade. "The apes?"

"Gone."

"Vivisection," Holmes said. My flesh crawled. "The lions will bring a tidy profit from an individual looking for an unusual pet. The apes are in high demand for medical studies, as well as the odd medicinal quackery. Do you recall the affair of the Creeping Man, Watson?"

"Yes," I said, feeling my face twist in revulsion. "But surely the other animals would be of equal value–"

"Hmm. No, the elephant was simply too large to steal. The wild dogs, despite their odd appearance, would be considered no more special by a thief than any alley mutt. *Dogs is dogs is dogs, innit?"* Holmes said the last in a Cockney accent, eliciting a grunt of humor from Lestrade.

"And the leopards?" I pressed.

"Too vicious. Male lions are notoriously lazy creatures. Quite fierce in the right circumstances, but these had been hand-reared by a dealer in Capetown. Thus, little threat to a careful man. But the leopards, ah," Holmes shook his head. "Leopards are uncontrollable, even when raised by man. And these were wild. No, no, even the most ignorant of men recognizes a dangerous animal when it glares at him, whether it be through leaves or the bars of a cage."

"How did you know all of this? About the animals?" Lestrade demanded. Holmes waved a hand towards the stack of newspapers sitting on the floor near the window.

"I read, Lestrade. If you have not done so, I encourage you to pick up the habit. It will serve a man in your line well." Holmes sucked on his pipe.

"Well," Lestrade said. I could tell that he was insulted, but, thankfully, not overly much. Indeed, he even smiled slightly as he caught my eye. He snapped his fingers. "Then how do you explain the cages?"

"Why, that is the simplest of all," Holmes said. He leaned back in his chair. "The cages undoubtedly have some form of identification etched into them. Thus, to cover their tracks, the thieves dispensed with them." He spread his hands.

"That simple, then?" Lestrade said.

"That simple."

"Well, my superiors will be pleased, I suppose," Lestrade said. He sniffed. "Though I believe they were hoping you'd lend that mind of yours to helping us track down the Crown's property, as you've done so many times before."

"No, no, I simply have too much to do at this moment, Lestrade." Holmes flicked his fingers. "Quite busy, you see. Besides, this is hardly a test of a man's cranial matter, Inspector. You should have the thieves in custody within days, if not hours."

Lestrade and I shared a look, then I rose and walked the Inspector to the door. As I opened it, he said, "I suppose I'll see you tomorrow then, Doctor?"

I looked back at Holmes, sitting hunched in his chair, basking in his cleverness. I looked back at Lestrade. "Almost certainly."

When Lestrade had left, I sat back down across from Holmes, lit my own pipe, and waited. When his eyes opened once again, I said, "How did you know?"

"How do you think I knew?"

"I presume you saw Lestrade approaching from your position near the window."

A smile flickered across Holmes' features for a moment. "And?"

"I also presume that you knew he had been down to the docks because of what he tracked in on his shoes," I said. Holmes nodded.

"We'll have to have clean that before Mrs.Hudson sees it, by the way," he said. "And the animals?"

"Animal hairs on his coat?"

"Lestrade owns a dog," Holmes said, simply. "You rely on your eyes overmuch, my friend." Holmes tapped his aquiline nose. "Lestrade bears about himself the faintest perfume of captive animals. Moldy straw, dung and the particular sun-baked odour which permeates the flesh of the inhabitants of Africa, be they man or beast."

"And the theft?"

"Simplicity." Holmes stood, abruptly. "Lestrade displayed little urgency and little inclination to be here."

"How is that any different from any other time?" I asked, before I could stop myself. Holmes laughed.

"Lestrade only comes bearing two gifts, my friend," Holmes said, holding up two fingers. "Murder and theft. Or some combination of the two. In the case of the former, Lestrade displays the urgency of a hound on the hunt. Despite his flaws, he attributes the greater sin to be the taking of a life. He displayed none of his customary urgency in that regard, thus I deduced it was a theft." Holmes shrugged. "Simplicity, as I said."

***

The next morning, Holmes awoke me with a sharp jab from his walking stick. I fumbled to a waking state, my vision blurred.

"What? What is it?"

"Will you sleep the day away, Watson?" Holmes said. "I weep for your patients."

"I weep for my *patience* as well," I snarled. Holmes turned and left my room without replying. He was dressed and ready for an excursion. I took my time readying myself, listening to Holmes stalking up and down through the sitting room, his cane tap-tapping. It was still dim outside, a blanket of blue light settled over the city. I felt a groan welling up as I examined my pocket watch. "Holmes, it's four in the morning!" I said.

"Would that it were earlier, I know, but we must press on," Holmes said. "You are a very sound sleeper, Watson."

"It's not even light out," I protested.

"All the better," Holmes said. He waved a rolled up newspaper towards me and I took it, reluctantly.

"Is this today's?"

"Early edition." Holmes' lips quirked. "Remind me that I owe Wiggins a shilling for services rendered," he said, referring to the leader of that rag-tag band of urchins he had dubbed the "Baker Street Irregulars" in a fit of creativity.

"Why, dare I ask, did you need an early edition?"

"Front page, Watson, front page." Holmes swatted the paper with his cane. "Read while we walk, please."

I skimmed the page as we headed down the stairs. I blinked as something caught my eye. "Holmes, there's something about the animal thefts in here!"

"Not that," he said. He closed the door behind us as quietly as possible though I knew Mrs.Hudson was well up by now. Holmes was an early riser, but Mrs.Hudson could safely be said to rarely sleep.

"What, then?"

"Bottom corner. Does anything strike you as odd?"

"Everything strikes me as odd this early in the morning, I'm afraid," I said. Holmes gave a sharp laugh.

"A murder, Watson."

"A murder?"

"Quite an unpleasant one as well," Holmes said. "A man was killed near the docks."

"Hardly unusual, I'm sorry to say."

"Cynicism does not become you," Holmes said, as he walked briskly down the street, one hand behind his back. I didn't reply, as I instead read the article Holmes had indicated. "Holmes, this doesn't say anything about a murder!"

"No?"

"No! It says here he was savaged by wild dogs."

"Death by misadventure, then?"

"It's certainly not murder."

"I wish you wouldn't come to such conclusions so early, Watson."

Holmes shook his head, frowning. "It implies that you have yet to absorb my methodology."

"I-"

"A man may be savaged, it is true. Especially if he was besotted at the time," Holmes said. "Alley dogs are pestiferous in London as they are in any great city. But when have you ever known them to hound and kill a strong man?"

"The article doesn't mention anything about him being strong or weak, Holmes," I protested. "Nor whether he was drunk or sober."

"Exactly."

"I'm sure I'm missing the point," I said.

"It was on the front page, Watson," Holmes said. "It did not describe the victim in unflattering terms. From both of these we can gather that the victim was neither a sot, nor a sleeping vagrant devoured by the wolves of Londinium. And, being on the front page implies that it was considered unusual enough to bring to the reader's attention, but not titillating enough to be closer to the headline."

"Which means?"

"There is an ongoing investigation, of course!" Holmes looked up at the sky and squinted. "Hail a cab, my friend. We need to be at the Royal Albert Dock."

Some minutes later we were riding comfortably in a hansom cab headed for our destination. I looked over at Holmes, who looked serene.

"Why are we going to the docks?" I asked. Holmes cracked an eye.

"To investigate Lestrade's theft, of course."

"Last night you implied that you were done–"

"But then I saw the paper. I am allowed to change my mind, Watson. It does not happen often, but it can occur, I assure you."

"What does the paper have to do with anything?" I gave the paper a swat with my hand. I paused. "The murder?"

"I'll make a detective of you yet, Watson." Holmes opened his eyes and leaned forward. "Don't you find it intriguing, to say the least, that a man dies of an animal attack so soon after the theft of several exotic beasts?"

"I honestly didn't connect the two until just now," I admitted. Holmes smiled.

"Most wouldn't. Most will not. Including, I suspect, our friend Lestrade. But I have a suspicion," he said, rubbing his lip with the head of his cane. "The rough edge of a theory, one could say."

"I would be surprised at you, if you didn't."

"Ha! I wouldn't want to disappoint you," Holmes said.

"So, are we investigating the murder, or the theft?"

"One leads to the other, if only we decide to start at the beginning. Thus, the theft." Holmes leaned back. "I only hope the blundering of certain individuals has not irrevocably tainted the scene of the crime."

Remembering the brief exchange Lestrade and I had had the previous evening, I said, "I'm quite sure it's been kept in perfect order, as the investigation proceeds."

Holmes looked at me, then away. He smiled again.

"Yes, I'm sure."

***

L estrade was there when we arrived, uniformed constables scurrying this way and that under his baleful gaze. Holmes sniffed.

"Well. It appears you were right."

"Mr. Holmes! Doctor!" Lestrade bellowed, waving a hand over his head. Holmes raised his cane.

"Yes Inspector, we see you, never fear," he said, though not loudly. I restrained a chuckle as we walked towards Lestrade.

"Decided to come out then after all, eh?" Lestrade said, thumbs in his waistcoat. He smiled and gave me a wink. Holmes gave a quick smile.

"I merely wanted to watch you at work, Inspector," he said. Lestrade laughed.

"Oh really?"

"Truly," Holmes said, peering interestedly at the scene before us. "I take it this is where the beasts were unloaded?"

The Thames struck the docks only a few feet away, a spray of water decorating the rough stone and wood. The Royal Albert Dock occupied seventy-two acres of water, and extended some several thousand feet from shore. I was struck with a sense of vertigo as we stood amidst slapping waves and big-bellied ships steaming to their berths along the leviathan length of the dock.

"Yes. There's the ship." Lestrade hiked a thumb at one of the vessels bobbing in the tide. "There were porters waiting to move the cages-"

"Where?"

"Well, there." Lestrade pointed to a point between two shabby berths. "The dock is connected to several special railway systems-"

"Yes. I can see," Holmes said, jabbing at a heap of dung with his cane. "Tarps?"

"Tarps?" Lestrade said.

"To cover the cages," I said. "Were they doing this at night?"

"The early morning hours, yesterday. The ship arrived early, before dawn. The porters were rung up–"

"You said they were waiting," Holmes said. Lestrade paused.

"They were. There," he said, gesturing to one of the buildings. "When the ship docked, they came out, helped unload the animals and took them to the train that would transport them to the zoo."

"Did they not notice that several cages were missing?"

"No. The–ah–the thieves had substituted empty cages–"

"Which, due to the tarps, no one would be able to examine until they reached their destination." Holmes rubbed his chin. "This was not a crime of opportunity."

"Someone planned it?" I said.

"Yes," Holmes said. "Oh yes. And ingeniously so. Consider the effort, Watson, of secreting two faux cages, then switching them out amidst the chaos of the unloading. Surely the animals would have been uneasy..." Holmes trailed off, lost in thought.

He wandered towards the berths, lazily trailing his cane through the refuse and grime that any dock in the Empire accumulates.

Lestrade turned to me. "Footprints, do you think?"

"Anything, most likely," I said. "I dare say you missed something."

"I dare say we did," Lestrade said, frowning. "Else I wouldn't have called on you both."

"If you are finished gossiping, would you both be so kind as to come here?" Holmes called out, waving his cane. He was standing near a berth further down from the one where the theft had taken place. Lestrade and I dutifully made our way through the crowd of policemen and dock workers going about their business. Holmes tapped his cane against the edge of one of the sheds that lined the berth. "Cigarettes," he said. "Cheap ones."

"So?" Lestrade said.

"How long were they waiting, Lestrade?" Holmes said.

"The porters? No more than an hour."

"Someone sat here," Holmes squatted, to demonstrate. "And watched there," he continued, pointing with his cane. He looked down. "Two someones, I expect. Scrapes there, from hard soled work boots." He patted the edge of the berth. "Metal soled. Perhaps a brace of some kind. That would explain the discrepancy between the prints..." Holmes trailed off. Lestrade grunted.

"This is a dock—one of the busiest in London. Men wait here all the time!"

"Yes, Lestrade. But for hours on end? Doing no work?" Holmes traced the edge of a deep print gouged in the hard grime. "No, these men weren't porters. But they were waiting for them." Holmes stood. "Was this berth occupied on the morning of the crime?"

Lestrade squinted, frowned, and turned, calling for one of his officers. I looked at Holmes.

"What are you thinking?"

"These berths are covered, for storage. The perfect place—"

"To store fake cages!" I exclaimed. "You think they waited, rolled out the cages—"

"Not just that. The porters would have noticed," Holmes said. His face was taut, his lips compressed into a thin, harsh line. He stalked forward, bent low, eyes scanning the ground. I followed him, and signaled Lestrade. Holmes straightened, abruptly.

"Blood. Not much, but it's here. Lestrade!"

"Holmes?" the Inspector said. Holmes didn't turn.

"Where are the porters?"

"We—ah—"

"You haven't been able to find them, have you?" Holmes turned. Lestrade colored, slightly.

"No. No, we haven't. Seems the company hired them to meet here. Men with experience transporting animals."

"How many?"

"Six. One trained to handle the elephant, the others to roll the cages."

Holmes turned, eyes narrowed. "I would not be surprised to find that at every empty berth along the dock the night before last, we find similar evidence to the cigarette butts and scrapes. Evidence of men waiting."

"For the porters?" I said. Holmes nodded. He looked into the water. His cane flashed, tapping the edge of the dock. I bent, and sucked in a breath.

"Lestrade, look," I said. The Inspector squatted and followed my fingers.

"Damn," he said. "Blood."

"They waited for the porters. Killed them. Took their places and brought out the fake cages and put them into the proper berth. The crew of the ship never noticed because there was nothing to notice. They had been told that the porters knew what they were doing." Holmes' voice was rock sliding on ice. He trembled slightly, not from the chill coming off the sea, but the inner fire that possessed him in times like these. He gestured at the water.

"Their bodies are down there somewhere, perhaps weighted, perhaps they've become caught beneath the dock or rolled downriver. Lestrade, I would check to see who they were, and whether anyone is missing them." Holmes looked up, his face blank. "Watson and I have another appointment."

*****

Holmes was silent as we rode in a cab towards Scotland Yard. I knew, from long experience, that he would speak when he desired, and not before. Finally, he did, first releasing a hissing breath.

"Six men dead. For what? Animals?" Holmes leaned forward, eyes unfocused. He looked at me. "There is a motivation here, Watson, that I am not seeing."

"You said it yourself, Holmes. The money-"

"Was not worth the cost," Holmes said dismissively. "No, no, none of the criminals of our acquaintance, Watson, have ever killed for anything less than a king's ransom. But the price of those animals was, while large, hardly that."

"Perhaps they thought so?" I ventured. Holmes frowned.

"Perhaps." He fell silent. Then, "One of them wore a brace. Of that I'm sure." He looked at me. "I require your medical expertise once again, Watson. Why would a man require such a brace?"

"There could be any number of reasons…childhood ailment leading to a weakness in the bones, damage to the muscles and tissues, even a deformity."

"A deformity," Holmes repeated. He rubbed his chin with the head of his cane. "Yes." He looked out of the cab. "Ah. Here we are."

Lestrade had sent word ahead, and we were shuffled down to the morgue without hesitation. Holmes had not shared his suspicions with the Inspector, but Lestrade knew my friend well enough not to question his sometimes bizarre requests.

Holmes' assertion that all was not as the paper had posited seemed dead on as the attendant showed us to the body, laying on its table, waxy, bloodless flesh porcelain white beneath the false lighting.

Holmes gestured with his cane. "Watson, if you please," he said. I leaned over the body and pulled away the sheet that covered most of it. I sucked in a breath. Bite and claw marks covered the body, deep gouges and rips and tears. I had seen animals attacks aplenty in Afghanistan, and

"Their bodies are down there somewhere..."

the body before me seemed to have suffered a similar fate.

"He was mauled," I said. "Do you think one of the stolen animals did this?"

"The wounds are consistent with neither species," Holmes said, leaning over the body from the opposite side. "The bite marks are far too small," he continued, gesturing with his little finger. "Did the bites contribute to his death?"

"They must have. I–" I stopped, suddenly struck. Curious, I grasped the chin and gently tilted the corpse's head. "Holmes, his neck has been broken." I traced bruises between the rent portions of the jugular. "If I'm correct, he was throttled with enough force to snap his neck."

"Then the other wounds occurred post-mortem?"

"No. Not all of them. The jugular wound, yes. Minutes after, I'd wager. Are you sure a baboon couldn't have done this?"

"I would be surprised," Holmes said softly. He picked up a pair of tweezers from the instrument tray near the body and dipped them into one of the wounds. He stepped back, examining what he had found.

"What is it?"

"Nothing less than the hair of the dog that bit him, Watson," Holmes said. I plucked my handkerchief from my pocket and held it open. Holmes dropped the hair into it and I folded it carefully, stowing it back in my pocket.

"You still believe this is connected to the theft?"

"Of course. Have they left his clothes this time?"

"Ah–yes," I turned. The clothes had been dumped into a tub beneath the table. I picked it up, and Holmes began to rifle through it, looking.

"Ah-ha," he said. He held up a cigarette case, battered and rusty. "I thought I recognized the brand." He popped the case open and showed me the two remaining cigarettes. "The same brand as at the scene. Hand rolled by a certain old woman of my acquaintance in Limehouse. A pinch of some unidentified poppy mixed with the tobacco. They call them the Claws of the Manchu."

"What an odd name," I said. Holmes sniffed.

"Not at all. Quite apt, really. They are highly addictive. Whatever dark genius created them, they are indeed claws that pierce the souls of men." He closed the case and tossed it back into the tub. "I have often wondered..." He trailed off, shaking his head. "That is for another day, I believe."

"Anyone could buy those, Holmes," I said. "How do we know that this was the same man?"

"The smell, Watson, the smell." Holmes gestured above the body, as if partaking of an aromatic meal. He smiled at what must surely have been my incredulous expression. "Again Watson, you use only your eyes. Smell his clothes."

I did, and was struck by the low-key effluvium of animal waste and oil. I coughed. Holmes reached into the tub and pulled out a battered boot. He upended the sole and waved it under my nose.

"Too, there is the bottom of his boot, caked with the grime of the dock. As well as dung-smeared straw."

He dropped the boot and turned back to the body. He lifted one arm, carefully examining the fingers. "There's hair under his nails as well."

"Holmes, who-or what-killed this man?" I asked.

"Offhand, I would suppose one who did not want him to talk."

"Who was he? Do you recognize him from your files?" I said. Holmes kept numerous files on every criminal we had encountered, as well as files on those whom they had encountered, worked with, or even spoken to. True, some of these files were less than informative, but others were amazingly detailed, possessed of such information that I suspected Holmes of spending his nights trawling through the more disreputable areas of the city, looking for gossip.

"Scour Morris," Holmes said. "A hoodlum and petty thief. A good man with a straight razor. He had a drinking problem as well as an addiction to opium, the latter of which he mitigated with his favored brand of cigarette."

"All of that from your files?"

"Mostly," Holmes said, with a smile. "Some of it straight from the dragon's mouth, so to speak."

"Holmes!" I said, startled. He laughed.

"Calm yourself, Watson. I have not supplanted one addiction for another. In truth, opium would only exacerbate my occasional difficulties, not mitigate them, as does my seven percent solution." Holmes looked at me. "Or as it did, before your intervention."

"Holmes, I..."

"No matter." Holmes waved a hand and looked away. "Scour Morris was possessed of an easily flappable tongue. Good at his job, bad at keeping what it entailed quiet."

"You think that's why he was killed?"

"Of course. I would hazard that hours, if not minutes, after the crime was committed, Morris was telling someone, somewhere, everything."

Holmes smiled sourly. "That word of his indiscretion got back to his employer so quickly, I must either lay at the feet of a criminal organization to rival Moriarty's–" He paused, eyes clouding over.

"Or?" I prompted. I had seen that look before, and I did not like it. Holmes' confrontation with Moriarty had shaken something in him, something previously inviolable. Even now, a year or more after the fact, it could still strike at him. A dark mood that enveloped him for days.

He shook himself all over, like a dog, and said, "Or it was his employer's intent from the beginning to silence Morris and his associates."

"Six men," I said. "He intends to kill them all?"

"Twelve actually, if you count the real porters, whom Morris and his fellows obviously killed." Holmes smiled sourly. "And yes, I do."

Holmes and I left the Yard. Holmes was intent on visiting the scene of the murder, though I doubted in any state to yield much in the way of information. When I voiced my opinion, Holmes waved a finger in my face.

"Tut-tut, Watson. There are some elements which cannot be destroyed. Did you notice the bruising on his shoulders?"

I had, but hadn't mentioned it, thinking it the result of a struggle. When I said as much, Holmes laughed.

"In a way, in a way," he said. "No, I do believe if we were to go back and take another look, you would discover that those bruises are the result of someone crashing onto him from above."

"What?"

"Death from above, as it were." Holmes reached up with his cane and signaled the cab driver to stop. "We're here."

"Here" was a squalid side street, between a disreputable pub whose name I shall not bother to inscribe and a boarding house of equal character. Holmes, as always, seemed perfectly at ease in his surroundings. I found myself patting my coat pocket, where I had placed my trusted revolver before we left 221B earlier in the morning.

"According to Lestrade, this is where the body of Morris was found. Already picked clean of most of his valuables, of course." Holmes prodded at the filth that clung to the alley floor with his cane. He looked up, at the side of the pub, lips pursed, eyes narrowed. He pointed. "There."

"Where?"

"There," he said. He tossed his cane and hat to me and unbuttoned his coat. Tossing that to me as well, he stepped back, then darted forward. With a startling degree of agility, Holmes scrambled up the side of the brick wall until he reached a small ledge. With a grunt, he pulled himself up.

"Holmes, be careful!"

"Always, Watson, always," Holmes said, crouching like a gargoyle. Head cocked, he ran his fingers across the ledge. Then, he leaned back, fingers interlaced between his knees. "I postulate that our killer waited here–"

"Why there?"

"Morris would have come out here to urinate, of course." Holmes tapped the side of his nose. I looked around, feeling my flesh crawl.

"Of course," I said, through clenched teeth. I could smell it now, the pungent stench of a community latrine.

"He simply waited for the right man to step out. Which implies that his senses are quite good actually," Holmes said, his voice betraying a momentary surprise. "In the dark, on the instant when Morris' back was turned, he leapt–" Holmes spread his arms and stood. My heart seized as I imagined him duplicating the mad action he was describing. Instead, he simply climbed down, dropping lightly to the street when he was close enough. He turned, flushed with exertion and excitement. "And killed Morris, without raising a hue and cry. Or enough of one to attract attention, at least."

"Amazing," I said. Holmes nodded.

"Truly. Especially when you factor in the fact that he was wearing a leg brace when he did it."

***

I stared at Holmes incredulously. "A leg brace?"

"There were scrapes duplicate to those I found at the dock, indicating that the man with the brace is the one who was perched up there, waiting for Morris." Holmes rubbed his hands together. "Imagine it Watson! Imagine the sheer brute strength–the agility–it would have required to make that leap without trouble. To then, almost simultaneously kill Morris, and quickly, then vanish."

"You sound as if you admire our mystery killer."

"Admire? No. But I respect his abilities. We have on our hands a most superior form of criminal, Watson. One who, if his cunning matches his physical abilities, may prove to be quite the challenge!"

We left the alleyway and Holmes hailed another cab. He glanced over his shoulder at the alleyway, a peculiar look on his face. As we waited, he said, "Watson, did you notice a peculiar smell in the alley?"

I shook my head. "Moreso than human urine and the detritus of London? No. I cannot say that I did."

Holmes nodded, as if he'd expected nothing else. "There was a faint musky tinge to the air on the ledge. An odour of wet animal. It rained last night, did it not?"

"Yes," I said. I looked up. "As it will again this evening, most like."

Holmes made a sound, and I looked at him. He was holding up something, peering at it closely.

"Holmes?"

"Hairs, Watson. On my trousers. I picked them up on the ledge, it seems. Do they look familiar to you?"

"Holmes, I must confess that unless there is some discrepancy in color, most hairs look quite alike to me."

He smiled. "Of course, of course."

"Is there?" I pressed. "A familiarity, I mean."

"Perhaps. I will not state further without facts." Holmes clenched the hair in his hand and stepped to the side of the street as a cab stopped. "Up and in, Watson. I have evidence to examine in the proper surroundings."

Those surroundings were, of course, his laboratory at 221B. Despite Mrs. Hudson's complaints, Holmes continued to perform the occasional experiment beneath our roof, often filling the flat with the most ungodly smells. I had grown used to them, but out landlady would never become so insensitive, I feared.

She was waiting at the door, a message in her hand as we arrived. Holmes strode past her without stopping, leaving me to make apologies and inquiries. Mrs. Hudson shook her head, watching Holmes' long, lean form disappear upstairs.

"He's got that look again, him," she said, shaking her head. She held the message out to me. "Inspector Lestrade called. Said he had new information to impart."

"Mrs. Hudson you are a wonder and a queen," I said, scanning the message. She snorted and slapped me on the arm.

"Hush. I'll bring up some tea, shall I?"

"That would be delightful," I said. I ducked my head. "I have a suspicion that Holmes is soon to be at work with his chemicals—"

"Say no more," she said. "I'll bring it up in an hour, then."

"Thank you." I smiled and started up the stairs. As I walked, I read the message. Apparently Lestrade had discovered that no tools were used to wrench the switched cages to pieces. No marks, no scratches or dents. But a curious bending...

"Holmes, Lestrade left a message–" I began, as I closed the door behind me. Holmes held up a hand. I fell silent. He was hunched over his desk, a pair of heavy goggles on his face. I had seen them before. An invention my friend had crafted in a moment of necessity. Interlocking lenses that acted as a form of microscope that left the hands free. By sliding the tiny arms that held the various lens down, one could duplicate the effect of the more traditional microscope, and, Holmes assured me, outdo the magnification properties.

Holmes held two pair of tweezers, each trapping a single hair. He looked back and forth, then at one, then at the other, and finally both together. Putting them down carefully, he raised the goggles to his forehead and turned in his chair.

"Now, what were you saying, Watson?"

"Lestrade sent a message. The cages–"

"Were not broken open by any known tool, yes." Holmes waved a hand dismissively. He stripped the goggles from his head and stood, walking towards his bookshelf. "I gathered as much myself."

"Holmes?"

"While the bars are iron, the bottoms and tops are wood. Iron breaks wood. The bars were yanked loose by an immensely strong individual. Our friend with the leg brace again."

"And what of the bending?" I said.

"Bending?" Holmes turned, eyebrow quirked. "Is he that strong, then?" He turned back, frowning. "A veritable brute, then."

"This doesn't concern you?"

"I didn't say that. Merely that it doesn't surprise me," Holmes said, glancing at me. He tapped his lips with a forefinger. "We are dealing with a most unusual villain."

"I should say so," I said.

"Not him." Holmes gestured, fingers fluttering. "Whoever gives him his orders."

"Orders? You believe–"

"I know." He trailed a finger across the spines of the books. His eyes lit up and pulled out a particular one. "Ah. Yes, I know. The savagery of the attack on Morris belies the sort of calculation that the theft of those animals showed. No, our brace-legged jimmy is, while possessed of a frightful cunning, no schemer. He has the planning facilities of a beast. Ruthlessness combined with a sense of spatial awareness does not a master-criminal make." Holmes took his book over to the desk and dropped it, open to a particular page. "No. No, there is a more frightful intelligence at work here." His eyes narrowed. "Watson, come give me your good opinion."

As I crossed to the desk, he handed me the goggles. I reluctantly put them on–I had never gotten used to their capabilities–and leaned forward.

"Examine the hairs, if you please."

I did so, noting that, for all intents and purposes they were identical. "Holmes, they're the same!"

"Of course. Merely supplementary evidence. Now, look at this."

As I removed the goggles, he twisted the book towards me. The hair illustrated on the page was identical to the two physical specimens Holmes had been examining. I read the page, my jaw sagging.

"Holmes, is this–"

"Yes," Holmes said. "When I said 'hair of the dog' earlier, even I did not realize how much truth was in that statement!"

***

"A dog?" I said, my mind reeling. "You're not suggesting–"

"That a dog committed these crimes? Hardly." Holmes sat in his chair, fingers interlaced, legs crossed. He frowned and rested his chin on his fingers. "No, there is an explanation. Perhaps our killer owns a dog. Perhaps he works with dogs, or had one with him or even had a coat made of dog hair..." Holmes leaned back, throwing up his hands. "I cannot say at the moment. I can only churn the evidence in my dull mind."

"Hardly dull," I protested. Holmes grunted, his face cloudy.

"Perhaps." Holmes shifted, facing the window. "I sent Wiggins and his consortium to find any information on the recent sale or purchase of our missing beasts this morning before you awoke. With that in hand, we should be able to make more progress."

"One thing still troubles me, Holmes," I said.

"One thing?" he said. I smiled.

"In particular, yes. Morris' death. You implied that it was ordered."

"Yes, most likely." Holmes' eyes were closed. I took no offense, knowing that he was reviewing the facts of the case and not ignoring me, as it appeared.

"Then what is to stop this mystery killer from murdering the other four men involved in the crime?"

"Nothing," Holmes said. "I theorize that Morris' death was necessary. If our mystery mastermind deems the deaths of the others equally necessary, he will not hesitate to send out his *canis familiaris*."

"And you feel no urgency to warn them?"

Holmes was silent for a moment. Then, "Lestrade is looking for them. He suspects that Morris was involved as well, though he arrived at his reasoning through different methods than mine. And Lestrade, bulldog that he is, will trace who, when and where like any copper on the scent. He will drag a net through the deep shoals and perhaps catch the fish before they flop free."

"And if he doesn't?"

"Then they will, most likely, die. And I find myself only bothered in that each death removes a link in the chain leading to their master." Holmes glanced at me, his eyes dark. "I find myself possessed of little sympathy for killers, Watson. There is little artistry in the passing of a blade through innocent flesh. Give me a dishonest thief over an honest murderer any day."

I had no reply. I well knew Holmes' feelings, but I often forgot the vehemence of them.

Before I could compose a reply, there came a knock at the door. Holmes sat up and I stood. Mrs. Hudson opened the door.

"Mr. Holmes, Doctor Watson, Inspector Lestrade is waiting downstairs with a cab. He urgently requests your–"

Holmes was already up and moving, sliding into his coat, before Mrs. Hudson had finished speaking. I followed after a hurried apology.

Lestrade was waiting in the street. "Mr. Holmes! There's been another death–"

"Another?" Holmes climbed into the cab. "Then you believe Morris' death to be a murder?"

"Believe? No, I know," Lestrade said, slapping the roof of the cab. It jerked into motion and we were off. "Dogs do not break a man's neck."

"That was my supposition as well," Holmes said with a smile. Then, "A second, then?"

"Yes. In Limehouse."

"When is there not a body in Limehouse," I said.

"But this one was an associate of our unfortunate Mr. Morris. One who was seen in his company less than an hour before his death, according to the local citizenry," Lestrade said with a bitter smile. Holmes nodded.

"As I suspected."

Lestrade gave him a look. "Could have warned us."

"Why Lestrade, I had the utmost confidence in your deductive abilities, I assure you."

"Ha," Lestrade said. "Man's name is Jenkins. Had him some experience in India."

"As did Morris, one would assume." It wasn't a question, despite Holmes' tone.

"Yes, served in the same regiment. We're working under the assumption that—"

"—men who had experience with wildlife were chosen," Holmes finished for him. "Yes, obviously." He frowned. "How was he killed?"

"Same as poor Morris. Mauled. Neck broken before."

"Morris wasn't—" I began, but at a look from Holmes I fell silent. Lestrade didn't notice, or didn't care.

"We figure—I figure—our mystery killer is using animals for his dirty work. Cover up the evidence an' such."

"Intriguing supposition," Holmes said. His lips quirked, and I knew he was restraining a smile. Lestrade nodded.

"Intriguing is one way of describing it, I suppose," he said. "Bugger must have some sort of business going. Selling animals and such. Probably has all sort of exotic beasts to do his bidding."

"And the beasts involved here? Were there any witnesses?"

"Not as such." Lestrade looked away. "The—ah—usual assortment of suspicious individuals."

"Ah." Holmes pursed his lips. "I assume he was killed somewhere off the beaten path?"

"He was chasing the dragon," Lestrade said. "Hence the witnesses being somewhat…unreliable, as it were."

"Mm. Yes," Holmes said. "Still, the body has been left in place, I would hope?"

"Per your request, indeed it has." Lestrade glanced at me, then at Holmes. "I suppose you'll be wanting the doctor to give his expert opinion, then?"

"What other kind does he have?" Holmes said. I remained silent, not knowing whether to be insulted or complimented.

When we arrived, uniformed constables were lounging in the doorway of the disreputable drinking establishment within whose walls the latest victim had found his end. Lestrade barked orders and the constables snapped to attention and escorted us through the teeming detritus of humanity that made up the clientele of such a place. Holmes seemed to need no guidance, indeed he navigated the tables, heading for the hidden stairs at the back of the room as if he had been there before. A green curtain, decorated with the coiling length of a golden dragon, separated the sots from the addicts.

A pungent smell rose from behind the curtain as Holmes swept it back. We tramped down a flight of mold-ridden stairs and into a dismally lit sea of reclining forms, and opium induced whispers.

My flesh crawled as we picked our way through them. Holmes seemed unperturbed. The body lay sprawled on a battered cot, arms flung out and legs bent unnaturally. Holmes lifted his cane and pointed at a window set near the ceiling. The bars had been bent and pried free.

"Holmes, that window is far too small–"

"Where there is a will, Watson, there is almost certainly a way." Holmes sat on his haunches, examining the body, his head cocked, nostrils flaring. "As the evidence proves. There, and here." Holmes gestured without looking. I saw a scrape on the wall and another on the frame of the cot.

"Holmes, are these–"

"Scrapes from our friend's brace? I believe so, yes." Holmes leaned forward over the body. "Give me your opinion, Watson."

I reluctantly leaned over the body and began a cursory examination, as Holmes boosted himself up to peer through the window. "He hasn't been dead long. Same marks as before. More vicious, if anything. The sternum is…crushed." I leaned back and looked up at Holmes. "His attacker leapt on him?"

"From the window," Holmes said. "Truly, our assassin is a marvel. However, while he has silenced this man, he has not prevented him from talking, so to speak." Holmes grabbed one of the victim's hands and twisted it towards me. "Look here, at his hands. Smell his clothes. What are your conclusions?"

I did as he asked and drew back, my eyes watering. "Animal dung," I said. "He reeks of–"

"Ape. Baboon, I believe." Holmes dropped the stiffening limb and looked up. "What do you think of that, then, Mr. Wiggins?"

I turned, startled to see the grinning face of the leader of the gang of urchins and pickpockets Holmes had dubbed the "Baker Street Irregulars."

"I think, Mr. Holmes, you need to talk to this bloke I done found,"

Wiggins said, displaying gap teeth. "Boarding house across the street and down. I was planning on sending Sam to Baker Street but Tall Suzy said she saw you lot heading this way. Figured I'd cut out the middle man, so to speak."

"Ever industrious, Mr. Wiggins, I commend you. What have you discovered?"

"He's the one who dumped 'im here, the bruiser in the boarding house, I mean," Wiggins gestured at the body. "At least according to Suzy. Fellows got a room together, them being from the same regiment an all, she says." Wiggins looked over his shoulder. "Also said some other bloke was asking after them—"

"A man with a brace on his leg? Thick set?" Holmes said. Wiggins shook his head.

"No, some toff in black. White hair, looked like a lion, Suzy said. All mouth and eyes and fine way of speaking," he said. "Said she'd seen 'im down here before. Figured he was one of them as likes to slum—"

Holmes' face tightened. "The boarding house?"

"Across the street and up," Wiggins said. Holmes glanced at Lestrade. "Inspector?"

"I know the place he's talking about," Lestrade grunted. He looked at Holmes. "I'll send some men—"

"No. We'll go." Holmes rapped the floor with his cane. "A name, Mr. Wiggins?"

"Meaney. He's a rum one, sir," Wiggins said. Holmes nodded.

"Noted, Mr. Wiggins. I do believe I owe you a guinea."

"I'll add it to your tab, Mr. Holmes," Wiggins said, then, with a cheery wave, he disappeared from the window.

Holmes laughed and turned to me. "The game, Watson, is now most surely afoot!"

***

Several constables fell in around us as we tromped across the street, Lestrade in the lead, head bowed like a bull on the search for something to gore. Holmes followed quickly behind, his cane tapping a disjointed melody on the cobbles.

"We have him, Watson!" Holmes said.

"Who?"

"Our mastermind. The 'toff' that Wiggins mentioned," Holmes said, looking at me. "Surely he is the master of our assassin."

"How can you be sure?"

"I cannot. Yet." Holmes looked away. "The only question is why?"

"Why?"

"Why, if he has an agent in the field, so to speak, must he himself be out and about, especially around here, where he will most certainly be remembered?"

"Perhaps his agent is less trustworthy than we've thought?"

"Or requires a shorter leash," Holmes said, with no trace of humor. We reached the boarding house minutes later and Lestrade led us in. The common room emptied as we stepped inside.

The proprietor of the boarding house was a sullen man, his blind eye rolling wildly in a scarred socket. He allowed as how every room had been paid for, but he was less than forthcoming with names.

While Lestrade badgered the proprietor, Holmes sought the stairs, ignoring Lestrade's bellowed cry for caution. I followed, my hand finding the revolver that had become my constant companion in the years since I had first joined Holmes on a case.

"How do you even know what room it is?" I said in a whisper. Holmes smiled, then, raising his cane, began swatting the walls.

"Fire! There's a fire! I say, dash it all, fire!"

Shabby figures poured out of rooms, men of low morals and women of ill-repute. Holmes pressed me back against the wall with one long arm, his keen eyes searching.

"Holmes! Why would you–"

"There," he said, pointing. "The door at the end hasn't opened. No one came out."

"Maybe he didn't hear–"

"He heard," Holmes said. "But he is, perhaps, too busy to care." Holmes charged towards the door and rattled the knob. "Locked. Watson! There's not a moment to lose!"

Knowing instinctively what Holmes required, I stepped back and fired my revolver, blowing the lock off. Holmes pushed the door open and stepped inside, only to turn and tackle me to the floor as a Webley Bulldog barked, tearing a chunk out of the door frame.

"Get away, Aldo! You won't get me!" a man screamed. The pistol roared again and Holmes and I scrambled away from the door. "Get away!"

"Who's Aldo?" I asked. Holmes laughed sharply and slapped his leg, mimicking the outline of a leg brace.

"Need you ask, Watson?" He leaned back. "Where is Lestrade? You can never count on the man."

The sound of glass shattering caught our attention. Holmes frowned. "He's going out the window. Go inform Lestrade," he said, the last directed at me. "Have him send men around."

"But–"

"We will lose him otherwise, Watson!" Holmes hissed "But leave your revolver. Perhaps I can reason with him."

Wordlessly, I handed over my weapon with only a moment's hesitation, then hurried towards the stairs, to find Lestrade. Of what happened next, I must rely on Holmes' account.

Even as I descended the stairs, Holmes rose to his feet and swung around the doorway, aiming the revolver. "Mr. Meaney," he said.

Meaney, half in and half out of the window, turned and fired. Holmes responded in kind, catching Meaney in the hand, forcing him to drop his weapon. Even as the Webley clattered to the floor, a second shot sounded and Meaney toppled from the window, slid down the slope of the roof and fell to the ground.

Lestrade and I saw the latter as we rushed around the side of the building. For a moment, I thought Holmes had fatally shot Meaney, as I caught sight of him standing in the broken window, smoking revolver in one gloved hand. But Holmes gestured, shouting, "There!"

Lestrade and I turned to see a large figure clad in a coachman's coat and a squat hat rushing through the crowd. Lestrade waved a hand, yelling, urging his tardy constables onto the chase. Holmes, for his part, slid down the roof and dropped easily to the street. He tossed me my revolver as he knelt beside Meaney's body.

Gently, he turned the man over. "Is he–" I began. Holmes sighed and stood.

"Dead? Yes. A perfect shot."

"Was the shooter–"

"Our friend Aldo? No. He was moving too quickly, too smoothly. I believe it was the 'toff'. Inspector!" he said, motioning to Lestrade. "It is imperative that you track down Meaney's associates. I believe you will find that Scour Morris was among them, even as that poor dead fool in the opium den was. We must find the others–"

"Already found them," Lestrade said, slowly. "Constable Phipps here–" Lestrade jerked a thumb at a fresh faced constable behind him. "Found me a few seconds after you went upstairs. Two men were just killed not a few streets away."

"Two—" Holmes' eyes widened slightly. "How?"

"They were mauled. In the street." Lestrade's face was stone. "He killed them both in a few seconds. Savaged them like an animal. In full view of God and everyone."

"Was the killer caught?" I said. Lestrade didn't look at me.

"He jumped onto the back of a passing cab. Disappeared down a side street."

"Good God," I said. "They're all dead, then."

"He's cleaned up his loose ends, sure enough," Lestrade said hollowly. Holmes made a sound. I turned.

"Holmes?"

"No. Not every loose end. Aldo remains." He glared at us, his eyes blazing. "The mastermind himself remains. And I will find him!"

***

Holmes filled his pipe and smoked furiously, fingers massaging his temples, his eyes locked on the evening edition spread across his knees. Lestrade sat with us, sipping from a cup of tea. The room was silent, but for the sound of cups clinking against saucers and the fire crackling.

Wiggins and the other boys of the Irregulars had been waiting on us at the steps of 221B when we returned. Morosely, Holmes paid out Wiggins his reward, listening with half an ear to the boys excited babble. I led the Inspector upstairs, as Holmes made his gratitude known and finally followed us some minutes later.

We had sat in a strained sort of silence since, Holmes' mind whirring away almost audibly, while Lestrade and I contented ourselves with our tea.

Finally, Lestrade looked at me, then at Holmes. He cleared his throat.

"Yes, Inspector?" Holmes said, his voice low.

"It isn't your fault, you know."

"Did I say it was?" Holmes said, languidly. His eyes opened and he smiled thinly. "Your words of comfort fall on deaf ears, Lestrade. I have been an unmitigated fool." Holmes stood and began to pace, pipe clenched between his lips. He carefully folded the newspaper and placed it under one arm. "Yes. Quite the fool."

"Holmes, really," I began, but my friend held up a hand, silencing me.

"No Watson. Spare me your optimism. I have been hunting men, when

I should have been hunting beasts. The stolen beasts, in point of fact."

"But the men would have–" Lestrade started. Holmes laughed, interrupting him.

"So I thought. But why settle for the fingers when you can have the whole hand, eh?" Holmes spun on his heel, hands behind his back. His eyes blazed at us from beneath his sharp brow. "Those murdered murderers were simply tools of another mind's design. When he was done, he dispensed with them."

"Which leaves us at all ends," Lestrade said. Holmes' lips quirked and he removed his pipe, emptying it into the fireplace.

"Not quite."

"No?" I said. Holmes straightened, his pipe bouncing against his palm.

"No, Watson. I had the foresight to ask Wiggins to keep an ear to the ground, as it were, on the subject of exotic animals, if you recall. I had merely intended that he listen for gossip concerning our thieves dropping from the lips of dockside doxies, but Wiggins, in his masterful, all-consuming way, brought me everything he heard, regardless of source." Holmes turned towards us, smiling slightly. "Like a fool, I disregarded it in favor of the more immediate thrill of the hunt."

"It?" I said, comprehension beginning to dawn.

"What did I say earlier, Watson? A keen observer must use all of his senses. Sight, touch, scent, taste and, of course, hearing." Holmes shrugged out of his smoking jacket. "Wiggins sent me a runner earlier, or, say several rather, all bringing word on the subjects of exotic beasts in London. Strange fish in the Thames, prowling panthers in the commons, a giant bat in Highcross."

I started, wondering when Holmes had spoken to any of the urchins that composed his rough and ready intelligence network. "When did you–"

"Watson, you are a marvel. Observance, Watson." He tapped his forehead. "It takes but a moment for a message to be passed, a phrase to be spoken." He smiled. "As I was saying, one of those phrases was simply, 'strange noises in Limehouse'."

"Strange noises–" Lestrade sputtered. "But that's not even–"

"Holmes, Limehouse is a den of iniquity! There are always noises!" I said, giving tongue to the Inspector's protests. Holmes clapped his hands together.

"Yes, Watson. But, what kind of noises would it take for a denizen of that place to classify them as 'strange'?"

Having no answer, I looked at Lestrade. He shrugged, narrow face pinched in thought. Holmes rubbed his hands together, his face lit by a devilish glow.

"The unnatural annoys me, Watson…it defies appropriate categorization and thus makes my work quite nearly impossible." Holmes turned back towards us. "But, at times, it does lend a bit of a thrill to things, does it not?"

"By unnatural, I trust you are referring to the crime, rather than the perpetrator," I said, remembering the canine hairs Holmes had found.

"Both, I think. The animals have vanished into the steamy guts of Limehouse, but why? Neither Wiggins nor his circus of the streets heard mention of toffs buying big cats for pets, nor of apes being sold for the doctors' knives. No, the profit of the theft was not monetary. That much I'm sure of."

"What of our gentleman murderer?" I said. "The man who shot Meaney?"

"He is the mastermind, I'm sure of it," Holmes said. "The devilish brain behind this crime. And he lairs in Limehouse."

"How will we find him?"

"Simple. We follow our senses," Holmes said.

***

A phalanx of blue-clad officers followed us back into the depths of Limehouse some time later. Bright colors and opium stink stretched past our coaches as they rumbled across the cobbles. We had not been to Chinatown in some time, since the Affair of the Man with the Twisted Lip. Lestrade was, while not without confidence in Holmes, unsure of his certainty in this matter.

"He's got to have cleared out by now," he said to me, sotto voce. Holmes turned, sharp ears catching every word.

"Not at all. Does the lion leave his lair? Our mastermind is not afraid of us. Something other than fear drives his actions in these endeavors. He will not run, not unless we threaten him with captivity."

"What did you mean before, about following our senses?" I said.

"Wiggins' message concerning the strange noises pinpointed them rather loosely around Chinatown. The same area where Scour Morris acquired his particular brand of cigarettes, and where men like Meaney tend to congregate. It is such a hodgepodge of the exotic, I don't know why I didn't see it before," Holmes said. "Think Watson, if you wanted to hide a menagerie of foreign beasts in London, where better than Limehouse, and Chinatown in particular?"

"But why hide at all? Surely a country estate would be better..." I protested. Holmes shook his head.

"Too far from the sea, Watson. Too far from the source of his menagerie and too far from his method of disposal."

"Disposal?" Lestrade said. Holmes tapped the paper he had brought with us from 221B.

"Another point in favor of literacy, Lestrade. Do you recall the unpleasant carcasses found floating in the river near Wapping last week?" Holmes unfolded the paper. "Dogs, cats, some malign breed of large rodent. All bearing the marks of the vivisectionist upon their clay. At first, I assumed it was simply the work of the usual cutters societies, but this clenched it." He tapped an article. "Last evening what was thought to be a child was found washed up near Regent's Canal Dock. Within minutes, it had been identified by a knowledgeable bystander—a sailor with some experience in South Africa—not as a child, but as an ape. A baboon, to be precise." Holmes looked at us, eyes narrowing. "It's all the work of the same man, Watson. The marks described are too similar, the patterns of cuts sound too much alike."

"But you said Wiggins had not heard of any vivisectionists—" I began. Holmes snorted.

"Of course not. This man did not buy the animals, Watson. He organized their theft!" Holmes gave a crowing laugh. "I thought that our mysterious ringleader was nothing more than a Moriarty-in-the-making, but instead he is a scientist in truth. Methodical, brilliant and ruthless. He organized a seamless theft to acquire what he needed and no more and then cleaned up after himself, tidying up all of his loose ends, and all for no monetary gain that we could see. Because there was no monetary gain to be had. The animals are for him!"

"But why?"

"That I do not know." Holmes fell silent. "But he lairs in Limehouse to hide the secrets of his house of pain, that much I'm sure. Easy access to materials, the peculiar smells and sounds will waft unnoticed through an area such as this, and a man can come and go as he pleases, unseen and—ah!" Holmes gestured. "There!"

A young boy hung from a lamp post, gesticulating urgently. With a start, I recognized one of the Irregulars, a sallow-faced youth who often acted as Wiggins' second in command.

"Holmes–" I said.

"Where he indicates, Lestrade," Holmes said. He looked over at me. "Yes, Watson?"

"You knew," I said. Holmes cocked his head. "Before we sat down, you knew."

"Knew, Watson? No, merely guessed. Disparate clues adding up to a unified theory."

"Then why not tell us?"

"Why…I wanted to make sure that our mastermind was at home when we called on him, of course." Holmes tapped the roof of the cab with his cane. "An intelligent man would keep well away from his usual haunts, especially after murdering others so close to his home. But not for long. Not this man. He is impatient, Watson."

"Impatient?"

"Why else would he have his cronies followed? He did not wait for them to spill their sins. No, he was in a hurry to clean up his loose ends. His impatience to acquire those animals lead to the death of the six porters, and his impatience in dealing with his hired help led to them being murdered so quickly and so brutally that we could not help but see the pattern." Holmes snapped his fingers. "And his impatience will be his undoing. Listen!"

As we stepped out of the cab, we heard it. Far below the hubbub of Limehouse in the evening, below the omnipresent sound of the Thames, there was something else. I strained, looking around. I could just make it out, but only just. Lestrade looked at me, his face gone suddenly pale.

"Is that–"

"Screaming," Holmes said.

***

The house had the look of a down at the heels *fan-fan*, gaudy colors and indistinct images. Lestrade motioned his officers forward and the door was knocked open. There were no patrons, or servers or anyone at all. Tables sat silent, dust and mold growing on them. There was a horrible silence there, a muggy stillness that clung to everything.

A peculiar odour touched my nostrils and I was reminded of my service in India, of the field hospitals and the cries of dying men. I could taste sour meat and blood on my tongue. Lestrade had a handkerchief pressed to his mouth.

"What is—"

"It smells like a butchers," one of the constables muttered. Holmes stood in the center of the room, head cocked. Listening. Then, with a peculiar hopping motion, he moved across the floor, tapping with his cane. He stopped. "Here!" he said. We hurried towards him. "Footprints, in the dust," he said. "Including the peculiar dragging mark I have come to associate with our friend Aldo." Holmes sank down, spreading his hands inches above the floor. He looked up. "Air. Rising from beneath the floor."

"Stand back," Lestrade said. He waved a hand and two of his constables moved forward, clutching pry bars in their hands. Lestrade had obviously had the foresight to believe their use might be called for. With grunts, the constables shoved the pry bars into the gaps Holmes indicated and, with a creak and a shriek, the trapdoor slid up and back, revealing the yawning maw of a hidden stairwell. A noxious odour rose up through the hole, stinging our eyes and noses.

A careening shriek greeted our ears a moment later, the cry of an animal being given over to the most unholy agonies. Holmes darted down the revealed stairs moments later and we dutifully followed after. For once, Lestrade didn't even try and stop him.

The tunnel beneath the *fan-fan* lead to what had once obviously been an opium den, but was now something much, much worse. We followed the ululating shrieks as they bounced off of the walls and rebounded from floor to ceiling.

Holmes stopped, abruptly. I hissed, "Holmes, what is—"

Holmes held up a hand, and I fell silent.

"Damnation Aldo, hold the brute still!" snapped a rough voice. Another scream and creaking of restraints. Holmes stepped around the corner and slammed the tip of his cane upon the rough floor.

"Doctor Moreau, I presume," Holmes said. I stepped up behind Holmes, followed by Lestrade. A scene out of a penny dreadful stretched out before me. Cages full of grimly silent beasts covered the walls and a red-stained basin stood in the center of the room, near an operating table. A guttering electric light hung from the rafters, giving the entire scene an unearthly glow.

On the table, what had once been a lion lay, limbs spread, skin red and raw. Bandages stained pink covered its form and tubes of blood and serum extended to it from half a dozen medical drips scattered around the operating table. It's skull was…there are no words. Suffice to say that it was wrong. It had been…bisected. As if someone were attempting to what? Shorten it? Rebuild it in some fashion? God only knew.

It screamed again, and thrashed against the twin grips of a broad shouldered man of indeterminate years, his white hair flaring out around his fleshy face in a fairly leonine fashion and an even more thickly built brute with a hideously elongated jaw and oddly sloping skull. The brute snarled at the sight of us and stepped around the table, the brace on his leg clanking.

"Holmes, his leg–" I whispered, despite myself. The brute's leg was not only deformed, but in the most hideous way possible. It bent in the wrong direction, giving the impression of an animal's slender limb grafted on to the body of a stevedore.

"I see it, Watson," Holmes said.

"You have the advantage of me, sir," the white-headed man said. He jammed a syringe into the lion's neck and the creature's screams descended into mewling whimpers as whatever concoction he'd injected took effect.

"You are Doctor Alphonse Moreau, late of the Royal Medical Society and London society in general, thanks to that hideous business with the Duke of Eltsham's daughter. And I, I am Sherlock Holmes. I trust I have renounced my advantage?"

"Quite," Moreau said, tossing his syringe on the instrument tray nearby. It landed with a clatter and he stepped around the table. I saw a pistol holstered in his arm pit–the same pistol he had undoubtedly used to shoot Meaney earlier in the evening–and drew my own.

"Holmes, he's armed," I said, aiming my trusty Webley. Moreau smirked.

"Of course I am…Doctor Watson, I trust?" He tossed his head. "My patients are no longer Society toffs and widowed matrons, Doctor. No, they are instead the very clay of God's hand. And a fierce clay they are."

"So I see," Holmes said, gesturing with his cane towards Aldo. Aldo bared hideously sharp teeth, so sharp I wondered whether Lestrade could add unlicensed dentistry to the list of Moreau's crimes.

"Settle, my friend," Moreau murmured. He met Holmes' eyes with his own glacial pair, a twisted smile forming on his red features. "You have heard of me then? Are they still selling those detestable penny dreadfuls with my caricature on the cover?"

"Not that I am aware. No, I read your monograph on organ transplants. And, of course, heard of your change in fortunes last year. By the by, the girl did not survive."

"As I said at the time. Without my constant attentions she was doomed."

Moreau said it coldly. "It is hardly my fault that the dunces in the Royal Medical Society didn't believe my theories, is it?"

"Perhaps you should have considered that before you removed her heart and replaced it with that of a chimpanzee, Doctor Moreau?" Holmes said. He leaned forward on his cane. "But then, you were never one for waiting, were you?"

"My late wife–God rest her soul–always said that my impatience would be my undoing," Moreau said. He smiled, displaying tobacco stained teeth. "May I ask what has led you to my doorstep. I am quite busy as you can see…" He swept his arms out, indicating the den of horror around us. At his movement, the beasts in their cages went wild. The baboons shrieked and rattled at the bars while the remaining lion roared madly, clawing at the floor. Aldo jerked, as if physically struck and turned slightly and gave a bark of warning.

"Yes. Quite the cutter you've become, Doctor," Holmes said. His face betrayed no emotion, but I, through long association, could see the revulsion in his eyes.

"Cutter. What an ugly term. I am no mere vivisectionist, Mr. Holmes," Moreau said harshly. "I simply intend to prove my theories one way or another, as any true man of science would do."

"But this–" I said, indicating the doped up abomination on the operating table. "This is nothing more than torture!"

"Blood must be spilled, if science is to prosper," Moreau snapped. "If you have milk in your veins, Doctor, fine. But do not seek to do the same to me!"

"You–" I began.

"Enough of this," Lestrade said, shoving past Holmes and pointing a finger at Moreau. "You, my son, are nicked."

"On what charge, pray tell?"

"Murder, for starters. Theft, unlicensed medical procedures, and whatever the hell you're doing here–"

"Giving birth to the future of evolution," Moreau said, stepping back. His eyes were alight with a sudden fire. "As good a descriptive phrase as any, I think." His hand began to reach upwards.

Holmes lunged forward, his cane lashing out. "Watson! Stop him!"

"Holmes! What–" I said, raising my pistol but too late. Aldo lunged forward, fingers spread, and crashed into Lestrade, bowling him over even as Moreau pulled his pistol and raised his free hand, grasping one of a series of pull-chains that dangled over the operating table.

With a grating cough, the cage containing the remaining lion opened wide and the beast lunged out with a shriek of fury. Moreau fired and a police constable stumbled back with a groan. Moreau then grabbed the other pulley chains and yanked hard even as he turned and ran for a door at the far end of the room. Baboons spilled out in a tornado of simian fury and I found myself pressed against the operating table, firing my revolver until it was empty as the maddened creatures boiled towards our shocked group. Lestrade's constables were equally assaulted and I saw one officer fall to the floor, covered in shrieking apes.

The electric lights were pulled down and some exploded in a shower of sparks. Flames caught at the curtains and wrappings.

The brute known as Aldo was slowly throttling Lestrade even as Holmes raised his cane like a cudgel and struck him on the back of the skull. Aldo reared back with a growl that could not have come from a human throat and swung a fist at Holmes, but he sinuously avoided the blow. Even as Aldo surged to his feet, teeth bared, the lion that Moreau had freed charged into the fray, crashing into Aldo and bearing him backwards with a scream.

I watched in horror as man and beast battled with brutal abandon. Even as the lion pressed Aldo down, the thug forced himself up, grasping the cat's paws in his hands and lunging for its tawny throat with his teeth! The lion staggered back and brought a paw down atop Aldo's head, dropping him like a stone to the floor. The lion followed, dropping atop him with an eager snarl.

Holmes grabbed my arm, shaking me free of the hold of the gruesome scene. "Come Watson! Moreau is escaping!"

I needed no further urging. I stumbled after Holmes, re-loading my pistol as we followed Moreau through the door he had taken. The walls became stone as the floor angled downwards and I fancied I could hear the press of the Thames beyond.

"The river, Watson. It coils around us," Holmes said. "Moreau chose his lair well. Easy access for certain materials and an inbuilt escape route..."

"Holmes, how did you know his name?"

"I recognized his face from the scandal sheets, Watson, as you yourself would have if you bothered to read them more closely." Holmes glanced at me as we followed the curve of the corridor. "I have always said that when a brilliant man turns his brain to crime, the result is the very essence of horror. And Moreau is a horrorist of the first order."

"Not so bad as all that, I'd hope," Moreau said, even as we rounded the bend in the corridor and came out into what looked to be a dock of some sort. A dinghy was tethered to the moldy wood of the jetty that speared out from the stone floor and into the dark waters of the Thames. Moreau stood on the dock, his revolver aimed at us.

"Drop your weapon, Doctor," Moreau said. "Or I will be forced to perforate your companion's stunning brain."

I did as I was bade and my Webley clattered to the floor. Moreau smiled.

"I fear your own companion is quite likely dead, Doctor," Holmes said. "The lion made short work of him."

"No matter. I can always make a new one," Moreau said, with a shrug. "A better one." His words sent a chill through me as I grasped their meaning. I understood then, at that moment, what he had been attempting in his torture of the brute on the operating table when we interrupted.

"You animal," I said, before I could stop myself. "You pitiless, godless demon."

"Ha! Demon, am I? No more so than Galileo or Da Vinci, Doctor! And science is the only god I require!" Moreau gestured with his pistol. "The science of Darwin, Doctor! Surely you can see the merit!"

"Merit? There is no merit in vivisection!"

"I am no vivisectionist, Doctor, as I said earlier. Rather, I am an evolutionist!" Moreau shook a fist at the ceiling. "What separates man from animal, Doctor?"

"Reason. Charity," I said. Moreau laughed.

"Hardly! There is more charity in the smallest insect than in the greatest man of our age. More reason. Only their wretched beast flesh prevents our four legged cousins from joining us in the great human race!" He grimaced at us, his teeth clicking together. "But I will strip them of that flesh and replace it with the stuff of man. I will do evolution's work and make men of beasts!"

"Impossible!"

"Not so! You saw that it can be done! You saw!" Moreau chuckled. "My dear Aldo. Such a faithful companion. So loyal. So useful. Despite his excess of brute instinct."

"God," I said, feeling ill. I remembered the marks on the men Aldo had killed and the strange deformity that gripped his leg…no deformity at all, if Moreau was to be believed, but rather the last remnant of the wretched flesh Moreau sought to flay away…

"Yet you abandon your companion, and your experiments so easily,"

He swung his pistol up, taking aim at Holmes.

Holmes said, speaking up. Moreau glared at him.

"Only because fools like you charge in, ready to burn me for a heretic, Mr. Holmes."

"With good reason. Da Vinci never flayed an orphan, Dr. Moreau," Holmes said, stepping towards him. I hung back, my eyes finding my gun.

"Stay right there, Mr. Holmes, or else I'll–"

I confess that I flinched as Holmes slid forward, his cane sliding through his grip until the tip struck the revolver in Moreau's hand, knocking it askew. Moreau stepped back and I fell on my pistol, snatching it up. I fired and Moreau gave a cough and staggered backwards, towards the edge of the dock. He swung his pistol up, taking aim at Holmes. My friend swung his cane in a wide arc, catching Moreau on the wrist and sending his weapon flying even as I fired again. Moreau gave a great cry and toppled backwards, arms wind-milling. A splash, and then nothing. Holmes leapt to the edge of the dock and peered down, his face pinched.

"Holmes, do you see him?"

"No, Watson." Holmes stood. "Like the men he had killed, his body is lost to the Thames." He looked at me. "Quick thinking, by the by."

"Hardly that. Instinct, more than anything else, I'm afraid."

"Despite what Doctor Moreau would have had us believe, instinct has its place, Watson." Holmes turned back to the water and was silent for some time.

***

Later, back in the confines of 221B, Holmes sat staring out the window as I conversed with Lestrade. The morning light was creeping up over the tops of the buildings and I was soon to bed, for whatever sleep I could muster. Lestrade too looked exhausted, but I knew he had a long day ahead, cleaning up after things.

"No trace of him, then?" I said, stifling a yawn. Lestrade shook his head.

"Not a one."

"I doubt very much whether you ever will, Inspector," Holmes said softly. He looked over at us. "If he survived, then he is already beyond the reach of Scotland Yard, I'm afraid."

"You don't think he managed to survive two gunshots?" I said, disbelief coloring my words. Holmes laughed.

"I merely state fact, Watson. Nothing more."

"What will become of that house of horrors?" I said.

"It burned, most of it. We had to put most of the animals down," Lestrade said. He swallowed. "That thing on the table, too."

"For the best, I suppose," Holmes said, waving a hand. "And Aldo?"

"Dead as doornails. Lion chewed him up but good." Lestrade shook his head. "Couldn't have happened to a nicer bloke."

"I find it hard to place much blame on that poor creature now that the full facts are before us." Holmes turned back towards the window. "It was, after all, only doing what a good dog does…following the whims of its master."

Lestrade and I had no reply. The blank, mad impossibility of it gnawed at the edges of our consciousness like rats in the hold of a ship. Lestrade, I knew, would most likely forget, in time. I was not so fortunate. In later weeks, I often found myself looking into the faces of the crowd, looking for some hint of Moreau's devilish hand.

It will remain with me for many years, I think, this affair of the wretched flesh. And, despite his assurances to the contrary, I know it remains with my friend Sherlock Holmes.

***

From Comics to Holmes

I'm not the first person to attempt a literary mash-up of the type you've just read. Others have done it (and better), and still more are waiting to do it. All I can really hope for is that I'm the first one to hit on this particular idea.

Probably not, but I'll pretend otherwise until someone corrects me.

Really, this story begins over a decade ago, when I first read Wells' *The Island of Doctor Moreau*. It wasn't the satire that struck me, or the creeping horror of the story, but rather one, brief, bland passage concerning Doctor Moreau having to flee England because of his experiments. Just a little thing, really, but it was the sort of thing that I'm always on the look out for in my reading.

See, comic books taught me to read. I wasn't a big reader as a child, and the usual children's books weren't really of interest to me. So, my parents being infinitely sensible people, bought me a selection of comic books, reasoning that the bright colors, action sequences and slender format might prod my dormant reading ability into full bloom. Which they did.

But what it also did was to engender in me a lifelong sensation of coming into the middle of the story. Comics being what they are, it should be no surprise to anyone reading this to say that I was both intrigued and confused, as, invariably, my first comic (and many subsequent ones) were quite literally the middle portions of already ongoing stories. Thus, now, when I start a new book, I immediately begin wondering what happened before chapter one. I can't help it.

Back to Moreau. Passages like the one that caught my eye are intriguing to me because of the implications inherent in them. Immediately, I began wondering what had happened to cause Moreau to flee. Or, rather, who...

Thus, the preceding story. It made perfect sense to me at the time. Of course it was Sherlock Holmes. Who else would it be? Granted, I briefly entertained the idea of Dracula being the cause of it, but that's just silly, really. I mean who would read that, right? Dracula versus Dr. Moreau is just nonsensical.

Isn't it?

And, owing to my unrequited hetero-crush on Jeremy Brett, it would have to be Brett's Holmes at that. Some like Rathbone, others prefer Cushing, but me, I prefer Brett. Something about the eyes, that whip crack of a voice, the way he only rarely wears that damn deerstalker (those are only for the countryside, damn it!), eschewing it for the more traditional top hat.

And so, "The Affair of the Wretched Flesh". I hope you enjoyed it.

***

JOSHUA M. REYNOLDS – is a freelance writer of moderate skill and exceptional confidence. He has written quite a bit, and some of it was even published. For money. By real people. Some of those people being *Dark Recesses Press*, *52 Stitches* and *Not One of Us*. And now, of course, *Airship 27*.

Feel free to stop by his blog, Hunting Monsters [http://joshuamreynolds.blogspot.com/] and cast aspersions on his character.

SHERLOCK HOLMES
CONSULTING DETECTIVE

"The Problem of the Western Mail"

by
I. A. Watson

W hen I look through the cases of my friend Mr. Sherlock Holmes with which I assisted during that beastly hot summer of 1890 I am always reminded of the problem posed by the portly gentleman from the railway company, a problem that may never have been solved without such intense and unbearable temperatures.

The sweltering heat had driven many people out of London. Between the stink from the Thames and the lack of any kind of breeze, I was unfavourably reminded of my time in Afghanistan. Indeed, my own dear Mary had taken refuge in the country and I was again a guest in my former lodgings with my closest friend.

Holmes was unaccustomed to the weather and it made him rather irritable about interruptions. He sought solace in his studies and combated the sweltering heat by bending his attentions to the penning of another of his brilliant monographs on the science of detection. "Oh really!" he complained as Mrs. Hudson announced Mr. Sidney Clover, "How can the canon of criminal research be advanced if one is to be constantly interrupted?"

I hastened to assure our visitor that he was indeed welcome at 221B Baker Street and assisted him to a chair and a drink. "Holmes is just now completing an article of some interest to him," I explained. "Recent development in chromatography have enabled new means of discerning the contents of certain kinds of stains, and my friend is eager to detail the fruits of some lengthy and comprehensive research."

Holmes responded by pushing the whole mass of paperwork away across the table, displacing some few volumes that were haphazardly stacked on the far side. "It does not matter for now," he said with one of his characteristic mood changes. "Mr. Clover is a man who is used to punctuality, and we must not keep him from his job for too long." He looked our visitor up and down and added, "I presume you come here with the full permission of your employers, the Great Western Railway Company?"

Mr. Clover started to get to his feet, his face flushed with amazement, but I was ready to calm our nervous guest. Holmes was apt to vent his peevishness at interruption with assertions of his intellectual gifts. "Please, Mr. Clover, do not disturb yourself. My colleague is merely using his methods to draw information about you from your clothing, manner, and personal appearance. For example, he has noted the small medallion on your watch-fob that bears the GWR crest."

Holmes nodded curtly. "That and the excellent timepiece you bear, the bulge in your lower left jacket pocket suggestive of a small silver whistle, the callosities of hand suggesting a man who does substantial paperwork, the worn soles of otherwise well-kept shoes indicating a job that requires some degree of walking and other details which are merely trivial. It is no work after that to suppose that we are being visited by a platform master in the employ of the Great Western Railway."

"No great work?" gasped Mr. Clover, "Why Mr. Holmes, it is nothing less than a marvel of detection. A masterpiece! I can see that I was right to convince my masters to let me bring our problem to you!"

Holmes sat back again, his expression becoming more austere. "Mr. Clover, if you are so easily impressed at this merest chain of deductive reasoning I have little hopes that your problem can warrant an interruption from the completion of my monograph."

"Oh come, Holmes," I felt compelled to interject, "Mr. Clover has struggled here to see us on this terrible hot day. At least let him lay his problem before us before we decide on its merits."

"You are right, of course, Watson," my friend admitted. "My apologies, Mr. Clover. The weather and my close studies are making me peevish and I am being far from a good host. Pray hand me the letter in your pocket and tell me what matter brings you to our door."

Mr. Clover's hand darted to his inside pocket in surprise that his letter's presence had been detected. Then he caught himself and handed over the manila rectangle for Holmes' examination. "This note is from my employer, sirs, and it authorises payment for your services if you can assist us to avoid scandal and disgrace. Never before has..." The platform-master broke off suddenly. "I assume that what I say here is strictly confidential?" he checked.

"What must be kept secret shall be," Holmes assured him. "You are probably aware that Dr. Watson here keeps a journal of my work and occasionally publishes popular accounts of my cases, but in all of these narratives identities are obscured to protect the innocent. In some cases of national importance or extreme delicacy his notes have been sealed away and will not be published for many years."

"You may speak freely and without fear," I assured Clover in my turn. "Now what troubles the Great Western Railway?"

The portly Mr. Clover mopped his brow and told his tale. "I am, sirs, as you have discerned, a senior platform-master, responsible for Platform 5 of Paddington Station. Platform 5 is most often used by the mail trains, which of course take priority over common traffic, so the platform-master there must be a man of seniority and experience."

Clover paused as Holmes swept from his chair and stalked to the bookcase, but the great man called out "Proceed," as he hunted amongst the myriad stacked volumes and journals that cluttered the shelves.

"Well, sir, first amongst those trains is the daily 5:17, travelling direct from London to Bristol without stopping. The mail is sorted as the train travels, with additional mail being brought on board by use of special hooks as the express passes through Slough and Maidenhead."

Holmes had opened *Bradshaw's Threepenny Railway Guide* and had already found Mr. Clover's mail train. "And it arrives at Bristol at precisely 9:13," he read. "Very well."

"In addition to the post cars," Clover continued, "there are also some passenger compartments and a general guard's van. Goods that are urgently needed in Bristol can be loaded into the guard's van and collected at the other end. And…"

"And what?" I prompted as the platform-master hesitated.

"And every Thursday – that is yesterday, sirs – every Thursday the Great Western Railway ships its payroll for the staff at our Bristol depot, a sum of several thousand pounds."

Holmes turned from the bookcase with the first signs of interest.

"Mr. Holmes, I watched as always yesterday when the notes and coin-bags were loaded into the heavy standing safe in the guard's compartment. I locked the safe door myself and the guard spun the combination dial. I watched the train leave the platform and steam off down the track. The van itself was locked whenever the guard was not present in the car. And yet, Mr. Holmes, when the train arrived in Bristol and the safe was opened, the contents had completely vanished!"

I raised my eyebrows in surprise. "Had the train halted at all?" I suggested. "Some unforeseen incident requiring an emergency stop?"

"None at all, Dr. Watson," Clover replied. "I assure you that such a thing would have been noted, by driver and fireman, by the guard, by the postal employees labouring in their sorting cars, by the passengers themselves. And the 5:17 is an express, so it is very carefully timed. Fifty men in signal-boxes along the way can attest that there was no deviation in its travel timings."

"Well then, we must assume some clever thief with great skill at picking locks," I decided. "Some master-cracksman."

"I will need to examine the safe, of course," Holmes cut in, "but I am doubtful about this master-thief of yours, Watson. As I recall, the Great Western Railway tend to use the Mattheson & Arbutt Floor Safe with its patent dual-lock nine-tumbler system. Mattheson & Arbutt have a standing challenge to pay a thousand pounds to anyone who can overcome that key-and-combination lock system of theirs in less than one hour – and so far not a man in England has come forward and won the prize!"

"There is no possible way that any burglar could have been alone in the guard's van for more than ten minutes," Mr. Clover assured us. "None whatsoever. In fact Tom Leddick - that is the train guard - left the van on only two occasions, once to check the tickets of the passengers in the third class car and again to watch the postal workers bringing aboard the mail as the train passed through Slough. For much of the journey he was also kept company by a passenger, an elderly clergyman who was feeling unwell and who sat with Leddick in the van."

Holmes returned to his chair and sat with his fingers cradled to his lips. From long familiarity I could see the signs that his mind was beginning to dissect the problem. I knew before he spoke that he would take the case.

The platform-master leaned forward, fingering his hat nervously. "Mr. Holmes, my employers are horrified at this theft, appalled at the possibility that word may get out that the contents of the mail train are not secure."

"Then we must discover what really happened yesterday on that mail-train," decided Sherlock Holmes. "Come, Mr. Clover, take us to your platform."

***

The sun was beating down on the glass roof of Paddington, reflecting off the steel girders and polished wood and combining with the heat from the steam engines to turn the interior of the station to an inferno. I was sweltering by the time we reached the mail-train and even

Holmes was less than his usual cool self.

Mr. Clover had sent a runner ahead. Two men awaited us on platform five beside a train that had newly been shunted into place. Carew the Station Master doffed his top hat as he was introduced and in turn made us known to Mr. Franklyn, an investigative agent on the GWR payroll.

"Ah'm mighty pleased to meet you, Mistah Holmes," Franklyn bade my friend, betraying a broad American twang. "I guess I've been following your adventures with some interest."

"There is much in my work that might be of value to a former employee of the Pinkerton detective agency," Holmes told him briskly. At a glance he'd recognised the American cut of the man's suit, the state of his shoes and trouser-cuffs, the tell-tale bulge of a weapon beneath Franklyn's jacket and the slight powder-scarring on his fingers. What other clues had helped him derive the security agent's history, he never thought important enough to explain.

"I apologise for having to hurry you, Mr. Holmes" Mr. Clover told us for the third time, "but if you wish to examine the very train that carried the lost payroll you must look at it now, before it leaves again on its night run."

Holmes wasted no time in replying but hoisted himself up into the guard's van. I followed with Franklyn and Carew. Mr. Clover came after us.

The interior was divided into three areas by wire-mesh partitions. A section at the rear was reserved for animals which could not travel in the passenger carriages and for bicycles. A lone dog was penned in a travel-kennel and it lay panting, the bowl of water set out for it already half drunk. The largest section was being packed by the porters with boxes and bags, some belonging to the passengers in the first class compartments, others the parcels and packages for delivery to Bristol. Forward was a small area reserved for the comfort of the train's guard.

Holmes prowled over to the desk where the guard kept his papers. So intense was the heat in the closed van that the candle on the desk had sagged drunkenly to one side. My friend glanced at an open ledger that recorded cargo, then at the roof ventilation grill which allowed air into the compartment when the train was in motion, then at the door that connected the guard's van with the rest of the carriages.

"The safe is in the middle section over there," offered Mr. Clover, but Holmes held up a hand to silence him.

"Best let him undertake his observations in his own way," I advised the platform-master. To keep him out of Holmes' search I drew the others aside and asked them to explain in more detail about the procedures of the money transfer.

"A representative of the company and a police guard go with me to the bank each Wednesday afternoon," Franklyn told me. "The cash is counted and withdrawn, then taken to the offices of the Great Western Railway Company right here at Paddington. The money's kept overnight in the company safe, then around five o'clock the station master and a senior clerk count out the payroll and we all bring the bags down here to the platform in a strongbox."

"You didn't actually see the money as it was loaded aboard, then?" I asked eagerly. "The strongbox might have already been emptied?"

"The money is taken out of the strongbox and transferred into the safe in this car," Holmes called out from behind a pile of boxes. He was down on his hands and knees, peering at some scratches and stains through his magnifying glass.

"That's how it is, yes," agreed Mr. Clover. He pointed to the safe, a heavy metal box some three feet in each dimension, clad with teak. "The strongbox is opened by Mr. Carew whilst the guard and I open the safe. I hold the keys to the safes on each of the mail trains. The guards know the combination of the lock on the specific train each of them looks after. That way I can't open the door without them nor them without me."

"Very sensible precaution," I agreed.

"On this occasion there was rather more cash than usual to load," explained Carew. "There has recently been fitting-out works at some of the branch stations near Bristol and payment was being sent for the additional labourers and material costs, nigh on five thousand guineas total. I can assure you that the stack of banknotes and bags of coin were definitely loaded into the safe. Then Clover locked the door, Leddick scrambled the combination, and Franklyn and I observed and signed that all was done according to regulations."

Holmes had begun to inspect the interior walls of the carriage. "There have been many people in here since the theft occurred," he complained.

Franklyn shrank before his accusing stare. "Well, when the loss was discovered as soon as the express arrived in Bristol there was a good deal of alarm," he excused his company. "The station master there took control of the situation and the Bristol Depot Manager had to be summoned. He insisted on questioning the guard and then the whole train was searched."

"But passengers would have already left the station by then," I pointed out.

"There have been many people in here since the theft..."

Mr. Clover winced. "And Bristol is a very busy station. By the time the theft was found, the travellers would mostly have passed through the ticket barriers and disappeared. And of course we could not call in the police. Such a scandal would damage our business even worse than the loss of the payroll."

"The money would be bulky and heavy, though," I said.

Franklyn nodded. "Why yes, Dr. Watson. Eleven large bags of silver in varying denominations and two thousand in five pound notes. It took two of us to carry the strong box down from the offices to the train. But there's ways for cunning criminals to conceal even that amount of money about their persons before leaving the train. For sure there was no sign of the payroll left though we searched every compartment."

"You searched thoroughly and there was no clue at all?" I checked.

"Only some lost luggage that had been handed in and that hasn't yet been claimed," Carew noted.

"They searched clumsily and made finding clues near impossible," growled Holmes. "This carriage was piled high with boxes and crates, stacked against the wall here, tied and netted to keep them from toppling. Here are the scrape marks where they were hastily dragged away. Here are traces of the sawdust packing where they were unceremoniously opened for searching. This discarded bent nail was drawn from the top of a tea-chest and not replaced. There were ten, twelve searchers each working without proper direction. The whole affair was allowed to descend into chaos."

"It'd have been a whole lot worse if ah hadn't happened to be on the train myself, Mistah Holmes," Franklyn objected. "It so happened that I had business at our Bristol office so I was able to help with the search. I can guarantee you that nothing left this van without it was taken to pieces and thoroughly checked."

Mr. Clover felt the need to defend his Bristol colleagues. "The whole mystery was something of a shock, Mr. Holmes. Poor Leddick was held to blame in the first instance. He claimed he had only left the van twice, and that for the latter part of the journey he had been visited in this very carriage by an elderly clergyman who was suffering from heart palpitations and required care."

Holmes rose sharply. "Indeed. Where is this clergyman, and what does he have to tell of the affair?"

So fervent was my friend's tone – how well I knew what Holmes could get like when the hunt was on! – that the platform master took a step backwards. "I... I..." he stammered. "Sir, it was only Leddick who claimed to have seen this parson. He describes a man in the full rig of a non-conformist preacher, with black robes and a broad-brimmed floppy Breton hat, a gentleman with prominent white whiskers and pince-nez spectacles."

"But," added Franklyn, "no such passenger has been found, and the ticket collectors at Bristol have no memory of seeing so singular a passenger yesterday."

"So this Leddick is under suspicion," I summarised, "and there is no sign of this clergyman he claims as an alibi?"

Carew hesitated. "Only one. One possible thing, as I said. While a search was made for the missing money throughout the train, a satchel containing coins was actually being handed in at the lost luggage counter. It was an old leather scrip such as men of the cloth often use for carrying their possessions, and in addition to a bible and some odd sermon notes it also held a tea-jar with some eight pounds, six shillings and elevenpence in change. But this was clearly not the missing money we were looking for."

"It is clearly the very thing you were looking for!" Holmes barked. "Blind fools, the lot of you! Have them send the bag to me at once, by the fastest means possible. Do you not see that what you describe is the key to the whole affair? That and the varnish stains on the floor by the safe here, and the fact that it is so hot in here that even the candle on the guard's desk has melted?"

"I don't see how, sir," Mr. Clover admitted, more flushed and flustered than ever. "But if you wish to see the scrip then of course arrangements can be made to..."

"Our first priority, however," interrupted Sherlock Holmes, addressing me now rather than the harried platform-master or his colleagues, "our first priority now is to interview this Leddick. Come, Watson, come!"

***

Tom Leddick and his family lived in a walk-up flat in Leinster Gardens off Craven Hill, not very far from my own Paddington practice. His was a humble but respectable address, a second floor apartment of five rooms suitable for a reputable and trusted employee of the Great Western Railway.

The door was answered by a neat woman in her early thirties whose red eyes betrayed that she had been crying. A pair of small children clutched at Mrs. Leddick's skirts and peered worriedly at the latest alarming visitors to their besieged home.

"You're more men from the company," she guessed. "Here to accuse my Tom of terrible things."

"We are here to discover the truth, Mrs. Leddick," Holmes assured her. "Only those who seek to conceal it are at risk."

The worried woman stepped backwards to allow us access to her modest domain. I tried to use Holmes' methods to discern something of the place. The décor was clean but aging, the furniture cheap but polished. Mrs. Leddick's garb was carefully mended. I concluded that here was a young family on a humble but regular income trying to raise children as best they could.

"Tom's this way," Mrs. Leddick said, leading us to the parlour.

Tom Leddick rose when he saw us, his eyes darting from Holmes to me then back again as if uncertain which of us he should most beware.

"Be at ease, Mr. Leddick," Holmes told him. "My name is Holmes and my companion is Dr. Watson. We're here to pursue the missing payroll from yesterday's mail train, and the quickest way for you to get back to work is to tell me everything you can about what happened."

Leddick closed his eyes. "I've told what happened to a dozen different men now, Mr. Holmes."

"But not to me," my friend insisted. We accepted the chairs proffered to us and waited until Mrs. Leddick had left the room to make some tea.

"Nobody will believe me!" the train guard blurted suddenly.

Holmes raised one long finger in caution. "Do not draw such conclusions based merely upon what has gone before, Mr. Leddick. That is poor reasoning and poorer logic. Kindly tell us your experiences and forebear from deciding what use or judgement we shall make of your account until the facts have been laid before us."

"You were there when the money was locked away, we understand," I prompted the man.

"Of course I was. I'm always present for that on the days I do the Bristol run. It's written in the manual." He described the procedure again as Clover and Carew had outlined it.

"And you can attest that the payroll was placed into the safe and that the door was duly sealed," Holmes checked.

"Only I knew the combination of the safe, Mr. Holmes, and only Mr. Clover had the key."

"Others must know the combination too," I insisted. "In case of accident or illness…"

"The two other men who travel as guards on that train know it," Leddick answered, "and I understand that there's a sealed envelope somewhere in head office with the number in case of emergency. But there is no means that Mr. Clover or Mr. Carew could learn of it. We are always most careful."

"There were many other boxes in the guard's van on that occasion," Holmes observed. "Were any of them large? Large enough to conceal a man?"

Leddick snorted. "We had some tea chests in there, great packing crates that a man could curl up in perhaps. But all nailed down and stacked and netted, and I'd have soon seen a man a-creeping from a box. Besides, they were all searched at Bristol, every one of them."

"You're not suggesting that a cracksman could have hidden in the van and broken the safe in the few minutes Leddick was away from his desk, are you?" I asked Holmes.

The great detective shook his head. His lips seemed to betray some amusement at my naiveté but he continued questioning the guard. "You left the van on two occasions," he noted.

"Yes sir. First off to check the tickets. That would take about ten minutes, for there were only seven corridor carriages not counting the mail sorting cars that are locked and no-one can enter. I went forward again as we came towards Slough. That's where the first of the moving mail pick-ups takes place, and I generally likes to watch to make sure there's no difficulties."

"Moving mail pick-ups?" I prompted.

"The mailbags are extended on a special frame," Leddick clarified. "As the express steams past an automatic mechanism catches the bags in nets so they can be taken aboard. A similar mechanism in reverse delivers the local mail that has already been sorted. The engine doesn't even need to slow down too much."

"So the money could have left the train there!" I reasoned.

"Only if there was a massive collusion between ten or a dozen employees, my dear Watson," Holmes scorned. "The bags are sorted in a carriage occupied by several employees, packed under mutual scrutiny. Likewise, when the mail is left behind on its hook it is taken and distributed by a whole squad of mail staff."

"That's right," agreed Leddick, obviously grateful that he didn't have to explain this self-evident information to an outsider again.

"There is a second such exchange at Maidenhead," observed Holmes. "Why did you not move forward to observe that also, Mr. Leddick?"

The guard stiffened again. "Well, I normally would have. Except by then this 'ere parson had turned up with his chest pains. Regulations are quite clear that I can't leave anyone unaccompanied in the van."

Under Holmes' careful questioning the guard turned to describing his elusive visitor. "The old gentleman comes in just after Slough," he remembered. "He was sixty if he was a day, wheezy and doddery and very pale. Said he was given to occasional heart seizures and would I happen to have any brandy? He was a temperancer normally – I mentioned he was dressed all in parsonical black except for his white Wesley bands? – but his doctor had instructed him to take a tot when his chest was paining him. 'A little wine for his stomach's sake,' was how he put it."

"You keep spirits in the first aid box," I remembered. I'd been making my own inspections while Holmes had been busy.

"For that very purpose, sir," Leddick confirmed. "So I gave him a thimbleful and then another and he seemed to steady. But he showed no signs of getting up and returning to his compartment, and I couldn't hardly insist he went, him being a man of the cloth of advanced years."

"And he was with you how long?" Holmes persisted.

"Nigh until Bristol, sir," Leddick assured us. "We were perhaps ten minutes away when he said something about having to return to his seat. I saw him as far as the door between carriages and watched him make for the toilet, and that was the last I saw of 'im. But if you can find him he'll attest that there was nothing going on in my van, that there was no way anything could have been taken away from it at all."

The man sounded sincere to me. "And yet there was something taken," I pointed out. "Over five thousand pounds vanished from the safe."

Tom Leddick looked very unhappy. "As to that sir, I can't help you. I was there when that door was shut. I was there when the door was opened. How all that coin and notes could just a-vanish in between times I cannot say."

**

As night fell Holmes took me along Lambeth Road, under the shadow of Bedlam Hospital, and from there through squares and alleys into the squalid parts of London that he knows so well but which seem to me like another country. The reek of the Thames was especially thick down there and the night was not much cooler than the day had been.

"Do not complain about the heat, Watson," Holmes chided me as we pushed our way into one of the cheap public houses that are so common in Lambeth and Vauxhall. "When you chronicle this affair you will understand that the extreme weather was vital in leaving clues that resolved this case."

I followed Holmes as he selected a seat in an alcove away from the bar, a place where he could watch the door without being immediately obvious himself. "Then you have solved the mystery?" I asked. "You can say how an invulnerable safe was emptied on a moving express train and how a substantial cache of money was spirited away under the eyes of the guard and all the staff of the GWR?"

Holmes lit a bowl of tobacco and sat back. "Restrain the writer within you, Watson. There are details yet to examine. I am not yet ready to formulate my theory, but there are... indications. Yes, indications."

"May I then know why we are waiting here, in this unsavoury place?"

"We are waiting, Watson, for an unsavoury man." He pulled out the parcel that had been delivered just before we had gone there. "And while we wait we may as well examine the lost luggage found on the 5:17 yesterday."

"The clergyman's scrip?"

Holmes' nimble fingers made short work of the knotted string and peeled back brown parcel paper. "We shall see," he answered. "Now let us examine the evidence."

I knew that my friend would require some moments uninterrupted by conversation. He drew out a magnifying glass and began to examine every detail of the leather bag. He flicked through the Bible, checking that nothing was concealed within its pages. He looked at the notebook containing random snatches of scripture and some key notes for sermons then tossed it over to me. "What do you make of that, Watson?"

I looked over the scribblings and brief homilies. "It seems to be confirmation that this is the property of an elderly gentleman of a religious nature," I surmised.

Holmes snorted. "Not an elderly gentleman," he corrected me. "The curling and regularity of the handwriting betrays a writer who seldom sets pen to paper. A man of the cloth accustomed to the task regularly develops a more fluid and economic style. The form of the lettering suggests he was taught his letters some twenty or so years ago, given that the a's and e's use the more modern form, and the s and f are distinguished in the way that has only become common in the last two or three decades. In short, Watson, this is not the writing of an elderly man, or of a gentleman."

"Then what?" I frowned.

"Look also at the thickness of the ink. A man who writes as he thinks follows one pattern, refreshing his pen to the rhythm of his thoughts. A man who copies-out pauses to the inkwell at suitable break-points in the phraseology of that which he duplicates. The words in that common-place book have been copied. This is not a preacher's notes. This is meant to look like a preacher's notes."

"To what purpose?" I wondered.

Holmes lifted out the tea-tin that had the money in it. He showed me the coins in the interior, a collection of crowns and half-crowns mixed with shillings and a lot of copper. "A parson's collecting tin, would you say?" Holmes asked me. "The careful gathering of charitable donations for some worthy cause? Orphans or starving widows or the like?"

I examined the money tin. "If it is, then the vicar who lost it will be sorely put out. What could have happened to make him abandon such a sum?"

"A sum of money?" Holmes asked, taking the container from me and replacing the lid. "What money would that be, Watson?" He opened the tin again and the money had gone. He turned the caddy upside down and shook it but nothing fell out.

"Holmes!" I gasped, rising from my chair. "But the coin was there!"

"And still is," my friend chuckled, delighted at getting such a response from me. He closed up the container once more, and when he lifted the lid again the collection was back in place.

"A conjuring trick," I realised. "Some kind of sleight of hand."

"A very simple mechanism, indeed," Holmes agreed, "but ingenious in its construction. A false bottom that conceals the money, even when the tin is upended. As long as the person doing the trick holds the box to conceal that it still weighs the same as when it was full, the illusion is quite satisfactory."

I took the box from Holmes and examined it so I could fathom the mechanism for myself. "It's all done with mirrors," I realised. A diagonal glass fell into place, concealing the coins and making half a container look like a whole one. "But why?"

***

olmes stirred. "I believe the man who can answer that question has just come into his regular pub for a drink on this hot thirsty night!" he told me. "Mr. Terrence Crouch! No, don't bolt, Reverend. You know I'll be able to find you wherever you go, so you may as well save us both the trouble."

The stick-thin man who had just entered the public house looked nothing like Leddick's description of the elderly clergyman, but when I thought back over what we'd been told things started to make sense. Whiskers and glasses were easy to add as ways of deceiving the eye. During my time with Holmes I had seen my friend perform amazing feats of disguise with just such properties. Add in a broad Breton hat and full parson fig and this Crouch could well pass for an aged man of the cloth.

"Mr. 'olmes," sighed Crouch. He received a pint from the landlady and came over to join us. "I don't suppose there's much point in running from you, now is there?"

"Who is this?" I asked. "I don't suppose he really is a Reverend?"

"The Reverend is Mr. Crouch's pseudonym on these streets," Holmes explained to me. "Mr. Crouch is much given to dressing himself as a minister or presbyter in order to part people from their money."

Crouch winced. "I'm a poor man trying to make a living, Mr. 'olmes. I don't do nobody no 'arm."

"You are a confidence trickster," I told him coldly.

"Mr. Crouch's *modus operandi* is quite simple," Holmes instructed me. "He meets a stranger as they travel. Perhaps they share a compartment on a long train journey. The stranger is soon drawn into talk with the genial old clergyman, to hear about the great project the Reverend is undertaking. A new school for destitute children. A home for crippled old soldiers. Missionary work amongst the lost tribes of Borneo. Whatever is in fashion."

"Decent work for fallen women," grinned Crouch irrepressibly. "That's what's popular right now."

Holmes continued. "In any case, that's what the Reverend enthuses about. And at some point in the conversation he confides in his fellow-traveller how much he has now raised for his cause. He even shows the old tea-tin in which he carries such a handsome sum."

"They often makes a donation, right then and there," Crouch admitted.

"But then the Reverend has to go away, to visit the public convenience or to buy a paper or some such reason. The trusting old pastor asks his new friend to guard his scrip, to keep an eye on the money. He shuffles off and returns ten minutes later. He ventures to enquire if the kind stranger would be so good as to help him count his collection. And when the tin is opened again..."

"It's empty!" I interjected. "Then the old man gets very distressed, his victim feels responsible, there is the whiff of calling the police, of scandal... and so the traveller handsomely offers to reimburse the clergyman for his losses!"

"Works most every time," smirked the Reverend. His face sobered as he looked at Holmes, "Well, until now."

"And that was your business on the Bristol express," Holmes told the thief. "Except something happened that forced you to change your mind. Instead of preying upon the goodwill of an unsuspecting traveller you took refuge in the guard's van on pretence of heart problems and did not even return for your scrip and your own seed money. Why was that?"

Crouch's sly face wrinkled. "Well, you're the great detective, Mr. 'olmes, so why don't you tell me?"

"You were interrupted in your intrigue," Holmes replied. "As you left to refresh yourself in the bathroom you spotted someone you knew, coming along the train corridor towards you."

"Monroe Franklyn!" spat the petty thief. "Him as was a Pinkerton and works for the railway companies now as their investigator. He's well known and marked amongst them of us who work the lines, Mr. 'olmes. He learned his trade in the brutal West of the United States, and he's not above breaking a limb or two to deter a private operator."

"You saw Franklyn and panicked," Holmes told him. "You assumed the enquiry agent was looking for you. You abandoned your scrip and took refuge in the guard's van, hoping to avoid an encounter with a man who would surely recognise you."

"He gave me a nasty fright, and that's for sure," Crouch admitted. "So I kept the guard a-talking nigh all the way to Bristol, then changed back to meself before the train came to platform." He looked wistfully at the scrip in Holmes' hands. "It was a grievous blow to me to be losing my stake like that."

"Consider yourself lucky to lose only this," I ticked off the thief. "As it is—"

"As it is, you have been able to offer another confirmation of what happened yesterday on the 5:17," Holmes interrupted me. "And now there remains only the matter of delivering the solution."

***

We all assembled again in the stuffy crowded guard's van of the Western mail train. Holmes had called together Carew, Clover, Leddick, and Franklyn, and had also invited along but not introduced young Jones of the Yard. He had asked Jones and I to come armed.

When we were all assembled Holmes led us to the safe. "Let me first say," he began, "that the extraordinary hot spell that we are currently enduring has made the solution of this case somewhat simpler. Likewise, an unexpected misunderstanding has thwarted the criminals in their endeavours and denied them their spoils."

"Denied them?" Mr. Clover puzzled. "But the money is gone, Mr. Holmes."

"You're saying you know where it is?" Franklyn demanded. He glanced accusingly at the train guard Leddick.

"If you have a solution then pray reveal it to us quickly," pleaded Carew the station master. He glanced at his watch. "It is now four thirty and this mail train will leave in less than an hour. The packages for delivery have not yet been loaded into this van."

Holmes ignored all the commentary and went on with his revelations. He clasped his hands together, arching his index fingers and gesturing to smears on the wooden carriage floor. The varnish marks were still sticky because of the heat, and were not in front of the Mattheson & Arbutt safe but beside it. "You ask how this lock and combination safe could have been cracked in the time available, when the carriage was left unattended for less than ten minutes at a time? I suggest to you that if this is impossible then there has to be some other solution."

"It's possible if Leddick had an accomplice," Franklyn argued. "Leddick had an hour or more at the start of the journey when he could have let a locksmith ply his trade. The cash could have been hurled from the train and picked up from the tracks."

Holmes nodded in acquiescence. "But that does not explain the varnish marks, nor the candle," he replied. "I have a different idea, Mr. Franklyn."

"Tell us, Holmes," I urged.

Holmes gestured around the guard's van. "Note that this space was reportedly very crowded with boxes and packing cases at the time the safe was filled. Some of those crates were large enough to contain a man – or a safe."

He gestured to the smears on the floor. "The varnish tells us that something recently stood adjacent to this safe. Indeed, the stain is of the same colour as the wood surrounding the safe itself. How, then, if a second safe was placed beside the first, identical in every way, and the actual safe was covered by some box to conceal it?"

"A newly-constructed fake whose varnish had not dried because of the hot weather!" I cried.

"Exactly, Watson! A safe which could have so simple a set of tumblers that any key might open and close it and a combination lock which would yield to any combination. Hence guard and platform master might open and seal it in the normal way and never know anything was amiss, yet the box's creator could access the contents easily."

"Why sir!" interjected Tom Leddick, "that would mean the theft could take place in but a few minutes!"

"The few minutes whilst you collected tickets as per your regular routine," confirmed Holmes. "The counterfeit safe could be flimsily constructed to disassemble easily, along with the crate covering the real safe, then be cast out onto the tracks as Mr. Franklyn mentioned earlier. Such debris would be little remarked and could be easily removed later."

"But how could such a fake safe be installed?" Mr. Clover demanded. "And what has become of the money we entrusted to it?"

Holmes allowed himself a thin smile. "Ah… there our criminal faced some bad fortune. His intention was to cast the coin-bags from the train, but at some pre-determined point where an accomplice could collect them. I'd suggest somewhere near Maidenhead, when the train slows somewhat for the second time to exchange mailbags and the guard is absent to watch the transaction. But that delivery of stolen payroll never occurred."

"Why not?" asked the station master Carew, still plainly baffled.

"Because a disguised petty confidence trickster named Crouch was alarmed at the sight of the feared railway investigator Monroe Franklyn on the train and sought refuge with the guard."

"The clergyman!" growled Franklyn. "That was Crouch?"

"And with Crouch and Leddick in the car at all times the thief could not return to claim his ill-gotten gains," I realised. "But then… where are they?"

"Yes indeed, Mr. Holmes?" drawled Franklyn. His lips had an insolent sneer. "Every crate and box was searched. Eleven bags of coins could not have been concealed."

Holmes indicated Leddick's melted desk candle. "It has been warm in here," he noted. "Hot even for this weather. Almost as if the ventilation was blocked." He looked upwards at the grill covering the roof duct.

Leddick was the first to understand. "There is a space up there," he realised, "between the outer and inner grills!"

"The train has been in constant use," Mr. Clover realised. "The thief has had no opportunity to return for his concealed prize!"

Holmes looked over at Franklyn. "I believe your security man was planning to travel again on the 5:17 today, though," he noted. "Mr. Franklyn, who was the only man involved who was aware in time that a particularly large money shipment was to travel on Thursday; Mr. Franklyn who has every right to board a loaded guard's van before a train rolls and could unpack and assemble a counterfeit safe."

Mr. Carew looked shocked. "Franklyn...!"

The former Pinkerton man's sneer was now a snarl. He whipped the pistol from his jacket ready to fight, but Jones and I were already prepared. We overcame him in an instant and wrestled him to the floor.

Jones straddled the villain and produced handcuffs. "Monroe Franklyn, I arrest you in the name of the law for the crime of theft..."

As soon as Franklyn was properly secured, Leddick clambered up to the ventilation grill and undid the screws. As the last clip came free the grill hinged open and the heavy coin-bags tumbled down and clanked to the floor.

Clover and Carew were amazed, gratified, effusive in their thanks. Holmes brushed them off with the barest courtesies. I could see that massive mind had already moved on from a problem solved to his waiting monograph.

"I'll get a full statement from Franklyn down at the Yard," Athelney Jones promised. "A full confession, given what we've seen here today."

"You've vindicated me, sir," Leddick told Holmes. "I owe you every-thing!"

Holmes was already sweeping out of the guard's van. "To Baker Street, Watson," he called. "There are many things we have to do."

***

T he following morning the weather broke, with a great squall of Westerly rain that swept away the heat and the smell and returned London to normal. I was so distracted at breakfast by the patterns of rain streaming down the window that I almost missed the item in the newspaper before me.

"Holmes!" I called out, shocked and surprised by what I read. "Have you seen this?"

My friend was ahead of me as usual. He was already pasting the clipping into one of those great files he keeps of any and all events that bear relevance to his profession. "Monroe Franklyn," Holmes said, "found hanged in his cell overnight, presumed to have committed suicide?"

"Yes. Poor fellow. A cold-hearted thief, but all the same..."

"Not clever enough to have come up with a crime such as that," Holmes opined. "Not without help. Not without... consultation. But he is dead now, and that avenue of investigation is closed."

And on the matter of Monroe Franklyn's unknown accomplice Holmes would say no more at that time.

***

I.A. Watson

I.A. Watson loves stories, whether he's reading them, writing them, or telling them. He's authored, produced and directed four stage productions, written a long-running newspaper column, and contributed to several anthologies of stories – but his most lucrative writing remains the business plans and feasibility studies he does as a management consultant (and they're not really supposed to be fiction). His children Rhiannon and Alexander love stories too, so now they're setting him deadlines for more writing. His next published work will be his novel *Robin Hood: King of Sherwood* and a story in the anthology *Gideon Cain: Demon Hunter*. Neither of these include cashflow projections or cost/risk analyses and are all the better for it.

Sherlock Holmes
Consulting Detective

"The Case of the Missing Engine"

by
Bernadette Johnson

I do, from time to time, when delicacy and the privacy of innocent individuals does not prevent it, recount the exploits of my good friend Sherlock Holmes. This is one that happened some time ago, but the departure from this earth of the last of the guilty parties scarcely a week ago, and a lull in work at my private practice as a physician, enables me to tell the tale of a most unfortunate situation at Cambridge, involving the theft of a device which, if it truly existed and performed in the way that its maker and my friend seemed so certain, makes it one of the most astounding of any that I have seen or heard of.

This tale began some years ago, before the case that introduced me to my future wife, so at the time I was still sharing lodgings with Holmes at 221B Baker Street. I was reading a medical journal and Holmes was sitting, smoking his pipe, and beginning to exhibit the symptoms of boredom that tend to lead either to him sedating himself with opiates or taking a turn at the violin, the former to my chagrin as a medical professional, and the latter to the chagrin of our landlady, Mrs. Hudson.

We were both sitting in utter silence except for the occasional drag from the pipe or flipping of a page or any of the various and sundry noises of city life outside, when we both heard the noise of a carriage coming to a stop at what sounded to be just outside the window. Holmes, obviously ready for any distraction, sprang up and looked out.

"Ah, Watson," he said. "If I am not mistaken, I may have a new case within minutes."

"What makes you so certain that the person or persons are coming here?" I inquired of my friend.

"The youth looks decidedly nervous upon exiting the carriage, as one might if in need of my services."

I stood myself and looked out. A young man hovered just at the edge of the street for a moment, scanning the nearby buildings, and then as Holmes predicted, he appeared to pick our address, or one very near it, as his destination and disappeared from sight as his transportation pulled away.

"As fine a carriage as I have ever seen. The lad must be of some means."

"That is unlikely," said my friend. "We will no doubt find him to be of moderate means, and that the carriage belongs to someone of a much higher station."

I could now hear the sound of the bell ringing, and Mrs. Hudson going to answer it.

"Ah, as I suspected. He is coming here," said Holmes.

"Good, good," I said. "I can tell that you are in need of a case. Would you like me to retire to my room to give you and the potential client some privacy?"

"No," he said. "Only time will tell, but you are often of so much help to me on my cases, and it remains to be seen if that might be true in this instance. Stay where you are."

"As you wish," I said, closing my book and waiting for the inevitable knock at the door. I had, during this exchange, heard the muffled conversation of the young man and Mrs. Hudson. Soon enough, there was a knock, our landlady entered at my friend's consent, and presented a Mr. Harold Smythe. Upon his entrance I could see that he was a very young man, indeed, of not more than nineteen years in my estimation.

"Thank you," he said to Mrs. Hudson as she left. He was a very nervous lad, holding a hat in both hands as though his life depended upon it. "Mr. Sherlock Holmes?" he inquired, looking back and forth between the two of us.

"I am Sherlock Holmes," replied Holmes. "And this is my associate, Dr. Watson."

The boy looked at me again a little nervously, and as answer to his unasked question, Holmes stated, "Dr. Watson is my oldest friend, and any word you utter to me may be heard by him. He will guard your troubles with a confidence as strict as my own, if the situation warrants it."

"Yes, you may be sure of my secrecy," I added.

"Please, have a seat," said Holmes. "I'm curious to see what possible trouble a student of your age and standing could have to warrant seeking my help. You cannot be more than a second year at university, I would say, though perhaps a bit ahead of most of the others due to your above average intellectual capacity. On scholarship no doubt, with the patronage of a rich man who is not a member of your family."

The young man breathed a sigh of relief, and took the seat proffered to him, while Holmes seated himself with the suddenness that attends so many of his actions when on the case. But upon this last statement of my friend's, the young man sprang back out of his chair.

"How could you possibly know all of that?" said the lad, as shocked as I, although I am used to Holmes's eerily accurate deductions based on what appears at first to be no evidence at all.

"Mr. Smythe, please do not be alarmed, and pray, seat yourself again," said Holmes, motioning toward the chair. "It is a mere demonstration of my powers of deduction, which should at least alleviate any doubts as to whether you have sought out the most effective help for your case."

Smythe sat back down, now more curious than shocked. "How did you know all of that?"

"Simple observation," said Holmes. "You have the impression of a fountain pen, quite deep on the outside of your right index finger, as one who has been writing with few breaks for days. Plus there are ink stains on most of your fingers, your right shirt cuff, and the outsides of your hands. I believe I even detect the shape of handwriting on your right hand, as though you have been up nights writing carelessly, perhaps pausing in between to consult books and leaning on your most recent and undried work. Are you in the middle of exams, perhaps?"

"Yes!" cried the lad. "I have just completed all but one. But how do you know I am a student and not a clerk at a bank, in the middle of balancing the accounts?"

"Another matter of simple deduction. You are of the age to be of either avocation, to be sure, but your dress is a little too fine for that of a lowly bank clerk or other skilled laborer. Your speech is also of slightly higher a nature, more educated. From your accent, I would say that you had been reared at Somerset, and are currently attending Cambridge."

"Amazing!" said the young man.

"I have studied the various English dialects," said Holmes. "Such knowledge can be quite useful in my line of work."

"Of course. And the patron?"

"Your dress is well tailored and not inexpensive, but it is showing some signs of age. Your shoes, especially, are alarmingly worn and in need of replacement. I even detect traces of mud at the edges of your soles, and the type of wear that would make me not at all surprised to find that you go home during the holidays and help out on the family farm. You are obviously not poor, but were your family rich, they would not hesitate to replace your garments and footwear more often, especially when they must know you are surrounded by wealthy schoolmates. And to attend a school of such stature, your intelligence must have caught the attention of some rich but unrelated patron, who would care more about the improvement of your mind than about your outward appearance."

The boy had a momentary look of embarrassment, perhaps at the comments which could have been interpreted as slights to himself and his family, but he seemed at last to take it in stride and his expression changed to one of awe at my friend's obvious deductive prowess.

"I say," said the boy. "I was definitely directed to the right person for the job."

"Ah, to that," Holmes said. "Please, relate your problem, in as much detail as possible."

"Well," said Smythe, obviously a little unsure of where to start. "I suppose I should begin with a little about myself. You are right on all counts, Mr. Holmes. I am considered quite intelligent, by my family, at least, though I wouldn't count myself as more than a quick study. I enjoy reading, and mathematics, and I have a special fondness for engineering, as well. Even when a mere boy with a governess and no prospects of attending school, I read every book on arithmetic and engineering that I could gain access to and began writing out proofs and creating blueprints for fanciful machines. My father is a gentleman farmer, of neither low nor high stature, but educated enough himself to see some potential in me. He must have talked me up quite a bit in the neighborhood, for about two years ago an older gentleman, who was visiting friends in the area and whose name I will withhold for a moment until it is more pertinent to the story, came to call and inquired about some of the plans I had drawn up most recently. I showed him the blueprints for an automatic calculator somewhat based on Colmar's arithmometer. Do you know of it?"

"Yes," said Holmes, "A quite useful device for simple calculation. Pray, continue."

"I had even started a physical prototype, which I also displayed to him, but I lacked the resources to build a working model. I then showed him some of my more theoretical unfinished work. This man seemed greatly impressed, and put it to my father that he would support me at university. The only conditions seemed to be that he wanted me to go to Cambridge, Trinity College specifically, and that he would utilize my expertise for certain projects of his own in the future. This was not objectionable to myself, since I wanted to go to college more than anything, or to my father, who did not want me to waste my talents at farming and dealing with tenants. So we struck up a deal and I have been at Cambridge ever since."

"Was there any reason given for the choice of school?" inquired Holmes.

"It was the college attended by his father," replied the boy.

"Ah, yes. Please continue."

"I was accepted, no doubt with the recommendation of my patron, and began school at the beginning of the next year. Approximately nine months into my studies, my patron asked me to look into the building of a certain machine for which he had the plans. I did and it was a project that I had hoped he would ask me to work on. The gentleman, you see, is Mr. Henry Prevost Babbage, and the plans were for his father's Analytical Engine."

"Ah, yes," said Holmes. "A most noble enterprise, envisioned by Charles Babbage, though never constructed."

I must admit that I was at a complete loss for every proper name and device mentioned in the the boy's account thus far, but I was certain that Holmes would explain it all to me on the way to the scene of the crime or at some juncture after he had solved the mystery, whatever that may turn out to be. So I sat silent and listened to the rest of the story.

"Yes, Charles Babbage's theoretical machine, the ultimate in automatic computation. And commissioned by his own son, in possession of all existing plans! I am at a loss to understand the timing of the matter or why attendance at Cambridge was necessary. Not that I am complaining, mind you. It has been a dream of mine for a long while, and of my father's. No one in our existing family has completed a university degree. But with the right resources I could have begun aiding Mr. Babbage immediately when he first introduced himself and perused my own designs. And indeed, aside from the availability of a multitude of books, which has made all of my schooling worthwhile, the university has been as much of a hindrance as a help to my endeavours."

"How is that?" asked Holmes.

"Well," said Smythe. "For the most part, my professors have not approved of my course of study. Early in my schooling, some complained about my independent nature and firmly suggested that I stick to their assigned readings. I have of late been keeping up with my prescribed studies to quell their complaints, and tend to stay up late working on my private interests and projects on my own time. It is difficult on so little sleep, perhaps four hours a night. I am doing quite well this term, though I am certainly not excelling as much as a few of my more brilliant and less distracted peers. But I know from a few encounters that there is little support for my type of work. Perhaps they consider it too industrial in nature."

"Have you spoken to your professors about your work with Babbage specifically?"

"I did try to broach the subject with Professor Berkshire a few months ago, but only as a hypothetical engineering project, and as soon as I mentioned the Analytical Engine, he became livid and told me that I would be wasting my time on such a venture and should stick to my approved studies."

"But you started work anyway. In secret."

"Yes, at least partially. It would be nearly impossible to work on such a huge project without some people knowing and in fact helping. I have even spoken of it to one more sympathetic professor, Professor Hill, who is perhaps the youngest lecturer at Trinity, and a little closer to his students as far as modern ideas. But I have done all my work at night and have never mentioned it to Professor Berkshire or any other of my instructors again. I was afraid to. But to get back to the point, I set to work drawing up more detailed diagrams for the machine based on Babbage's plans, those of the Analytical Engine and his earlier Difference Engine, for his son had given me both. I even developed plans for some possible improvements to the storage and printing mechanisms, which I thought might offend Mr. Babbage on behalf of his father, but though it seemed to startle him at first, he saw the logic of it and approved my modifications. I then began sending him, through the post, specifications for everything I would need. From what I can gather, though I haven't asked him for all the details out of respect, he has been having the various parts built to my specifications at different machine shops depending upon the requirements for each piece, and he has them sent via courier to me at night at a workshop in town that Mr. Babbage had let for me. Sometimes I accept the shipments, and sometimes when I am indisposed with other work, I have one of two friends meet the courier at the workplace. I spent most of my nights in the early months of the project up in my room planning and writing and sketching diagrams to send to Mr. Babbage, but most of my nights these past few months at the workshop piecing everything together and running tests of individual segments of the machine. I was very close to having a working prototype of a simple version of the engine that could not quite do the range of calculations that the senior Mr. Babbage conceived, but one that could show the genius and necessity for such a machine. I believe my patron's hope is to take his father's idea once more to the government and get backing for a larger machine, or even for the production of a number of machines to be used in scientific calculation."

"Yes, one can see why he would want to do so. It would validate his father's lifelong work in this area," said Holmes. "Pray, continue on to the difficulty that led you here, for you would not be consulting me if all were going as planned."

"Yes, of course. One night, when I had intended to go after dinner to continue work as I had every previous night, I became inordinately tired. I retired to my room and fell into a deep sleep. When I awoke it was already morning, just after dawn. I was a bit muddled, but before classes, I walked to the workshop to get a little work in, or at least to plan for the coming night. When I went to unlock the door, it opened without the key. The lock appeared to have been broken. Inside, I found that the machine, and all of the most recently delivered parts, were gone! The chairs were scattered, and one of the work benches was overturned. There were muddy tracks all around on the floor. I ran to my friend St. John's chamber, one of the friends who knew of the project and provided help occasionally, and woke him. He, too had unaccountably fallen into a deeper than usual sleep. I had to surmise that we had been drugged so that during the night someone might steal the machine. Although I find it hard to believe that anyone would go to such measures to steal an unfinished prototype, and that they could have so easily made off with it without anyone noticing. Even this small version of the machine must weigh hundreds of pounds, and I have discussed possible ways to move it without harm after completion with Mr. Babbage. It would have taken many men to lift it, and even then they likely would have required pulleys and other machinery. It's a quiet area, but not unpopulated, and this must have taken place in the middle of the night. I think it quite likely that someone would have seen or heard a gang of men performing such work at such an hour."

"What was the exact day you found yourself drugged and the machine stolen?" asked Holmes.

"It was just three days ago. Monday morning," said Mr. Smythe. "I would have come away sooner, but I was scheduled to take an exam and turn in a paper. I sent a telegram to Mr. Babbage as soon as I could reach the wire office after discovering the theft, of course, and he advised me not to jeopardize my studies, but to make excuses to my professors immediately after completing everything of some family dilemma and leave for his house in London as soon as it was possible. I was impatient to leave and must have appeared ill to Professor Berkshire, who asked what was wrong. When I related to him my fabricated problem, he said that he would pass on my difficulties to whoever needed to know and bade me to leave and not worry about my exam until I returned, which was not quite what I expected of him. I also secured the plans, including Mr. Babbage's and most of my own, save a few sketches that had been in the workshop before the theft. I cannot tell you how thankful I was to see them still in my room when I returned from the workshop that dreadful morning, unmolested on my desk. I packed them away in my suitcase, and as soon as every excuse was made, I caught the next train to London and consulted with Mr. Babbage."

"You did not go to the police at any point?" asked Holmes.

"No," said the lad, a little downcast. "I had at first thought to do so, but what would I tell them? They would not understand the nature of the work, and would likely say it was a school chum's prank or something of that sort. And worse still, they would probably go straight to college officials. My professors would find out about my work, and I could be cast from school forever. My father would be heartbroken!"

Mr. Smythe looked quite worried at this prospect. Holmes's reply was able to give some reassurance, but with a caveat. "I will make every effort to keep your education out of harm's way, but in order to investigate this crime, I will have to go to the scene. We will do everything in our power to keep our intentions secret, but it may prove impossible depending upon what we find and who we have to question in the matter. If it comes to it, would you rather I abandon the investigation, or continue despite how much of your work may be brought to the attention of the school masters and other officials?"

"I...," started the poor boy uncertainly. After a moment he collected himself, and in a resolved voice said, "Please, Mr. Holmes. I would rather find out what happened and see if the machine can be retrieved than stay at the school for another day. The work is important, and without it and Mr. Babbage's patronage, I would not be at Cambridge anyway."

"Good!" said Holmes, springing from his chair. "I take it that it was Mr. Babbage who suggested me?"

"Yes," said the young man. "I told him everything I have just told you, and he put me in his brougham to come here straightaway and speak to you. I believe you helped a friend of his on a case, a Lord Waldemere."

"Ah, yes," I said, speaking up for the first time. "That was a most interesting investigation. You might read of it in 'The Case of the Truant Heir.'"

"I will endeavor to find a copy, once my current troubles come to a conclusion one way or another," said the lad.

"Is there anything else?" asked Holmes. "Anything you have neglected to tell me that might be of import?"

"Well," the lad said, obviously hesitant to continue.

"Have it out, boy," said Holmes with some impatience.

"Yes," said Smythe. "Regarding the drugging. I was not entirely truthful."

Both Holmes and myself looked at him with interest.

"At least, I omitted something. I did have dinner as usual, but one of my friends, William Fitzpatrick, convinced us to partake of a bottle of wine."

"Did he seem inordinately persistent?" inquired Holmes.

"No, indeed. I thought about this after realizing we had been drugged. He offered, and even drank himself, and the usual group of friends accepted. What schoolfellow would reject such rare contraband?" said the young man.

"Could it have been the effects of the wine that led to your sleep?" I asked.

"I do not think so. There was but one bottle and seven of us. Not even enough for one full glass apiece. So it really could not have been the small amount of spirits that led to the long sleep. It is not as though we had never imbibed before. And I have never felt so disoriented and exhausted as I did that morning."

"Those were most astute observations regarding the drugging, Mr. Smythe. You could perhaps one day turn your mind to detective work. But I will ask that you refrain from leaving out such pertinent facts in future, however embarrassing they might be to you."

"I do apologize, Mr. Holmes. I really didn't think it so important how I was drugged, just that I was drugged."

"Please, leave the importance of the data surrounding your case to me. It is difficult to judge without all the facts, and you never know which seemingly innocuous clue might lead to the solution." After his reprimand of the lad, Holmes asked, "Is there anyone you suspect at the moment?"

"I cannot think of anyone in particular. Perhaps some foreign power wishing the technology for themselves? It has occurred to me that I might be in some kind of danger, though thankfully I have not had much time to think about it, having been occupied with schooling and the more practical realities of the crime this whole time. Mr. Holmes, do you think I should be doing anything to protect myself, or Mr. Babbage?"

"I seriously doubt so. Please, strike such thoughts from your mind, for if you were in real danger, you would have been poisoned rather than drugged," said Holmes, quite startling our young friend.

"I suggest you take the most expedient transportation back to Cambridge," Holmes continued. "Did Mr. Babbage arrange for this?"

"Yes, I will have no trouble getting back."

"Then make haste, go straight to school and get back to your classes. Pretend that nothing is wrong aside from whatever family matter you gave as pretense for leaving. Try to do nothing to jeopardize your studies. Dr. Watson and I will follow within a day."

"Thank you, Mr. Holmes! Dr. Watson!" cried the lad, standing and shaking both of our hands violently.

"I will locate you at some point tomorrow or the next day, depending upon my findings."

The boy began to take his leave, but then said, "Oh, we haven't discussed payment."

"No matter!" said Holmes. "I'm sure we can come to a satisfactory arrangement with your benefactor. Put it out of your mind at once. Before you go, quickly jot down the location of your workshop and your room at school, and the names of anyone who knew about your work. We will have to look into them all to some extent, though again, we will be as discreet as possible."

"Yes, of course," said Mr. Smythe. He scrawled some lines on a paper I had managed to scrounge from my desk, and handing it back said, "Thank you, again, Mr. Holmes." And with that the boy left us alone.

"This is really a most extraordinary crime," said Watson.

"Really, my dear Watson, there is nothing quite so ordinary as simple greed or envy," replied Holmes. "I suspect this case to involve far less than Mr. Smythe is making of it. It is simple theft. What remains to be determined is which of the two vices motivated this crime the more."

"Do you have any idea what might have happened?" I asked, knowing that often Holmes has solved the crime in his own mind before even viewing the physical evidence.

"Some possibilities have sprung to mind, but it is useless to theorize until one has all the facts. I will, however, discuss some of the details with you tomorrow. Have I spoken amiss by promising your presence at Cambridge, or are you free at present?"

"There are no obstacles to my going that I cannot clear up in an hour or so, and I shall be glad to join you," I replied.

"Excellent! Please attend to your business. We will leave tomorrow early in the morning by train. I will make the arrangements. Have all of your luggage ready by seven thirty. We will have to make a quick stop before the station. Bring your best suit. And do bring your revolver. I hope it is not necessary, but we do not yet know what sort of people we are dealing with."

I gathered my coat and hat, took leave of my friend, and left to attend to business, saving the rest of my questions for the morrow. No doubt Holmes would be conducting his own business related to the case, judging by the length of time before our departure. I left anticipating a most interesting weekend.

***

I was up in plenty of time, and waiting for my friend in the study, having packed a single suitcase and eaten a light breakfast. Not having time to start any new work or reading, I was idly looking out the window. I expected Holmes to emerge behind me from his room, but instead, a hansom pulled up outside and out stepped my friend, obviously having attended to some early morning business. He saw me and beckoned me outside, which I thought best, as well. No need to disturb Mrs. Hudson. I had spoken to her the night before when returning home to let her know that there would be no need to serve us any meals over the next day or two, a nicety that my good friend, however much I respect him, might have neglected. Outside, the cabman helped me with my suitcase as Holmes ignored my cordial greeting and waved me into the cab.

"Where are we going before the train?" I asked when we were both seated comfortably.

"To visit Mr. Henry Babbage at his London house," said Holmes.

"I should have guessed as much."

The ride to the Babbage house was not a long one. We stepped out of the cab and Holmes instructed the driver to remain outside for however long our business would take, leaving him a hefty payment and promising double upon our return.

The home was large and stately. Mr. Babbage, or perhaps his father, had obviously done well for himself and his family. When we rang, we were ushered into the sitting room. And after a few moments, a gentleman came in, perhaps in his late sixties or early seventies, but as spry as a much younger man.

"Mr. Holmes," said the man. "I am Henry Babbage. It is an honor to meet you."

"Likewise," said Holmes. "And this is my friend and associate Dr. Watson."

"A pleasure to meet you," said Babbage, shaking my hand. Turning back to Holmes, he said, "I have been expecting you."

"I thought as much," said Mr. Holmes.

"Please, be seated again," said Mr. Babbage. "I will call for tea." He stepped out for a moment, and I could hear the muffled speech of the man and his serving girl before he returned.

"So," began Holmes before Babbage was fully seated, "What can you tell me of your father's work? Did he have any notable rivals, especially in regards to this particular project?"

"Ah," said Mr. Babbage, more resigned than surprised. "Straight to the point. You've drawn a conclusion similar to mine, perhaps."

'The boy thinks the device has been stolen, perhaps in some complex espionage scheme perpetrated by another country," said Holmes. "But I think it more likely a domestic affair."

"Yes," agreed Babbage. "There have always been those who did not appreciate my father's work, and a small number who downright opposed it. Do you know much about his accomplishments?"

"Yes," said Holmes. "I cannot profess to know the details of his work on the Analytical Engine or its predecessor, but I have read a little about them, and quite a bit of your father's work on interpreting ciphers. It is a special area of interest of mine."

"I can see why it would be," said Babbage. "My father delved into many areas of mathematics and physics, engineering and manufacturing, and was brilliant at all of them. He made many important contributions that are still in use today. But the Analytical Engine was the pinnacle of his life's work, and one that even he knew, given the failures surrounding the Difference Engine, that he was unlikely to see built in his lifetime."

"So you have sought to finish his work," said Holmes.

"Yes, and not just for familial honor, or any such thing," said Babbage. "That plays a part, of course. But I deeply admired my father's vision, and indeed shared it. This machine could be revolutionary. It would greatly reduce human error and speed the calculation of complex problems. Its possible uses are incalculable and it could be a great aid to research of all kind, hopefully freeing scientists from the toils of calculation to the extent that it will greatly increase the rate of scientific discovery."

"I have been expecting you."

"Agreed," said Holmes. "A more brilliant contraption was never devised."

At this comment, Babbage looked gratified. There was a short interruption as tea arrived, and once we all had our cups and we were alone again, Holmes resumed his questioning.

"Back to the matter at hand," said Holmes abruptly. "What can you tell me of your father's enemies?"

"I cannot point you to any one person, unfortunately," said Babbage. "But my father did not make friends with the entire scientific community. He had very public battles with William Whewell and George Airy, among others. He was most outspoken when he thought that someone was not considering the best interest of the scientific community. He did not hide his disgust with the inefficacy of the Royal Society in promoting science in this country, and even created and supported other scientific societies. This upset quite a few members of Royal Society, of course, all the way up to the president, who he publicly snubbed. This man is no longer with us, but I am sure many of its junior members are still alive, with knowledge of the rivalries, and perhaps some wish to carry them on. I even think the boy's professor, Berkshire, I believe, to have been affiliated with them in some way, and the boy did mention the man's anger at the mention of my father's machine."

"So you think he might have had something to do with the theft?" asked Holmes.

"I hate to libel someone not knowing all the facts," said the man, to my friend's obvious approval. "He is but one possibility. In an institution of such standing in the scientific community, and with a number of scientists in residence, there are any number of people who might be interested in the device, either with admiration or with malice. I do hope the machine was stolen for scientific gain. Then at least there is the possibility that it will be returned safely for further development. But the other alternative, that it was stolen to stop its production, seems just as likely to me."

"And you did not disclose any of this to the boy?" asked Holmes.

"No," said Babbage. "I did not want to alarm him. Though from what you have said, my omission caused just as much alarm."

"He is an imaginative young man," said Holmes. "He is bound to strike upon fancies and believe the case to be more than it is."

"Yes, of course," said Babbage.

"You were correct in your earlier supposition," stated Holmes. "We have drawn similar conclusions."

"It occurred to you that someone might be trying to stop the work?" said Babbage.

"Indeed, I think it the most likely scenario," said Holmes. "But we will get to the bottom of it. I have no doubt that I will be able to settle your mind one way or the other by tomorrow or the next day."

"Good," said Babbage, as politely as before, but notably less cheerful. "I will be glad to know the truth, however this unfolds."

"Was there any particular reason for placing the boy at Cambridge?"

"In my mind the boy's education was payment for his help on the project," answered Babbage. "As to the particular school, my father attended Trinity in his early years. And it was still easier for me to assist Smythe in getting into the same university where my father was Lucasian Professor of Mathematics for a time."

"Yes, a title once held by the great Isaac Newton himself. I think we have all the information we need," said Holmes. "I will wire you if I have further questions."

"I will of course pay you whatever you like," said Babbage.

"Expenses, including travel and lodging, plus a stipend of fifty pounds, should suffice," said Holmes.

"That is more than fair," said Babbage, as we all rose and shook hands once again. "Would you like me to wire ahead to arrange for your lodgings?"

"There is no need," said Holmes. "I have taken care of it."

"Well, then, please, be in touch," said Mr. Babbage. "And let me know if I can be of any more help."

We took our leave and returned to our carriage, where Holmes instructed the driver to head for the train station in all haste. We did not speak a word on the way, and when we arrived at the station, I noticed that Holmes had two cases, though I could not imagine that we would be staying long enough for him to use all of their contents.

We caught the train that would take us to Cambridge, and made our way to an unoccupied car. After putting away our things, we sat in silence for a moment, me perusing a paper I had picked up from a street vendor, and Holmes sitting with his fingers pressed together and eyes closed in thought. After a short while, the train engine made the usual noises and the trip commenced, at which point Holmes began to speak.

"What do you make of the case thus far, Watson?" queried Holmes.

"You have already stated yourself that you do not believe it to be anything as grand as espionage. If it is as simple as you think, and I will not deign to disagree with you on that point, as you tend to be correct about these things, then it was a local theft. Someone who found out about the machine's construction, drugged the boy and stole it to either sell or take credit for himself," I said confidently. "I will disagree with you on one point. I do not see why you think it more likely that someone stole it simply to stop its construction. It is only too bad that the boy came to us so late after the crime. I could perhaps have determined with certainty what drug was used on him."

"Yes, I fear that unless we find the bottle, we will only be able to guess based on symptoms. Though from the boy's story we do know how it happened, at least, and can look for further evidence of the source of the drug when we arrive. I worry that the scene of the crime may have been adulterated beyond repair and wish that I was able to see it the very next day rather than half a week later. Still, I did some prying and found that it has not rained in the area since the morning before the theft, so that, at least, would not have destroyed any footprints or other markings," said Holmes. "But I stand by my position that it was not stolen for personal gain, based on the evidence at hand."

"But Holmes, what other aim could there have been to steal such a device, especially if it is as important as you and Mr. Smythe seem to think? I cannot imagine that someone would take such a machine and simply do away with it. How could you know such a thing at this point and on so little evidence?" I asked, incredulous.

"Ah, but we do have evidence. You are ignoring the clues we already have from the boy himself. Mr. Smythe obviously never expected anyone to do anything of this sort. Despite the fact that college life is not what he expected, he still has the naivety of un-accosted youth. Or had, until a few days ago. He did not keep the plans hidden before the crime occurred, as he spoke of them still being on his desk when he returned from the workshop. From what we do know, I can tell you that the criminal, assuming we find that it is only one person, will not come after him, at least not for his papers."

"Again, how could you know that on so little evidence?" I asked. "For all we know someone is going after the boy as we speak to steal his plans."

"What could be easier than stealing papers from an already drugged and sleeping person in the night?" replied Holmes. "If the plans were part of his aim, even the dimmest of criminals would not have missed such an opportunity, and to have coordinated such an effort with such success, I doubt very much that we are dealing with a simple minded person."

"Perhaps he was too afraid to venture onto campus and into the dormitory? Not everyone in the building would be drugged and someone might have seen him sneaking about."

"True, Watson, but the culprit's very knowledge of the work and its location, as well as his ability to sneak the boys involved a drug, indicates that he had inside help, if indeed he is not someone working within the university itself. Even if the thief did not have the courage, an inside accomplice could have undertaken it easily enough. It would be far less risky than returning to the scene for the plans once the theft has been discovered. And if, as I think I have successfully argued, he was not after the plans, it is not likely a case of industrial or scientific espionage, since these documents would be necessary for successful completion and use of the device."

"But if it is as you say and someone wanted to stop production of the machine, would they not want the plans destroyed, as well?"

"That is possible, but even if the papers were destroyed, there is still the existence of Mr. Smythe. I have little doubt that he could replicate them with a little time. And as to Babbage's plans, I am sure the son would have not have been so foolish as to give the boy the originals. No doubt they are copies and the originals still exist. But with the time and resources the endeavor has already required, theft is an effective way to halt the effort, at least for the short term, and perhaps, in his mind, enough to discourage further work."

"I still fail to see how the simple matter of the papers not being stolen makes you so solidly believe someone wanted to stop work on the machine. As I see it, the matter could still be a case of theft for profit."

"There is one other bit of evidence of which we have knowledge. The weight and delicacy of the machine itself. I suspect, based on Mr. Smythe's description of the disarray in the workshop, that little care was taken in keeping the machine intact, if indeed it was lifted out in one piece. No doubt the mastermind of this plan, again, not a simple man, hired heavy thugs to perpetrate the actual theft to avoid implication or direct invovelment. And they would not have taken much care with the machine, even if they knew how."

"I have no further argument against anything you have said so far," I said. "Only that we shall find out soon enough."

"Right you are, Watson," said Holmes. And after that, he scarcely spoke until we reached our destination, and I spent the remainder of our journey reading my paper.

***

W hen we arrived at Cambridge station, it was already mid afternoon, so we caught a hansom to our lodgings. Scarcely having time to deposit our bags, Holmes retrieved some items from one case and rushed us out to the street once again, where we caught another cab to the workshop. Holmes had the cabman stop nearly half a mile from the scene, and knowing my friend, I surmised that this was to avoid adding our carriage's track marks to the existing evidence. We walked quickly to the location given us by the boy. It appeared a plain, though solidly constructed, stone building.

Holmes handed me his lantern, which was unnecessary at the moment. "We might need this later," he said, and proceeded to pull his looking glass from his coat and began scanning every square inch of the scene, starting with the road, then the doorstep.

As the boy stated, the lock was broken, and Holmes opened the door without issue. "Please, stand just outside the door for now," he said. "Do not let anyone in."

From my vantage point, I saw Holmes light several lanterns within the workshop. He then came back to me to retrieve his lantern and surveyed every spot in the room, from the floor to the tables to the walls, from corner to corner, no doubt seeing far more than I would have, for he made several noises of acknowledgement and retrieved several small items from the floor while I saw nothing but an empty room, aside from dust, furniture, and a couple of scattered papers. Holmes reached down into one corner, picked up a tiny item, and walked back over to me.

"It is as I suspected," he said proffering me the item, which turned out to be the gear of a machine. He removed several similar but differently sized gears from his pocket and held them up beside the one in my hand.

"They are just small gears," I said, not understanding what he was getting at.

"Note, my dear Watson, that four of them appear to be broken."

I did as he said and said, "Dear me, you are correct."

"Their presence in the shop, as well as their state, further supports my idea that they did not retrieve the machine with much care," he stated. "And I say 'they,' as I see evidence of at least two thieves."

"But it could just have been a moment of carelessness," I said, still hoping not to be proven entirely wrong so quickly.

"If that were the case, it only would have happened once, as they would have taken greater care once the first damage to the machine was done. And the pieces would have fallen in a more concentrated area rather than all about the room," said my friend. "I doubt even the rolling of gears could account for such a wide distribution."

"If they were trying to break it, why not just smash it up and leave it?" I said.

"They no doubt did smash it up," said Holmes. "The footprints outside and inside lead me to believe only two men were involved, ignoring a few older prints which are likely those of our students. They made many trips into and out of the building. There is another set of prints outside that I have not yet accounted for entirely. Perhaps that of a driver, but this man did not come inside, and I would think that even a driver would have been more involved, given that the amount of time necessary to complete the crime was only a few hours."

"Such as?" I asked, but was not answered. Holmes began examining the ground outside once more, this time more thoroughly, including the grassy areas surrounding the building.

"I suspect something much more grave than we previously thought has happened here," said Holmes returning to my position. But before I could ask what he meant, he stepped past me, and stated, "This is interesting. The machine, or its parts, were carried back toward the school."

"How do you know that?" I asked.

"There are much deeper tracks leading from here in the direction of the university," said Holmes. "Or from the university to here, but since we are dealing with the theft of a heavy device, we can eliminate the latter."

"I say," I said. "Why on earth would they carry it that way?"

"That remains to be seen."

"And as to the grave crime you spoke of?"

"There are tracks and markings that I doubt have much to do with the theft itself, but that seem to have occurred around the same time," said Holmes. "And they are accompanied by a small amount of blood."

I was quite shocked. "Really? To whom do you think the blood belonged?" I asked. "One of the criminals? Perhaps he cut himself on the machine?"

"I fear not, though that would be preferable," said Holmes. "I need to look for further evidence before coming to any conclusions on that matter."

I knew inquiring further would be useless. We walked back to town, not bothering to catch a cab as the weather was so mild, and once at our lodgings, Holmes said, "Go ahead and have your dinner. I will be going out again shortly, and shall not be back until late."

"Will you not need any help?" I asked.

"Not tonight, Watson," he said. "But tomorrow you will be of use." Holmes returned to his room, no doubt to prepare for whatever scheme he had devised.

I cleaned myself up, since this was my first chance on the long journey, and headed toward the dining room, hoping that a hearty meal, the evening paper, and a good night's sleep were in my foreseeable future.

***

I was awakened with a start by a man standing over my bed. He wore shabby clothes and smelled slightly of garbage. Noticing my state, he quickly said, "Do not be alarmed, Watson," and removed his beard, revealing my friend beneath. "I have just returned and wished to wake you."

Having seen my friend in all number of disguises, I was not the least surprised, and perhaps would have guessed it had I not been in such a groggy state. But a stranger hovering over you is not what you wish to see upon waking, and the specter of more serious business afoot than theft had left me having nightmares.

"Dear me," I said. "You scared the life out of me."

"I did not mean to startle you," he said. "Only to hasten our departure. We will have breakfast and return to campus."

"So you wish to leave once again in such haste, without even an hour of sleep?"

"I do not need it," said Holmes, no doubt temporarily enervated by the chase. "Although I will need to bathe."

"Speaking of which," I said. "What is that smell?"

"I disguised myself as a janitor, which gave me free access to all of campus."

"That does not entirely explain the odour," I said.

"Ah, that," he said. "Yes, I did go through a number of waste bins, and located the school dumping grounds as well."

"Of course," I said. Holmes would consider no possible receptacle for evidence out of bounds.

"Wear your better suit today," he said, and then rushed off to bathe as I readied myself.

Once downstairs, we were the first at breakfast, and felt at liberty to speak of the case aloud save the few moments when the serving woman was nearby. When the food was on the table before us, I ventured, "Did you make much progress?"

To my surprise, Holmes replied, "The case is all but solved, or at least I have some idea of the culprit. There are still several details to be uncovered."

"Not that I believe it impossible," I said. "But so quickly?"

"Mr. Smythe gave us quite a bit to go on," said Holmes. "Despite his reticence in some areas. In short, I was able to trace the wine bottle."

"Ah, that is a bit of good luck!" I said. And then quieted down when I noticed I had attracted the attention of the proprietress.

"Given its source, I believe I know who the perpetrator of the crime is, though I am as of yet unsure of his motivation."

"Who?" I asked.

"It would not do to mention him here, especially given that we still do not have all the facts. Tell me, Watson, was there anything interesting in the local papers yesterday?"

"How did you know I had read them?" I asked.

"They were still in your room this morning," he said.

"Ah, of course," I said. "The only unusual thing was a disappearance in this very area. There was news of the ongoing search. Seems somewhat frivolous to look into a theft when you could be putting your powers to finding a missing man."

"Since when has he been missing?" Holmes asked quite seriously.

"The papers said since Sunday night."

"Ah, this is quite serious," said Holmes, placing his hand to his chin in thought.

"You think this man might be connected to the case?" I asked.

"Yes, I am afraid he might be," said Holmes.

"Do you think he was one of the thugs?"

"Doubtful," said Holmes. "In fact I think he may have stumbled onto the scene and met with some harm."

"Good lord," I said, unable to think of any further reply, and we finished our meal in silence.

Holmes then said, "I withheld one thing from you, wishing you to enjoy your breakfast free of worry," said Holmes. "I need for you to perform a task alone, while I return to the school once again in disguise. This is even more vital, given the new circumstances."

"You have but to ask," I said, unable to hide a hint of worry, but willing to do whatever was in my power to help.

"I need you to go to Trinity, as well, in a separate cab, of course, under the pretense of touring the school with the hopes of enrolling your son. Would a small lie weigh too much upon your conscience?"

"No, my friend," I said. "I can only hope when I do have a son, that the same people are not here if I ever have the wherewithal to send him to Cambridge."

Holmes laughed. "Do not worry yourself," he said. "Given the involvement of someone in the school's employ, we will in the end have to reveal ourselves and our ruse before we leave. We will likely even have to involve the police soon. But given the circumstances, I think they will understand."

I did not inquire further about who he meant as the involved party, and instead asked, "What am I to do while there?"

"Just keep your eyes and ears open and report whatever you see or hear back to me, however inane it may seem to you at the time," said Holmes. "Please idle in the dining room for twenty more minutes, and then leave at will. I will depart shortly after."

"When and where shall we meet?" I asked.

"Do not worry," said Holmes. "I will find you when the time comes."

Holmes rushed back to his room to prepare his disguise, and after the requested delay, I departed through the front door and caught the attention of a driver. While on the way, I worked up the best story I could, and hoped that I was a better liar than I thought myself to be. Acting is more the forte of my friend, but he no doubt had more important work ahead of him.

***

I arrived at Trinity College in no time, and walked into one of its stately halls, asking directions until I was ushered into the office of the school master himself. I had not expected to speak to anyone quite so high, and this made me a tad more nervous than I would have been talking to a lesser administrator or professor.

"I am Mr. Thompson. What can I do for you, sir," said the man, who was portly but with a congenial face, as he waved me into a chair.

"My name is Watson. Dr. John Watson. I have a son, William, at Harrow, and he is interested in attending your fine college. Provided he makes the necessary marks, of course. I was just wondering if I might have a tour of the place, though I did not expect to gain entrance to see anyone so high as yourself. You must be extremely busy."

"Oh, it is quite all right," said the man pleasantly. "I am not quite so busy this week as usual. I have a meeting in half an hour, but I would be glad to show you around this building, and find a professor or tutor to show you around the rest of campus."

"Capital," I said. We both stood and he ushered me out of the office. We walked the halls of the building as he pointed out various artifacts and told their stories.

"I must admit," I said. "I've never visited Cambridge before, though I have always meant to."

"There is no time like the present." He showed me a splendid trophy case with many rowing awards. "You and your son should come up for a game. We are competing against Oxford a week from Tuesday."

"Ah, the boy would love that," I said, having forgotten momentarily the name I had given the imaginary lad.

We stepped outside the building, passing a lone custodian, and Mr. Thompson pointed out and named every building in eyesight before attracting the attention of a passing professor.

"Mr. Wilkinson, are you free at present?"

"Yes, sir," said the man. "I was just heading to the library."

"I do hate to disturb you, but I must leave for a meeting. Could you possibly show Mr... Oh, I am sorry, Dr. Watson around the grounds. And perhaps some of the residence halls. You could end at the library."

"Certainly," said Mr. Wilkinson, politely if not effusively.

"Splendid," said the school master. "And Dr. Watson, I'm sure we would love to have your boy here, but if you get the chance, there are many other fine colleges here at Cambridge. Do give a few more of them a look."

"Thank you very much for your assistance, Mr. Thompson," I said.

"It was good to meet you, sir. I leave you in good hands."

I shook his hand before turning to Wilkinson. "I do apologize for having waylaid you."

"Oh, it is nothing. I really was headed to the library to locate a book. But I am sure it will wait for me."

"Ah, thank you, sir," I said. And he proceeded to guide me around the campus. We stepped into many a stately Medieval building, most with ceilings higher and rooms more vast than I would have imagined, being used to more closed quarters in London.

At one point, I could have sworn I saw the custodian from the main building out of the corner of my eye, but I was paying as close attention as I could to Professor Wilkinson so as not to draw suspicion and to gather as much information as I could. Though there was nothing he said that I thought could be of the slightest interest to Holmes.

As we were touring another great building, we stopped midway down a hall.

"Alas," he said. "We can go no further. This wing is undergoing renovations and is shut off for the remainder of the term."

"Ah, it is no matter," I said. "I believe I have seen enough of the building to get the gist of the rest of it."

"Quite so," he said. We walked outside and after a tour of a dining hall and residence hall, we reached the library. After a quick tour of that building, he left me at the front of it after politely asking if I had any more questions or wished to see anything else. I had none and had seen everything of the campus that I wanted to, so he retreated back into the building. Moments later, as I was walking from the library steps and wondering how Holmes was going to catch up with me, I came face to face with the custodian from before.

"Good job, Watson," he said quietly. I should have guessed, once again, that it was none other than my friend. "You have given me a great clue."

"How could I have done," said I. "All either of the gentlemen and myself talked of was the grounds, the history of the university, the great environment for learning, and the like."

"Ah, Watson," said Holmes. "As usual you heard and saw a great deal and observed little."

"Were you with me the whole time?" I asked.

"Yes," he said. "I was within earshot for the entire tour, save the few minutes you talked to Mr. Thompson in his office."

"And I suppose we will be heading back now?" I asked.

"It is early, yet," replied Holmes. "And I wish an hour or two more advantage of my costume. I have a particular interest in one of the buildings you toured. The one under renovation. You will return to the village for luncheon, and I will join you later in the evening."

"Have you any more assignments for me for after lunch?"

"I believe we shall confront the professor tonight, provided I have found what I am looking for."

He strode off before I could say another word, just as two students passed by on their way to the library. I could only assume he meant Professor Berkshire, but could not imagine what he hoped to find in the building, which was as interesting as any other building on campus, but no different in my estimation.

On my trip back to town I congratulated myself on successfully pulling off the ruse, though I felt a bit bad about having been dishonest. Still, anything to help Mr. Smythe regain his lost machine was worthwhile.

***

Holmes entered the room at a quarter past eight as I was once again reading the paper and wishing that I had had the foresight to bring a medical journal.

"Ah, Watson," he said energetically. "Are you well enough rested and fed for what might be an unpleasant encounter?"

"As well as I will ever be," I said.

"Good," said Holmes. "I will change, and as soon as I am ready, we will depart."

I reread the sporting scores as I waited, and Holmes was out in no time in his normal attire. We caught the attention of a cabman and made our way to a residential area on the edge of campus. We approached a small dwelling, no doubt a professor's residence, and knocked. Holmes asked for a Professor Hill, which had me taken aback for a moment, as I was expecting this to be Professor Berkshire's home. Perhaps Holmes had planned a detour. The servant took our names and led us in, where we were seated while she inquired of the master of the house. Within minutes a man, rather younger than the two university staff I had spoken to earlier in the day, with unkempt blond hair and a rumpled and yet finely woven smoking jacket, greeted us and asked us to come into his study.

"You will have to forgive me," said the man. "I was not expecting company, or I would have dressed. Do have a seat."

"Thank you," said Holmes. "As you have no doubt been told, I am Sherlock Holmes, and this is my friend, Dr. Watson. Have you heard of me, by chance?"

"No," said the professor, a little suspiciously. "Should I have?"

"Unless you have run afoul of the law, or read any of the more sensational mystery journals, there is no reason for you to recognize my name."

"Ah, well, that eases my mind."

"I am a consulting detective, and I was hired to investigate a crime that took place near campus earlier in the week."

"Dear me," said the professor. "Nothing serious, I hope."

"Yes, it is deadly serious," said Holmes. "A matter of both theft and murder."

"You will have to forgive me. I was not expecting company."

Both the professor and I started at the same moment. I, of course, knew of the theft, but despite Holmes's mention earlier of a more serious crime and the missing man, had not allowed myself until now to truly believe it could be as serious as murder.

"You are surprised," said Holmes, not as a question.

"What reaction would you expect?" asked the professor. "Has there really been…a murder?"

"I'm afraid so," said Holmes. "Are you not curious about the theft?"

"The one is so trifling compared to the other," replied the professor. "Do explain yourself, sir. What could this possibly have to do with me?"

"You, my dear sir, were the cause, if not the mastermind, of the matter."

"What?" yelled Professor Hill, jumping from his chair. "How dare you?"

"Please, seat yourself," said Holmes. "I will explain."

The professor looked for a moment as if he did not know what to do, and then obediently sat.

"You know of a Mr. Smythe. A student of yours," said Holmes.

"Yes," said the professor. "Dear Harold. Brilliant boy."

"I agree," said Holmes. "He was in the middle of a most promising project. To build a machine the likes of which has never existed."

"Was he?" said the professor, nonchalantly.

"Yes," said Holmes. "You know he was."

"I haven't a clue what you mean," said Professor Hill. "And I have never stolen anything in my life."

"Perhaps that is technically true," said my friend coldly. "You may be able to make that claim, not having done the deed directly. But you orchestrated the theft, for a reason that I intend to discover."

I could tell that Mr. Hill wanted to protest once again, but Holmes's method of disclosure had done its trick. The professor had not the energy to make a case for himself after the mention of the more serious crime.

"Please, sir," said the professor. "You mentioned a murder?"

"Yes," said Mr. Holmes. "A Mr. Billings, a watchmaker in the town. No doubt you have heard of his disappearance in the papers or student gossip?"

"I believe I have heard something of the man," said the professor wearily. "But what does he have to do with the theft you spoke of?"

"He appears to have interrupted dismantling and removal of Mr. Smythe's machine from his workshop, which was very near his watch shop. One of them struck Mr. Billings on the head, killing him."

"Oh, dear," said the professor. "That is horrible. Have you found the men responsible?"

"No, Mr. Hill," said Holmes. "It is you who will tell us who the perpetrators were."

"But...," said the professor.

"There is no need to protest, sir," said Holmes. "There is enough evidence, however circumstantial, to point to you as the mastermind behind the crime."

"But this is a very serious accusation. And I certainly did not kill anyone," said Mr. Hill.

"No, you did not. I know you to be innocent of that crime, at least directly, just as I know you to be responsible for the theft."

"What proof do you have that any of this has taken place? That this fanciful machine you speak of ever existed?" asked the professor matter-of-factly.

At this, Holmes pulled a gear from his pocket much larger than any of those he showed me earlier outside the shop. "I found this in the walls of one of the school buildings. I was fortunate that some of the masonry was freshly laid and not yet fully dry. I was able to pry some bricks loose and fish it out along with some others. Someone had dropped them behind a wall under construction and bricked them in, no doubt thinking they could not possibly be discovered."

"And you think it to have been me?"

"I seriously doubt you to have done the masonry. You must have had accomplices, at least one of them a brick mason," said Holmes.

"I honestly have no idea what you are talking about," said the professor, though he was obviously nervous, casting his eyes about as though looking for a clue as to how he should proceed.

"Come now, Hill!" shouted Holmes. "A murder has been committed. You need to divulge the culprits or live with the consequences."

"But I..." the professor started, looking terrified.

"It will go better for you if you cooperate," said my friend more gently. "I will find out the truth sooner or later. But the sooner the better. There are dangerous criminals free in the town. Do you wish a murder to go unpunished?"

"No," said the man with resignation. "No, of course not. There is no point hiding my crime now. But I knew nothing of a murder. The police will have to be involved, I suppose?"

"Of course," said Holmes. "But we can keep them out until absolutely necessary. The theft is solved. I wish to solve the murder and deliver them the guilty parties."

"Right you are," said the man. "As you have guessed, it was I who hired the men to steal Mr. Smythe's machine. Ian Jameson and William Saunders, from the town."

"How did you find them? Had you used them for anything before?"

"No, no," protested the professor. "As you guessed, Mr. Jameson is a mason. He has been working on the recent renovations at the building where you found the gears. I caught him stealing. He was apparently going through the rooms in the building, as he had several valuables with him when I ran into him on a stroll. Quite literally. He was exiting the building at a rather late hour, past normal mason's hours, and I was taking a walk around campus, as I do from time to time, and bumped right into him. He dropped a bag and out fell a silver candelabra. In retrospect, it was a wonder I did not come to harm."

"But you did not turn him in," said Holmes.

"No," admitted the professor. "I thought to at first, as the man was begging me not to. I recognized him from his work on the building, having passed him in the hallways several times. I had even seen him at work when out of curiosity I visited the room that was most recently being worked on. But that night it occurred to me that he might be of some use. As a man with access to the grounds, a man of some strength, of dubious character, and a mason working on new construction, no less. That last fact is what gave me the idea. I knew of Smythe's project from his own lips, and wished to put a stop to it, but did not have a clue how, until the opportunity of destroying it and hiding the pieces behind a solid brick wall presented itself. I hadn't the strength to do the job myself, you see, or a hiding place up to that point. And I could not think of anyone who could help me that would not get me into trouble for even asking."

"So you told Mr. Jameson you would not turn him over to authorities in exchange for a favor," said Holmes.

"Yes, I presented the idea quickly so that he would not flee. He was a local and, of course, wished to avoid trouble that would keep him from work or land him in jail, so he complied. I also offered further compensation. I told him of my newly conceived plan, and he suggested enlisting his friend, Mr. Saunders, who I did not actually meet until the night of the crime on delivery of the machine. He assured me that he was the man for the job."

"So you bade the man and his partner, by proxy, to destroy the machine as thoroughly as possible, and bring the pieces to this building under cover of night, where they hid them behind the unfinished wall and laid fresh brick to hide them from the other workmen still working on the room."

"Yes, though I am still in amazement that you have figured this all out on what cannot be much evidence."

"I assure you, there were plenty of clues left behind, detectable to the trained eye."

"Whatever they may be, you have discovered every detail."

"There is one detail left that I can only hope you will consent to tell us," said my friend. "That is the motive for this crime."

"Ah, yes," said the professor wistfully. "I...I hesitate to say, as it all sounds so pointless now given the turn of events, but seemed so important to me at the time. This machine that Mr. Smythe spoke of, the one that the departed Mr. Babbage conceived—a brilliant man, I must confess—seemed a danger to me. A machine that can perform complex calculations, such a machine could perhaps in future conceive of formulas yet undiscovered. I am a mathematics professor, you see. My entire job is to teach arithmetic, perform calculations, derive formulas. If some infernal contraption can do the work for us, what will become of not just me, but my profession in general?"

"I see," said Mr. Holmes. "I do not think your fears were well founded."

"However that may be, it is no matter now," said the professor. "I have made my bed. I have to tell you that I had no idea of anyone coming to physical or mortal harm. If the notion had ever occurred to me as a possibility, I never would have proceeded with the plan."

"I believe you," said Holmes. "And I will relay this to the authorities when the time comes. Please, give a description of the two men, including any knowledge you might have of their whereabouts."

"The man, Jameson, is stocky with dark hair, a little taller than me, with a deep scar down his left cheek. I do not know where he lives, but he frequents the Boars pub. Saunders I have only seen once and it was rather dark when I rendezvoused with them for the unloading of the cart. He is taller, and a bit more slender, with ginger hair. I really cannot tell you much more."

"That will suffice for now," said my companion.

"But tell me, Mr. Holmes," said the professor. "How did you discover all this?"

"It was quite simple. A thorough examination of the clues at the boy's workshop led to tire tracks on the road. The deeper ones, of course, led me to campus, when the carriage was laden with the heavy machinery. But there was a particularly deep gouge where the carriage obviously stopped in the middle of the road and pulled off to the side. Tracks led me into the woods, and to a partially concealed body."

There was a sharp intake of breath from the professor, who had likely been struck with the reality of the terribly deed at mention of an actual body.

"Once my partner uncovered that a building was undergoing construction, I surveyed it, and the surrounding grounds. I found cart tracks and footprints outside the windows to one particular room that were similar enough to those around the workshop.

"I entered through a window close to where the tracks ended. With a lantern, I looked around and noticed the fresh masonry I mentioned earlier. The rest I have already disclosed."

"And how did you connect me with this matter? I assure you, I am not trying to escape blame," continued Mr. Hill. "I am merely curious."

"The wine," said Holmes.

"But of course," said Mr. Hill, smiling faintly. "I should have guessed it. A family label, you know. On my mother's side."

"Ah!" exclaimed Holmes, with momentary fascination. "That I did not know! As it was, it was easy enough to trace it from you to the dinner at which Mr. Smythe and his friends imbibed it. But had those details remained mysteries for much longer, I am sure I would have traced it via your ancestry eventually."

"Of that I have no doubt! You really are a most remarkable man, Mr. Holmes," said the professor in admiration. "Please, sir, find the men. It is of no importance what happens to me now. But I could not bear the thought of a murder, especially one for which I am partly responsible, going unpunished."

"Mr. Hill, assure me that you will not do yourself harm," said Holmes. "You will be needed at the inquest, and as you did not intend for this terrible tragedy to occur, I have no doubt things will go easier for you than for the other two, and you will recover in time."

"No, no," said the downcast man. "Do not worry. I will be here, as I am now, when you or the police return."

***

"**W**here are we going now?" I asked as we entered the cab, which Holmes had convinced to wait with the promise of a sovereign.

"The police," said my friend, to my surprise.

"I would not think that you would want them involved until you apprehend the criminals for them."

"But they may be of some help in finding the men, as we do not know where they live," said Holmes. "It will be quicker than spending the night at the pub."

"Ah, true, true," I said. "But tell me. I gathered from the interrogation how you found the body, and the gears in the walls, but how did you trace the wine bottle to the professor?"

"It was simple enough," said my friend. "As the custodian, I was able to enter the residence and dining halls unhindered. I already knew of Smythe's friends from our earlier conversation. I found the bottle in the room of a Mr. Fitzpatrick, and after following you around campus, caught back up with him at his quarters, where once I disclosed my identity, he told all, despite any trouble it might get him into. He was given it by Professor Hill, after receiving a vow from the boy not to disclose that he had done so. The boy thought nothing of it at the time but the act of a kind professor who did not want to get into trouble for contributing to their delinquency. They really do think of Professor Hill as one of their own."

"Remarkable," I said. "And here I was sure it was Professor Berkshire all the time."

"One cannot always judge by first impressions," said Mr. Holmes. "Oftentimes the most pleasant of men are the more vicious and clever con artists, and the worst curmudgeon is secretly tithing a percentage of his salary to the local orphanage."

"I say, the more I know of the criminal element from my forays on your cases, the more I begin to doubt my own judgment. How do I know that anyone I meet is not a criminal in disguise?"

"My dear friend, do not let these events sully your trust in your fellow man. Most people are, if not saints, at least relatively harmless."

I smiled at my friend's usual disdain for the common man, and with that, we arrived at our destination. We exited the cab and entered the station, where Holmes identified himself and asked for the man in charge. The highest-ranking constable on duty at this late hour was summoned, and my friend explained the situation up to this point, including the names of the suspected perpetrators.

"Are the men I am describing familiar to you?" asked Holmes.

"Mr. Jameson is known to me, and I believe I have heard Mr. Saunders' name, though I do not recall his face. You should have come to us at once," said Constable Jones, somewhat tersely.

"I assure you, sir, that the police would have been involved sooner had the murder been known to me earlier. But it was initially a matter of theft, and the victim consulted me rather than going to the authorities for his own reasons."

"He will have to be questioned regarding both crimes," said the constable.

"I believe at present the best course would be to find the perpetrator or perpetrators of the more serious crime, and I am certain the boy knew nothing of it, and indeed still does not, since I have not yet disclosed the matter to him."

"So you have found the body, and know for a fact that Mr. Jameson was involved?"

"Yes, from a confession from the man who hired him and his partner," said Holmes.

"How do I know that you weren't involved in some way?" said the officer. "You could be trying to lead me to the wrong people."

"I assure you, if I were involved, I would not be talking to you now," said Holmes. "But if you doubt me, you may wire an Inspector Lestrade of Scotland Yard, with whom I have worked many times, and we can wait until the morning to apprehend the wrong-doers. I have no objection, but fear that time is of the essence, lest the perpetrators hear of the discovery of the body and decide to flee before you can apprehend them."

"Very well," said Constable Jones. "I must admit, I have heard of you. I can contact this Inspector Lestrade in the morning if you give me any cause to doubt your story. Give an account to Constable Peters as to the exact location of the body. I will retrieve Mr. Jameson's address. I believe he's been brought in on minor charges at least once before. We had no leads whatever regarding Mr. Billings' disappearance, so it will be worth trying anything if there is a chance of solving the case. Although I was hoping we would find him alive."

Holmes spoke to constable Peters, one of only four on duty, and Jones returned with a slip of paper. He ordered Peters and another man named Miller to investigate the location Holmes described, and left the only remaining constable in charge, a young man of not more than twenty four or five, who looked a tad nervous at the prospect of being left alone in the station house.

"We could really use another man," said Holmes. "I would like to go in with Watson and confront Mr. Jameson before he knows police are involved."

"I am not sure I agree with you, sir," said Jones.

"I have many a time been able to elicit confession by laying out the evidence before the criminal. I am afraid if the police rush in, he will immediately claim innocence."

"Again, it is worth a try. We will stop by Inspector Anderson's home and bring him along. It would be well to have a higher ranking officer present."

"If it is agreeable to you and the inspector, please remain outside the suspect's door while we talk to him. He will either go with us willingly after our conversation, or try to escape. In either case, you can take him into custody if you are convinced of his guilt after our interview, however it may end."

"As you like," said Constable Jones.

We entered our waiting cab after getting the addresses of Mr. Anderson and Mr. Jameson, and the constable followed in the police wagon. At Holmes's instruction, the cabman halted at the address of Mr. Anderson and waited for him to come out with Jones and board their carriage before we resumed our journey.

Mr. Jameson's building was on the seedier edge of town, the buildings and streets more careworn than those nearest the university. At Holmes's suggestion, the police wagon had stopped a little over a block away with the hopes of not being seen should the suspect look out the window. We entered the building, went up one flight of stairs, and knocked on the door.

The man who opened it was a nervous man, rather shorter than myself, but stocky and muscular. I noted the scar described by Professor Hill.

"Yeah?" said the man, somewhat brusquely.

"I am Mr. Sherlock Holmes, and this is my associate, Dr. Watson. We need to speak to you on the matter of a theft."

The man looked stricken, but stepped aside and let us in.

"Theft?" said the man after a short pause. "What theft?"

"A rather large machine," said Holmes. "We have reason to believe you were involved."

"Look," said the man. "I am a brick mason. I aren't no thief. I don't know what sort of proof you think you have."

"I have physical evidence and a confession from the man who hired you," said Holmes.

The man began to look more nervous, but confessed more quickly than I would have expected. "All right, Mr. Holmes. I did it. Me and my friend Willie, we went to the building the professor told us to, and broke apart that big contraption. I didn't have no choice. The man was blackmailin' me."

"He has admitted to that much," said Holmes.

"Oh," said Mr. Jameson, taken aback. "Well, who are you, anyway? And what sort of trouble am I in?"

"I am a detective hired to investigate the theft, and you are in the most serious kind of trouble."

Mr. Jameson looked back and forth from one of us to the other, uncertain what to do. Finally, he said, "What do you mean?"

"A man has been murdered," said Holmes. "And I believe you did it."

"What?" yelled the man. "I am not a murderer."

"If you are not, then you know someone who is."

"What proof have you got? What right do you have to walk in here accusin' me?"

"I have all the proof I need, Mr. Jameson. The confession, the body, and various traces leading from the location of the theft to its location."

Mr. Jameson reached into his jacket, but I was faster and pulled my revolver on him before he was able to retrieve his. He stopped and my friend relieved him of his weapon.

"I never meant for no one to get hurt, mister," said the man in desperation. "But Willie, 'e panicked."

"Tell us precisely what happened."

"Well, we was in the building, bringing out the pieces. It was taking a long time. The man walked by as we were walking out with some of the gears. 'e asked what we were doin' out so late. I started making up a story. Can't remember what I said exactly. As I was talking to 'im, Willie struck 'im with a metal gear, on the 'ead, and 'e fell to the ground. We didn't know what to do."

"So you dragged him to the side of the building, resumed your work, and then carried him out to the woods at the edge of campus and buried him."

"Yeah," said the man, stunned. "How'd you know all that?"

"And you did not tell the professor of your additional crime?" asked Holmes, ignoring Jameson's question.

"No, sir," said the man, wringing his hands anxiously. "We thought it best to keep it quiet."

"Where is your friend now?"

"I 'aven't seen 'im since that night. I think 'e skipped town. But I swear, we never meant to 'urt nobody."

"I believe you, sir," said Holmes. "And had this remained a simple matter of theft, I might be inclined to have pity on you. However, a life was taken, and therefore yours and that of your friend are out of my hands now. You may make your case to the authorities and a jury and hope for the best."

Mr. Jameson made a move as though he was going to try to rush past my friend and out of the flat, but Mr. Holmes grabbed his arm and said, "Running will do you no good. The police are just outside, and you are less likely to come to harm if you go with them of your own free will."

The man's shoulders slumped in resignation, and he allowed us to lead him out, where the constables were waiting for him. They escorted him the rest of the way to the police wagon and he was, as Holmes said, out of our hands. We followed and my friend talked to the constable about Professor Hill and his willingness to cooperate. Constable Jones decided to visit the professor in a civilian cab to avoid creating a stir, and he assured us he would be as discreet as possible and try to save the boy and the university any unnecessary humiliation or hardship, being most happy to have the case of Mr. Billings nearly solved.

We retired to the inn, where Holmes said that we would be able to conclude our business on the morrow. I slept soundly, knowing that the case was nearly over, save the location of one assailant who was no longer in the vicinity. That one detail would likely be left up to the constabulary, so I had little doubt we would be back at our flat the next day, however late.

***

I awoke to find that Holmes had already been up for some time. "After breakfast, we are visiting Professor Berkshire." He explained that we were going to talk to the professor about the boy's future. The meal went by quickly and we left directly after. Holmes had already sent word to the residence of the professor and he was expecting us.

After the usual pleasantries, my friend got to the point. He explained the entire situation from the beginning and I watched as the professor's features shifted from curiosity to horror.

"Oh, dear me," said the professor. "This is all very serious business!"

"Quite," said Holmes. "And aside from relating the particulars, of which

I think the university should be made aware, given the serious nature of the crime, I have come here in hopes of ensuring that this whole business will not affect the education of Mr. Smythe."

"I am shocked that such a thing has occurred, especially within the hallowed walls of our university and our beloved town. But I can assure you, Mr. Holmes, that I will do my best not to impede Mr. Smythe's studies. He has done nothing wrong, from your account of it. Aside from lying to me, which, under the unusual circumstances, I can forgive."

"You are not upset at his involvement with Babbage?" said Holmes.

"I am a bit disappointed, but not surprised."

"The young man seemed to think that you would not approve, and was most afraid of you and your fellows finding out."

"I can see why he would think so," said the professor, after a thoughtful pause. "I do recall reacting badly when he mentioned the project to me. He spoke of it as a hypothetical, but I suspected there was more to it, by the manner of his speech. However, it was not disdain for the idea itself that caused my reaction. For one thing, though I do not consider such endeavors to be useless, an industrial project of this nature should not be the purview of a college student. And for another, the great Babbage himself never completed his work successfully and met with some opposition and many obstacles. A student, especially one of his age, should concentrate on his studies, passing exams, making friends. Despite what he might have thought, I really meant him no harm, but rather to save him from great disappointment."

"That is good to hear," said my friend. "He is a promising young man, though it remains to be seen what effect this episode will have on his aspirations. With your permission, I will impart to him that he is in no trouble, at least in your eyes."

"Please do, Mr. Holmes. I hope he stays with us," said the professor. "I could not have imagined the boy would actually make such progress. I must admit, I am impressed."

We parted amiably, and Holmes confessed to me on the return voyage to the inn that he believed the professor.

"Are you certain?" I asked, my faith in human nature having been shaken so many times on these cases.

"He seemed genuinely concerned and sincere," said Holmes. "But I agree with your line of thought, my dear Watson. That is not evidence in and of itself. But I did note a good many photographs of the professor's students in his study, some taken with the professor, but a few others obviously sent to him by graduates who had done well, many signed with notes of gratitude. He obviously engenders the affection and appreciation of a number of his students, and this may well be the case with Mr. Smythe if he allows himself to ignore his first impression and get to know Mr. Berkshire."

"I say, Holmes," I chuckled. "You really do have an eye for detail matched by no other."

"I do not see why it should be so. It appears so simple a matter to me," said my friend. "I pay attention to the details of my surroundings. Nothing more."

***

All that remained now was to talk to Smythe and Babbage, and when we arrived back at the inn, both were waiting for us. I gathered that Holmes had wired Mr. Babbage and sent word to the lad to meet us here. We retired to our rooms, where we would have more privacy, and Holmes, once again, explained the entire situation.

"Poor Mr. Billings!" said Mr. Smythe, to his credit, focusing first on the loss of life rather than on his personal loss.

"Yes," said Mr. Babbage. "It is a terrible thought that a man was killed over this."

"Indeed," said Holmes. "The loss of life was most unfortunate, and decidedly unnecessary, but had more to do with the professor's choice of criminal instruments than with the theft or the machine itself."

"Of course," said Mr. Babbage.

"I did, due to the serious nature of the crime, have to talk to Professor Berkshire," said Holmes to Mr. Smythe, to which the lad started a bit.

"It is no matter," said Mr. Smythe, recomposing himself. "I will face the consequences of my actions."

"You will likely find Mr. Berkshire far more sympathetic to your situation than you have imagined. I believe his earlier concerns over your project were for your well being and that of your education."

"If you say so, Mr. Holmes, I have no choice but to give him the benefit of the doubt," said Mr. Smythe. "You have been right about everything else."

"If nothing else, perhaps you have learned that your impressions of people based on demeanor alone can be incorrect."

"Never have I heard a truer statement!" said Mr. Smythe with animation. "I could not have been more wrong about Professor Hill, and hope to find that I was equally wrong about Professor Berkshire."

"Mr. Babbage, I suggest that you confer with university officials this afternoon, who will soon enough be informed of the entire situation by the good professor and the police. I am sure they will be obliging as to retrieving whatever parts of the machine can be salvaged, despite the requisite damage to their renovations."

"Right you are," said Mr. Babbage. "I will talk to the professor first. Perhaps he can direct me through the proper channels."

"And what of the work, Mr. Babbage?" asked Smythe. "I do not wish to press you on this at the moment. Please be assured I will abide by your wishes on the matter, even if it means going home this instant."

"I see no occasion for that, dear boy," said Mr. Babbage. "I would like you to continue on here at school. The degree will serve you well in future. As to the work itself, I will take it back to London with me, and continue work on it with my current assistant. If not much can be salvaged, I may work instead on the Difference Engine for a time. It is simpler and came closer to completion even in my father's day."

At the boy's slightly downcast look, Mr. Babbage added, "Do not worry. I do not mean to cut you out of it permanently. The project has benefited greatly from your work. After you graduate, you are assured a place on whatever projects I am developing, if you wish it. And I see no harm in you assisting during summers or holiday breaks."

"Oh, thank you Mr. Babbage!" said the boy, his spirits lifted. "And thank you, Mr. Holmes and Dr. Watson, for everything."

"Yes, thanks to you both," Mr. Babbage concurred, and he shook our hands. To Mr. Smythe, he said, "I suggest we both go talk to the professor."

***

"You seem always to be one step ahead of everyone else in knowledge of the crime, and on so little evidence," I said to Holmes once we were seated comfortably in our own sitting room, I back at my book and Holmes back at his pipe.

"Ah, but if only I could be ahead of the criminal! It is more gratifying to anticipate and prevent a crime before it happens than to solve it after the fact."

"But you have done both on many occasions," I said.

"Unfortunately, not in this case," said Holmes with regret. "The loss to the world of science and engineering has been great. And the career of a young professor, who had made important contributions of his own, was

*"It is more gratifying to anticipate and prevent a crime
before it happens than to solve it after the fact."*

thrown away on one serious fault in judgment."

"Not to mention the terrible loss of life."

"Ah, yes," said Holmes. "A needless crime. One so often perpetrated for so little reason. At least, in this case, I have no doubt the murderers will be brought to justice."

"And to think a professor, a scholar at such a noble institution, would hatch such a plan, even if he could have no idea it would lead to murder."

"Folly is not a trait confined to the uneducated. It unfortunately afflicts people in all walks of life."

And so ended the mysterious case of the missing engine. We learned a great many details of the aftermath through word from Mr. Smythe and Professor Berkshire, and even a few through the papers. The second criminal was apprehended in his hometown and returned to Cambridge for trial. He was hung for the murder of Mr. Billings, though Mr. Jameson was shown some leniency for his cooperation with authorities and given life in prison. Mr. Hill was forced to resign in disgrace, his career in academia destroyed, because, although his intentions were not murderous, the crime had gotten out of hand and become known to university officials and the local constabulary. The matter could not be kept entirely from the presses, though to the extent possible, the professor's involvement was materially lessened in reports, as Holmes had predicted. Mr. Hill himself, despite his ill advised and underhanded deeds, showed integrity after he was found out. From what Holmes relayed to me, he had a chance given him by the police, who wished to keep order in the town and stay on good terms with the university which provided so much of its income, to hush up his involvement entirely, except as the man who found out and let go the criminal at an earlier theft on campus, but he declined and suffered the consequences. He did, however, manage a lucrative enough career in one of the industrial fields. That fact, however, would be of little comfort to the family of the victim, and I have no doubt that the knowledge of his responsibility in the matter plagued him until the end of his days.

As I implied at the beginning of this tale, he passed away less than a fortnight ago, and I saw no further reason to withhold the story. Perhaps it can serve as a lesson to any otherwise upright citizen who may be considering crossing over into criminal activity.

***

Victorian Computing
The Dream That Never Came to Pass

I have been a fan of Sir Arthur Conan Doyle's Sherlock Holmes stories for years. I read *The Hound of the Baskervilles* when I was nineteen or twenty, and have since read and reread a good number of the short stories (though I have to admit that I have not read every single one yet). I've always loved the cold, analytical reasoning of the main character, who deduces things that no one else would be able to figure out on the smallest of clues, with the help of his warmer, more recognizably human friend, Dr. Watson, from whose point of view we hear the stories. It actually made me quite nervous to even attempt to emulate Doyle's style, and more specifically to attempt to recreate such a recognizable and beloved character. Even people who have not read the stories have some idea of the character through the Basil Rathbone movies, the wonderful Granada Television series starring Jeremy Brett, or numerous other adaptations and references in pop culture over the years. It would be quite easy to get it all wrong, so I immersed myself in the stories for a while to remind myself of the "rules." Another difficulty was coming up with clues and ways for Mr. Holmes to interpret them. Holmes is an early example of a forensic scientist, so mud and ink and various tracks and footprints often feature in the original stories, and they do here, as well. Perhaps next time I'll also work in his vast knowledge of tobacco ashes.

As to the plot, being a computer programmer, I thought it might be interesting to integrate the work of Charles Babbage into the mystery. He is widely acknowledged as having developed the concept of the modern computer in the early to mid nineteenth century, well before anyone was able to build one and before anyone started calling them computers (I was careful not to say the word at all in the story). Babbage was not alive at the time of the Holmes stories, but some of his progeny were, including Henry Prevost Babbage, who actually did attempt to build working versions of his father's Difference Engine with limited success. By all accounts, Babbage the senior really did have a tough time getting funding and support for his project, and a fully functioning model of his Difference Engine was not produced until the 1990s. The Analytical Engine was never built, although Babbage spent years plotting out its design, and you can see its principles at work in every modern computer, including the one on which I am writing this essay. Several of the names mentioned in passing in the story were real people with whom Charles Babbage had dealings or issues, but all of the main characters, save Babbage the younger, were fabricated, and every event in the story is wholly fictitious.

I hope that I was able to capture Doyle's style tolerably well, and hope that you enjoy the story.

BERNADETTE JOHNSON - is an author from the Southeastern United States, as well as an avid reader, an obsessive watcher of movies and television, and a recent grad school graduate. Her daytime occupation is computer programming, but she has been an aspiring writer ever since she penned (or crayoned) and bound (with yarn) a short book about her mother at the age of seven. Despite critical acclaim from its sole reader, it never saw the light of day. "The Case of the Missing Engine," is her first published work, though she has many more on the way.

SHERLOCK HOLMES
CONSULTING DETECTIVE

"The Last Deposit"

by
I.A. Watson

Holmes rarely speaks about his cases once they are concluded, but if he can be coaxed on the subject his accounts are always informative and enthralling. Over many years of acquaintance I have managed to draw comment from him on most of the many investigations we have shared and some few which my friend has undertaken alone; but I have never broached the events at Merrow's Bank to him and I never will. I offer this account of the sad affair now to illustrate that my friend took the only course he could and served justice the only way it was possible.

The long summer of '90 was finally fading when I received a telegram from Mr. Sherlock Holmes – Come at once, Merrow's Bank, Throgmorton Street. Bring medical examination bag. I closed my practice somewhat early and hurried to respond to the call.

Merrow's is one of those old private banking institutions that cluster around the Stock Exchange. It stands foursquare on a corner, its Georgian frontage stern and symmetrical conveying its gravity and permanence. The effect of the solid reputable edifice was somewhat marred by the constables swarming around outside and the presence of a black police dray.

Holmes met me at the door and waved me in past the officious sergeant who was blocking passage to the idle and the curious. "This way, Watson!" my friend called. "I have managed to prevent these bumblers from disturbing the scene too much, but their eagerness by far outstrips their understanding."

"Some mystery is afoot, then," I surmised. "The police have no objection to your presence?"

"Atheney Jones knows better than to bar me from the scene," the great detective replied, "and the Chairman of the Bank has contacted the Chief Constable himself to request my involvement. Of course I would not think of tackling a case like this without my Boswell at my side!"

"Then lead on!" I cried. "What's the cause of all this furore?"

For furore there was; inside the bank the tellers and cashiers were clustered together behind the polished oak rail that separated customers from staff. Young Jones himself was with them, questioning the chief accountant and taking down replies in his little yellow notebook. Beyond that two constables were laboriously poring over ledgers, looking very much out of their depth with the task. A nervous man in a black business suit hovered over them wringing his handkerchief.

Holmes ignored them all and swept on through the back offices, down a flight of stairs and into a private room. This chamber was luxuriously appointed with leather-topped desk, two wing-backed chairs, a sofa, and a curious trestle on which rested a large steel security box. The walls were decorated with watercolour tints and lit with cut-crystal gas lamps, but there was no window at all.

A dead girl was laid out on the floor. Havers, the police surgeon, was examining the corpse.

"Dr Watson!" the bewhiskered pathologist called to me. "The very man! Holmes said you might be coming."

"And here I am," I agreed. I bent down beside the cadaver and opened my medical bag. "What do we have?"

Havers glanced at Holmes, but Holmes gestured with his fingers that the police surgeon should explain. "It's a girl of between fifteen and nineteen years of age who has been dead some three or four days. She is dressed in male clothing. The cause of death appears to be the penetration of a thin blade into the aorta – as evidenced by the bloody state of her clothing and the crate itself."

Havers' mention of the crate caused me to look up at the metal box on the trestle. The steel cube was as large as a packing crate, a little over a yard square, constructed very much like a metal cupboard. Its surface was polished to a pleasing patina. Handles protruded from its sides. A small card slipped into a wire frame identified box number A17. The front face hinged to the side and its door now hung open. The leather-padded interior had grooves on the edges where shelves could slot.

It was just large enough for a woman of diminutive stature to be pressed inside. The interior was almost entirely matted with crusted blood. Sinister brown stains suggested that she had already been confined there when she had been stabbed through the heart.

I glanced over at Holmes.

"Yes," he replied to my unspoken question. "Patterns of blood spray, the accumulation on her clothing, seepage stains all indicate that she was already in situ when the deed was done. The blade which our enthusiastic constabulary have removed from the scene is also encrusted. Its dimensions are consistent with the wound upon this poor unfortunate."

"This makes no sense, though," Havers declared. "No sense at all. How could a young woman simply appear inside a locked crate inside a sealed bank vault? How could her murderer do the deed and then escape unnoticed?"

I regarded the box. Its only remaining contents was an empty one pint beer bottle.

Holmes looked carefully at the open metal door, holding his magnifying glass over the lock, then lost interest in the container.

I examined the dead girl. She had a sweet, innocent face, frozen in death into an expression of utter despair. In life she would have been very pretty; her young frame had the promise of maturing to great beauty. That promise had been stolen from her and I suddenly desired very much to find out why and by whom.

Once again my friend read my expression. "There are more things to examine before justice can be served," Holmes told me. "We must speak now with Sir Edmund Pennick, the owner of this strongbox. He is waiting with a constable in the next room."

Holmes led me away from Havers' ongoing examination into the adjacent chamber, the chief clerk's office.

***

Sir Edmund was a heavy-set florid man with old-fashioned mutton chop whiskers to match his old-fashioned temper. "More questions?" he thundered as Holmes and I joined him. "I do not enjoy being treated like a criminal, sirrah!"

"Quite so," I soothed him, "but it's the duty of every upstanding citizen to help in a criminal investigation. Especially when there's a young girl been murdered."

That calmed Sir Edmund down just enough for Holmes to begin his examination. "You were present when the corpse was discovered?"

"A fine thing when a man goes to his bank box and finds it stuffed with dead girls!" growled the old man. "Not the thing at all. I shall be closing my account, make no mistake!"

"The facts," Holmes persisted. "When did you arrive at Merrow's?"

"Twenty-five minutes to twelve," replied Sir Edmund precisely. "I checked my pocketwatch with the clock above the exchange counter. I filled out the usual slip to access my box and was taken to the private room where the container is brought."

The constable guarding Sir Edmund chipped in helpfully. "They brings them there boxes up from their vaults so'as nobody from the public needs to go in there."

The peer gave the young policeman a withering stare. "The vault clerk had me sign his docket then left me alone to open my box. The bank doesn't keep keys to the largest containers, so nobody can access them except the owners."

"A typical procedure," Holmes agreed. "Did you apprehend anything unusual before you opened your box?"

"Nothing whatsoever. A man doesn't expect to find a corpse hiding where his possessions should be."

"And then you opened the box," prompted Holmes.

"Well of course I did. That's when the girl fell out."

Holmes clasped his hands and pressed his index fingers together. "Think carefully now, Sir Edmund. How was the corpse folded up into the space? She'd have to be bundled into a ball to fit, but was that head or feet to the door?"

Sir Edmund appeared nonplussed by the question. "How the devil should I know? She tumbled out, that's all, and I... there was a sickening crunch as her head hit the floor." He reviewed his experience. "Head first, then. Her head was by the door."

"And the knife?"

"It clattered onto the tiles beneath the trestle when she fell."

"When had you last accessed your strongbox before today?"

"I called in exactly a week ago at the same time," the knight answered. "It is my regular custom." A new thought occurred to him. "My possessions? What has become of the things I stored here?"

"What is missing from your box, sir?" I enquired, but received a fierce glare.

"What I choose to lock safe in my own bank is no-one's business but my own, sirrah," Sir Edmund growled. "It's a fine day when a man can't keep his personal possessions secure in a British vault!" And Sir Edmund refused to be drawn further upon the contents of his strongbox, even when it was pointed out to him that recovery of his treasures would be far more likely if it was known what was being hunted.

Holmes shook his head and moved the investigation on. "Let us speak to the chief vault clerk, Mr. Gould. The next part of this story is his."

***

Holmes regarded Mr. Gould with that eye for detail which meant he was already forming judgements about the man's habits and character. He took in the aging functionary's ascetic appearance, the slightly dated cut of his conservative business suit, the much-handled pocketwatch on his grey-striped waistcoat, the brass-rimmed monocle hung from a lapel chain. "Mr. Gould, be so good as to outline for us the procedure for accessing a strongbox from the vaults of Merrow's Bank."

It was clear that Jones and his myrmidons of the law had already posed that enquiry. "As is usual when one of our depositors wishes access to his private box, Sir Edmund was taken into our viewing lounge where you interviewed him lately. The junior vault clerk on duty – Mr. Corrington today – would have him fill out an identification card and to inscribe a pass-word or code-phrase he had previously agreed. This would be done even if the customer was well known to staff, as with Sir Edmund Pennick."

"You have records, then, of every visit made by every customer," I noted.

"Of course. Mr. Corrington brings the card to me in my office where I check signature and code-phrase with our card index to verify identity. Once I am satisfied as to the provenance of our client, a porter is given the card to fetch the numbered box from the secure vault and wheel it to a private room."

"The porter is alone in your vault?" Holmes interrupted.

"Mr. Partridge has been with the bank for forty-two years, Mr. Holmes," Gould responded. "He has my utmost confidence."

"Your Mr. Partridge isn't too old now to handle heavy metal vault boxes?" I wondered.

"The boxes rest on roller-shelf drawers and slide out onto a trolley. Mr. Partridge is hale and hearty for his years and will serve out his time until his retirement. Merrow's will be fortunate indeed to find another man of such diligence and integrity."

"Partridge brings the box to the private room," Holmes prompted.

"Viewing Room 1 in the case today," agreed the chief clerk. "There are three rooms, although they are rarely all in use. We are an exclusive establishment and have only one thousand and thirty strongboxes, and but one hundred of the size Sir Edmund uses. Once the box is delivered to the viewing room the porter and clerk withdraw allowing the client his privacy. A bell summons them back when the client wishes to return his property to the vault."

I considered these security precautions. "A box cannot be opened unless the client is present," I summarised, "and a client cannot access his box without it being brought out by bank staff."

The self-controlled Gould showed his first signs of agitation. "That is what I was trying to tell that brash young policeman," he replied, gesturing through the open door of his office to where Athelney Jones was questioning an accounts clerk. "The bank protects its clients. We will not give police the names of other depositors without their consent. We cannot open their boxes to check for…" He paused in distaste as he recalled the inspector's line of questioning, "to find if similar deposits have been made in their containers. We would have to force the locks in any case." He closed his eyes as if living a personal nightmare. "There is no way that unfortunate young woman could be placed inside that strongbox. None whatsoever."

"Patently there is," Holmes replied. "One cannot deny the evidence." He pointed to a walnut-wood cabinet resting on the corner of Mr. Gould's desk. The drawer was unusual in having a small keyhole. "This is the index file for your vault box depositors," he observed. "Dr Watson and I are not officers of the law but have instead been invited by your Chairman Sir Abraham Shenney to investigate the matter. I trust you will share with us the vital information of who has accessed their property in recent days."

Gould demurred at first, but given the implicit backing of the Chairman of the Board Holmes was soon able to convince the chief vault clerk as Jones had not.

Mr. Gould produced the relevant access forms and I quickly copied the details into my notebook:

Sept 3rd 11.35-11.40am: Sir Edmund Pennick – box A17
Sept 3rd 12.10-12.20pm: Mr. Daniel Browning – box A84 – new client
Sept 3rd 1.10pm–1.50pm: Mr. Francis Routledge – box A66
Sept 4th 10.15-10.55am: Dr. Clement Underwell – box A30
Sept 4th 11.55am-12.35pm: Chumley & Sons – boxes A11, A22 & B293
Sept 4th 1.55-3.10pm: Dame Margaret Gouvenier – box A45
Sept 5th 11.40am-12.00pm: Mr. Frederick Sanderson – box A98
Sept 4th 11.55am-12.05pm: Chumley & Sons – boxes A11, A22 &

B293
Sept 4th 1.10-1.20pm: Mr. Daniel Browning – box A84
Sept 5th 1.45pm-1.55pm: Sir Michael Harrier – box A68
Sept 8th 11.10am-11.55am: Mr. David Coppard – box A22
Sept 8th 11.30am-11.55am: Mr. and Mrs.. Lesley Kerwell – box A73
Sept 8th 2.25-2.45pm: Lindstock & Fezzy Ltd. – box A3
Sept 8th 2.30-2.50pm: Dame Margaret Gouvenier – box A45
Sept 9th 10.45-11.05am: Mrs.. Amelia Pagitt – box A82
Sept 9th 1.50pm-2.50pm: Major Sir Joshua Courage - box A27
*Sept 10th 10.10-10.25pm: Drew, Potter & Bainbridge – box A72 &
B144*
Sept 10th 11.35am: Sir Edmund Pennick – box A17

Holmes requested a few points of clarification. "The alphabetical prefixes of the box numbers refer to whether the container is one of the largest crate-sized strongboxes or your more regular smaller ones? Some clients possess one or more of each?"

"A number of firms use our vaults to store both documents and items of value," Gould confirmed.

"And where a company leases a box there are named employees who can access it?"

"The arrangement varies from firm to firm. Generally if an employee gives the correct code-phrase and has the key that suffices. Many companies prefer to send two staff to visit their strongbox to reduce the opportunities for mischief – as with Chumley and Sons on the list before you."

"You mentioned a Mr. Corrington as being on duty this morning," Holmes went on. "Is Mr. Corrington always the person present when a client inspects their box?"

"Not at all," Gould replied. "There is a rota, with each of the intermediate clerks responsible for a half day at a time. It could have been any of a half-dozen such men – Mr. Corbett, Mr. Matthews, Mr. Sutton, Mr. Brown, or Mr. Timson are the others."

Unsatisfied with the list of those accessing the largest containers Holmes also insisted on perusing the entire register of visitors to the viewing rooms, a considerably longer list.

"We shall inspect your vault now, Mr. Gould," Holmes announced abruptly.

***

The gloomy vault of Merrow's Bank was old and capacious, the lower half constructed of ancient London stone, the upper portion and barrelled roofs of dusty red brick. Ignoring the bars which separated off the establishment's money and bullion Holmes strode directly to the area containing the strongboxes.

The elderly chief porter Mr. Partridge trailed behind him, squinting myopically in a mild state of panic. "I don't see as how this could have happened," he worried. "Nothing like this has ever happened in all my days here, sir."

Holmes swept his gaze over the first room where small drawers lined the walls, the eight hundred and thirty smaller deposit boxes held by the bank. He passed through a wide metal door to the chamber where the hundred large containers were racked against the walls. The heavy strongboxes were slotted in steel shelving like drawers in a gigantic filing cabinet. Only one surface of each container was visible, the side where the handle and identifying number were. The strongbox one row down and seven across on the right was missing from its cradle.

"No further," Holmes instructed us, barring our entry. He dropped to his knees and began a minute inspection of the room. Partridge fidgeted nervously, but I was accustomed to my friend's habits.

I engaged the old porter in conversation to ease the moment. "This is where your customers store their treasures? What kind of things do people keep in these strongboxes?"

The old porter shrugged. "It's hard to say, sir, being as mostly we're not in the room when they opens their chests. Some keeps valuables, of course, money or jewels or portraits or statues. A few preserve family heirlooms and the like. Others store legal documents, deeds and titles and contracts too important to be lost. Some just keeps things with sentimental value, safe from fire or loss I suppose."

"No client ever enters the vault proper? You always take their strongbox up to them?"

"Oh yes, sir. There's a trolley that we hoists the box onto – they're mighty heavy, those biggest boxes there – then we wheels it out to the visitors rooms."

I looked to the vaulted ceiling where a block and tackle waited to hoist the metal crates. "And afterwards you have to lift the boxes back into their cradles?"

"Well, not by myself, sir," Partridge admitted, "not at my age. I stacks them against the wall there and someone helps me with the handling after closing time."

"It was you who brought the box to Sir Edmund this morning?"

"Yes sir. Me and Mr. Corrington, the duty clerk. We wasn't but halfway down the corridor from the visitor's room when we heard the gentleman cry out and swear."

"You rushed back there immediately?"

"Of course, sir, not knowing but what Sir Edmund might have hurt himself or the like. And then we saw that poor girl all sprawled across the floor and covered with blood."

"You have no idea who the child is?"

Partridge shook his head. "Some poor soul gone before her time, and murdered they say. All the staff peered in when word passed as to what had happened, before the police came and shooed them all away."

"And none recognised her?"

Partridge paused. "None said so, no."

"But?"

The old porter shrugged. "Young Timson went pale and went off to be sick - but he has a weak stomach and little experience of the world."

I noticed Holmes' head move imperceptibly as he eavesdropped on our talk. I was sure that young Timson had just joined the list of people to be interviewed.

My friend seemed keen that I keep Partridge occupied so I continued on with the conversation, ensuring that the porter was facing away from the room where Holmes investigated. Thus I saw, but Partridge did not, how Sherlock Holmes removed a thin needle from his inner coat pocket and deftly probed one of the strongbox locks. It took my friend less than half a minute to turn the tumbler and break in. Satisfied with his experiment, he refastened strongbox A11 and resumed his general search.

***

A thelney Jones was a rising star of Scotland Yard and one of the few inspectors of police whom Holmes regarded with confidence. The young man knew better than to pester my friend for his conclusions but was eager to hear Holmes' opinion as soon as Holmes was ready to offer it.

It was by now late in the afternoon. The unfortunate girl's body had been taken away to the coroner and most of the bank staff were waiting to be dismissed to their homes. Sir Edmund had stormed away long since, threatening to call upon his member of parliament.

"I have a summary for you of the case so far, Jones," Holmes announced. "We are far from ready to untangle this tragic business, but the points are indicative."

"I should be glad of your observations, Mr. Holmes."

"The girl," Holmes began, "I should say the young woman, since she bears upon her left hand the slightly lighter marking where a wedding ring might have been worn."

"She wore no ring," I observed. "Did the murderer steal it? Or take it to conceal the fact of her marriage?"

Holmes shook his head. "The ring has not been worn for a number of weeks, long enough for the signs of its previous brief existence to have almost faded. Otherwise: the victim has worked outdoors and has engaged in hard manual labour which has left its mark upon the colour and coarseness of her skin. Her calluses are consistent with someone familiar with domestic service, including marks upon her knees from much scrubbing of floors. I also noted a thickening of the fingertips consistent with a childhood occupation of picking at hemp."

"The sign of an orphan," I concluded. Many such children were put to work unpicking old rope for their daily crust.

Holmes nodded. "Her clothing is also of interest. It is, as you could not fail to observe, an inexpensive suit such as are worn by many junior clerks and office boys in the city. They have been carefully and recently cut down and resewn to fit her, possibly by the young woman herself. Formerly they belonged to a young man of irregular habits with a tendency to overfill his pockets and a liking for Oates' Tar Tobacco. Her undergarments were her own."

"That's useful," Jones admitted, but I could see from his furrowed brow that he was uncertain how to put such information to actual use. "There are things I don't comprehend, though. Sir Edmund will not tell me what is missing from his box. I can't learn who else might have visited the vaults in the four days since the body was put there – or was murdered there."

"Definitely murdered there," I confirmed, remembering Holmes' earlier comments to Dr. Havers. "Although why and how…?"

"Remember the beer bottle, Watson," Holmes advised me. "Recall also the advancing years of the chief porter."

Jones' frown deepened. "Do you know who the girl was, Mr. Holmes?"

he pleaded. "If we can find that we can start to look for suspects."

"A diligent questioning of orphanage-keepers might turn up a lead," Holmes admitted, "but I suspect a far quicker route might be for us to now interview the junior clerk Timson. Be so good as to have him in, Watson."

***

C harles Timson has been questioned along with all the other bank staff, but as he was ushered into the managers office again to face Sherlock Holmes and the Scotland Yard inspector his alarm was evident. A sheen of sweat broke out across his forehead and his face went so pale that I feared he might faint once more.

"You have nothing to lose by now telling the truth," Holmes assured him. "Your lack of skill at dissembling and your obvious shock at seeing the girl's corpse have already betrayed you. Now you must help us in resolving this unpleasant affair."

Timson trembled visibly. "I know very little," he promised. "But I am afraid. I am afraid for my position. I have been… indiscreet."

My speculations of a secret marriage with a pauper orphan girl had hardly formed when Holmes burst them. "You recognised the dead woman. You have seen her before but do not know her name."

"Yes," Timson swallowed. "She came here three, four times, some months ago. I noticed her because, well…"

"Because she was very noticeable," I understood. Timson was a young man and the dead girl had been fair to look upon.

The junior clerk nodded. "She was a maid, I think. She came with her master, dressed in servants' uniform. He came to his strongbox and she carried a case for him."

"A manservant would have been more usual," commented Athelney Jones.

That sweet despairing face haunted me. "Who was her master?" I enquired, eager to get to the bottom of the mystery.

Timson didn't know. "It was months ago now. So many people come to the bank. I wasn't looking at her employer."

"You saw her since then, though," Holmes discerned, "under other circumstances?"

The clerk confessed. "I met her by chance as I went home a few weeks ago," he admitted. "It was raining and she had no coat. We sheltered beneath a tree at Finsbury Circus until the squall had ended."

"Did she tell you her name?" Jones demanded.

"We had not been introduced; but we did enjoy a conversation to pass the time."

"And you were indiscreet," Holmes reminded the clerk.

Timson shuddered again. "I suppose I was showing off. I wanted to impress her with how important I was. I told her about my work at the bank. She was interested so I told her more."

"About the vault?" suggested Jones.

"She had visited Merrow's with her master," Timson replied, "and she was curious about the strongboxes. I described the procedure of how they are stored and brought out to clients. I explained about the precautions. It didn't seem wrong at the time. I didn't mean any harm by it. I never saw her again until today, when I saw – that!"

Then Timson was overcome and I was compelled to administer a stiff tot before he could muster himself again.

***

W hen we left the bank it was growing dark. The pavements were all but deserted and the gaslighters were at work along Threadneedle Street. A coach and pair passed on the way down to Southwark Bridge but otherwise London was strangely quiet after another dog-day afternoon.

Holmes was in a pensive mood as well. "The next part of this case will make poor reading for your audience, Watson," he told me. "There are no leaps of deduction to be made, no sudden discoveries to unfold the plot; merely a series of lengthy and detailed enquiries to confirm certain points which an observer would find tedious."

"I'm willing to accompany you, Holmes. I confess that I'm quite disturbed by the thought of that young lass dying in that cramped metal box in that dark dreary bank vault. I want to find the man responsible and see him hang."

My friend regarded me with a sad gaze. "It was not a single man who was responsible, Watson, and I doubt we can hang the most deserving of them all."

"You apprehend then what has happened to that poor girl?"

"I have the beginnings of a solution; but much must now be determined before I can offer a comprehensive answer. I shall bid you good-night, Watson. Perhaps you would be so good as to attend me again tomorrow

"And now I'm away to the hostelries that sell Black and Swanson's Mild Ales."

afternoon at Merrow's Bank and I will try to satisfy your questions?"

"I would be glad to, Holmes," I agreed. "Can you tell me nothing more to help me understand what I have failed to see today?"

"You have written the principal material with your own hand," my friend told me. He shrugged off his black mood and hefted the beer bottle from the strongbox interior. "And now I'm away to the hostelries that sell Black and Swanson's Mild Ales," he announced, "to search for apprentices of Chumley and Sons."

***

I spent a restless night haunted by the vision of that blood-stained girl. I woke early and found my hand unsteady as I shaved. I was distracted at my surgery and finished as soon as I had attended to the needs of my patients.

I have witnessed many unpleasant things in a lifetime marred by war, and in the course of Holmes' investigations. Few have perturbed me as much as the sight of that sweet child sprawled across the bank's plush carpet, nor the expression of despair upon her pale dead face.

It was early for my appointment at the bank so I found myself wandering down to the coroner's office for a conversation with Havers.

"Your friend has already visited," the police surgeon told me as I entered the pathology room. He pulled a pair of rubber gloves from his hands and dropped them in a bowl beside the washbasin. "Amazing fellow, that Holmes."

"His powers of deduction are remarkable, his character moreso," I agreed. "I take it you were able to confirm whatever observations he made?"

Havers gestured to the half-written case notes on the girl's autopsy. "He was correct in every degree. The girl has known long and sustained hunger and she has worked hard with her hands. There is a faded mark as of a wedding band on her left hand, and she had known a man. Indeed, there are signs that she may have recently been with child but if so she miscarried at an early stage. She died of blood loss from the wound upon her breast."

"Did Holmes say more about her?" I wondered.

"He examined her clothing once more and he suggested a name," Havers reported. "Annie Carter."

"Did Holmes describe how he had come to that name? Or infer anything further from his inspection of the male garments this Annie wore?"

"He noted that the clothes had formerly belonged to a young man of careless habits who had worked as a clerk, probably in trade that involved objects packed in wool and wrapped in canvas. The former owner was right-handed and brown-haired and had occasion to visit the streets around Elephant and Castle." Dr. Havers scratched his head. "Why your friend might assert such things I cannot know."

"You do not know his methods," I replied. "The man's jacket would betray much. Minute ink stains might indicate a careless clerk and the wear on one elbow whether he wrote right or left handed. Tiny fibres on the collar could indicate hair colour. Other traces, of the soft wool dust used in the packing of valuable and delicate items and of the oiled canvas used to protect others might suggest the kind of things with which the wearer would be in contact. Any fleck of mud would also be telling as to where in London it originated. These are but the minor refinements of Holmes' art."

"Holmes also examined the murder weapon," Havers informed me. "He has arranged for it to be taken back to the bank for a briefing he has called. He said that the tale it had to tell was conclusive."

***

My good friend Mr. Sherlock Holmes is often diffident to the point of rudeness; but sometimes when the mood is upon him those months he spent on the stage with the Sasanoff Shakespeare Company[1] tell upon him and he can be as theatrical as any side-show barker. Hence when we were gathered together once more behind closed doors after Merrow's Bank had finished its business for the day Holmes drew in his audience with a performer's skill.

Inspector Jones watched closely like a man waiting to see how a conjurer might produce a rabbit from a top hat. Also present were Dr. Havers, the chief clerk Gould, and the bank's Chairman Sir Abraham Shenney.

Holmes cradled his fingers and touched them to his lips. "Let me say first that what I describe today is a tragedy. I see no way of attaining justice for what has occurred, so I will content myself with at least revealing the truth."

He turned abruptly and strode into the visitor's room where Sir Edmund Pennick had made his gruesome discovery. We all trailed behind him.

---

1 Holmes' American stage tour is described in *The Musgrave Ritual.*

"Are you ready now to reveal the name of the murderer, Holmes?" Athelney Jones asked urgently; perhaps he too had been haunted by Annie's countenance.

"There was no murder," my friend replied. "That was evident from the beginning. The splash-marks upon the girl's dress, the prevalence of blood upon her right hand, the matching stains encrusted upon the dagger – these were the unmistakable marks of suicide."

Mr. Gould snorted sceptically. "Are you suggesting that this person somehow crawled into a Merrow's strongbox for the purpose of destroying herself?"

"I am suggesting that finding herself trapped in such a strongbox with no means of escaping, confined in a vault with limited air, unable to summon help because it was the weekend and nobody was around to hear her she succumbed to the despair that was all too evident upon her face and she sought an easier end to her existence than the starvation or suffocation which she thought her only alternatives."

"That is horrible, Holmes!" I cried.

"There is another reason she may have had for ending her life of which I will speak shortly," the great detective replied.

"But who is she?" demanded old Shenney. "How did she come to be in our most secure strongbox?"

"Secure?" Holmes challenged. "I was able to pick the lock on your 'secure strongbox' in under a minute. Any competent locksmith could do so using nothing more than a thin-bladed needle-knife."

"Such as Annie used to kill herself!" I exclaimed.

"Annie?" Inspector Jones asked. He and the others had not yet learned the name of the dead girl.

"I perceive that Dr. Watson has been investigating me as I have been investigating Annie Carter," Holmes noted. "Doubtless Dr. Havers here has told him of my identification of Miss Annie Carter, born 19th June 1876 in Brook Street, in the shadow of the Bethlehem Asylum where her mother ended her days."

"You know her, then!" Jones exclaimed. "How?"

Holmes summarised his conclusions from the medical evidence and from a study of Annie's clothing much as I had earlier. He called upon Havers for occasional technical verification. "Given Kent Road as a starting point for my investigations it was no great matter to locate the church orphanage on Hampton Street and have the governess there identify the image of an inmate who had left her charge less than one year ago."

"But how came she here?" demanded Sir Abraham, "And into Sir Edmund's box?"

"All will become clear," Holmes assured us. "Indeed, the whole solution suggested itself once I observed Watson's helpful listing of when and by whom the vault had been accessed."

"How so?" Gould could not resist asking; after all, the same information had been available to him.

Holmes obliged him with an explanation. "It seemed to me that Miss Carter had gone willingly into that box." He deferred to Havers for confirmation that there was no sign of bruising to suggest that she had struggled when she was fitted so tightly in a foetal position inside the container. "You will remember also that she took with her sufficient water in an old beer bottle to keep her hydrated for a long wait, yet not so much as to prompt her to other natural functions."

"She chose to hide, then," I agreed. "To rob the bank?"

"How could she rob the bank?" objected Gould. "Even if Mr. Holmes' scurrilous suggestion that he could break our locks is correct, there is no way to reach the lock from inside the box."

"Nor any need to," Holmes replied, "if the box was returned to the vault unlocked."

"Are you suggesting that Sir Edward Pennick was an accomplice to this deed?" demanded old Shenney.

"I am not."

"The whole plot is nonsense!" objected Gould. "Even if the girl got into the vault she could not escape her box. When the containers are stored there is no way to open the doors – only the side with the handle on it remains exposed on the shelving."

"But before they are stored away each night they are left on their trolleys by the far wall!" I remembered. "Left unattended all day – a fact revealed to Annie when she 'accidentally' encountered a young clerk she had noticed noticing her on her previous visits to this bank. A small girl concealed within an unattended unfiled container could slip out and get to any of the boxes in the vault!"

"And one who came prepared with the right instrument and sufficient training might open any of them and extract their contents," Holmes agreed.

"A robbery, then!" Jones cried. "But... we found no stolen goods in Sir Edmund's strongbox."

"Nor would you," Holmes answered. His triumphant explanations seemed suddenly to let him down. His face became graver, colder. "Annie

Carter never intended to get into Sir Edmund Pennick's strongbox."

"What do you mean?" I wondered. "Holmes?"

My friend stirred from whatever bitter thoughts assailed him. "Annie Carter left the orphanage as she approached her fourteenth birthday," he told us. "She was found a domestic position based on the recommendation of the governess who accounted her a good girl, kind, diligent, and honest. She went to work in the household of Mr. Daniel Routledge of 65 Stratton Street."

Gould looked up sharply. "Mr. Routledge is a client. He visits his strongbox every Wednesday – except for yesterday, when we had been forced to close."

Holmes went on. "It was during her time in Routledge's service that Annie Carter acquired a wedding ring – and a child."

"A secret marriage?" I wondered. "But..."

"A pretend marriage," Holmes replied, "perpetrated to convince an innocent young girl new to the world to go to the bed of an accomplished seducer. I have found two other young women who now live sordid lives of shame in the East End who testify that Mr. Routledge used similar methods to convince them to surrender their virtue."

"That cad," I growled; now the despair in Annie's eyes had cause.

"I doubt their evidence would gain a conviction even for breach of promise," Holmes warned. "In any case, Annie Carter found herself carrying a child and blaming her employer. Shortly thereafter she was dismissed without references and cast onto the street. I have interviewed other of Routledge's staff to confirm the circumstances."

"How does that bring her here, though?" Gould demanded.

Holmes turned to Inspector. "You have the judge's warrants to allow us to open two of the strongboxes, Inspector? I trust you raise no objection to this legal process, Sir Abraham?"

"I'll stand aside for the law when the law has due process," agreed the Chairman of Merrow's Bank. "May I enquire which boxes you wish to open?"

Holmes answered him as Gould unlocked the vault for us and led us to the chamber where the large boxes were stored. "The first container is that of Francis Routledge, which I expect to find empty. The second is the container wherein Miss Carter transferred the contents, and there I am not sure what I will find."

"But which container?" persisted old Shenney.

"Watson?" Holmes prompted me.

"Box A84," I ventured, "the one taken by a new client, one Mr. Browning, on the day Routledge last visited his box."

"The same," agreed Holmes. "And can you venture to tell me how Miss Carter came to be concealed in a strongbox in the first place, and therefore who Mr. Daniel Browning is likely to be?"

I confessed that I could not.

"When Annie found herself destitute she was rescued," Holmes revealed. "She was taken in by a young man she had known at the orphanage, a young man who had been apprenticed at Chumley and Sons Antique Dealers at Elephant and Castle."

"The clothing!" I recalled.

"Cut down to disguise that the second man sent to deposit in Chumley's box was actually a girl. You mentioned that Chumley's was amongst those companies who prefer a second visitor for integrity, Mr. Gould?"

Gould was stiff and icy. "I rather think that the duty clerk who attended the visitors would notice if one of them had vanished, Mr. Holmes."

"Not if the visit took place over lunch-time, when the rota changes and a different clerk lets the visitor out than saw two visitors in," Holmes suggested. "Nor would Mr. Chumley be aware whether the clerks he sent both attended or if one of them slipped away to visit his young lady, allowing the other to instead take Miss Carter in disguise. I have a confession from one Stephen Williams that was induced to slope away and call upon the object of his desire on both occasions he was recently sent to the bank. He saw it as a kindness that his fellow clerk Thomas Winney was so willing to assist his romance."

"Winney was the lad who took in Annie?" I surmised.

"And formerly something of a street Arab with a talent for locks," Holmes replied. "A talent he clearly passed on to Miss Carter."

Jones was struggling to keep up but he tried manfully. "Annie Carter and this Winney conspired to rob the bank?"

"To rob Routledge," I guessed. "After Routledge had robbed Annie of her virtue and perhaps cost her a child. Annie knew what Routledge kept in his strongbox. She'd accompanied him here several times when he'd visited it."

By now Holmes has located box A66. He opened it with the same disconcerting deftness he had demonstrated before, to the dismay of Gould and Shenney and the discomfit of Jones. His instrument was the dagger that had ended Annie's life.

And for once my friend was wrong: Routledge's box was not empty. It contained nothing except a simple cheap wedding ring.

"Ahh," sighed Sherlock Holmes. "Annie Carter was more than I allowed." He turned quickly to the second box. "You may be interested to know that banns were published two weeks since for the marriage of Miss Carter and Mr. Winney. Likewise travel papers were applied for and passage booked on the steamer Laurence to Canada. They clearly intended to use the proceeds of their theft to escape their current life and begin anew."

Jones could not contain himself any further. "But how?" he exploded.

Holmes opened box A84. It contained a treasure trove of bank-notes, golden sovereigns, and plate. My friend closed his eyes sadly.

"Holmes?" I prompted.

"Winney came disguised as Browning to take a strongbox here," he said. "He returned again in his role as Chumley's clerk and accessed not only the small strongbox he'd been sent to maintain, B293, but also the larger and less frequently used ones, A11 and A22. He had to pick the lock of those, of course, for he'd not been provided with the keys. He transferred all the contents to A22 and hid Annie in A11 so she'd be taken back to the vaults. There she could remove the contents of Routledge's box to Browning's. The next day he returned to retrieve Annie from A11 and then later in his guise of Daniel Browning to withdraw the stolen goods from A84."

Jones shook his head. "Your theory does not stand, Holmes. This Annie was not in the Chumley box. She was in Sir Edmund's."

"Ah, Sir Edmund... You will find Sir Edmund's missing property, a collection of exotic Parisian lithographs, in A11, where Winney replaced it believing it to be the original contents of that box. Of course it was not."

We all exchanged puzzled glances.

Holmes looked tired and dispirited. All his earlier flair was gone. "The porter Partridge is of advancing years. His eyesight is failing. When given the card to bring the strongbox to the viewing room on 4th September he read the request as being for box A17 instead of A11."

Suddenly it all fell into place for me, the whole tragedy. "Annie thought she was getting into the Chumley box, but wasn't. The next day Winney came back to fetch her but the actual Chumley box was brought, and of course she wasn't in it. She was trapped in Sir Edmund's box, now replaced in its drawer from which there was no escape."

"Who knows what those two young people thought?" Holmes reflected. "He wondering where she had gone – and yet the proceeds of the crime were waiting for him in Browning's box. She wondering why her rescuer did not come, fearing she had been betrayed again, struggling in the claustrophobic dark against a growing suspicion that she had been abandoned to her fate; until despair and horror overcame her and she took her life."

Jones, Havers, and the bankers looked sober at this chain of reasoning.

"Winney could have come forward," Jones suggested.

"And face certain arrest," I realised. "Yet he did not take the haul."

"And that suggests," Holmes told us soberly, "that Thomas Winney too has no further need of mortal goods."

***

We found Winney hanging in his rooms, the seedy single-bedroom slum he'd shared with Annie Carter. Their desperate struggle for escape from their lot had taken them out of this world. Nothing could be done against Francis Routledge. Holmes curtly declined the man's offer of a reward for the return of his treasure. I gave the cad a piece of my mind; had Routledge dared to demur I'd have gladly thrashed him within an inch of his life.

Holmes never mentioned Annie Carter again and it is only with the utmost reluctance that I now commit this account to paper to illustrate that sometimes even the brilliance of my friend can only explain and not prevent human tragedy. Even Sherlock Holmes may be hurt by the suffering of stained innocents; as can we all.

The Mystery of Mr. Holmes

There's a mystery behind Mr. Sherlock Holmes; beyond the canon stories of precise detection and fantastic obfuscation, past the "missing episodes" with which Watson tantalises his readers; further even than the speculations about Holmes' secret months after Reichenbach "under the name of Sigerson".

The character fascinates and resonates. Holmes is analytical and precise in his thinking, he seeks to restore justice, he aids the desperate, yet suffers from character defects of untidiness, rudeness, callousness and antisociability that would usually render him a most unlikeable fellow. He makes it hard for a reader to empathise with him, because the very act of watching Holmes' thought processes destroys the heart of the detective stories in which he features. Yet he continues to inspire and enthrall new generations in his original canon, in new literary ventures, in film, on stage, and beyond even that in the wider consciousness of popular culture. Why?

In writing additional Holmes stories, the author has to grapple with these questions. If one cannot understand the broad appeal which Holmes satisfies one must at least intuit it enough to offer more of the same.

One key is John Watson, M.D. As our usual point-of-view window upon the Great Detective – and indeed often our narrative interpreter of his moods and motives – Watson offers the humanising, compassionate picture that tempers Holmes' otherwise intolerable arrogance. We love and admire Holmes because Watson does.

Another is that Holmes almost inevitably assists those being oppressed by evil against those who would perpetrate it. He's a very devil, but he's our devil, set on against fiends far worse than he who are guilty of crimes far greater than being careless with a slipper full of tobacco or inconsiderate in the matter of late-night violin playing. A kinder, gentler consulting detective would not be so much fun when the game is afoot.

Credit, too, to Conan Doyle, who quickly identified that Holmes' negative traits could be used in positive ways to keep the character compelling. How much of Holmes' behaviour is eccentric and how much a calculated pose to aid his detection is left to the reader to decide; in fact reading and judging Holmes for oneself is part of the Sherlock reader's experience

Additional Holmes fiction can too easily pass into pastiche and thence into satire. If we simply invoke the trappings – the pipe, the deerstalker, Lestrade and Jones and Mrs. Hudson, the familiar tropes of brougham and country house, the hackneyed phrases of "Remarkable, Holmes!" and "Elementary" – then we miss the heart of Holmes' mystery. More than the furniture of his stories, Sherlock Holmes depends upon the enigma of his own self to address the enigmas laid before him. We depend upon Dr. Watson to offer us up the clues to solving Holmes as Holmes solves his cases. A mystery solves the mystery, and readers are invited to ponder both.

It is a privilege for a new writer to be allowed to venture into the mystery and offer another small strand to the tangled affair. Fortunately Holmes can always be counted upon to make the mystery turn out well.

IW
Yorkshire, England, 30th December 2009

SHERLOCK HOLMES
CONSULTING DETECTIVE

"The Adventure
of the
Phantom Raiders"

by
Andrew Salmon

A s I write these lines, I am once again reminded and astounded by how much civilization has progressed in the intervening years since I first crossed paths with the inestimable Sherlock Holmes. I can recall vividly dashing hither and yon on some adventure in a rollicking hansom along streets choked with humanity and now we have automobiles, great lighter than air craft in the sky and telephones to span the miles. However our progress has come also with a terrible price. The Great War left its black mark on us all, and the harsh cruelty of death lingers in our eyes. In poring over my notes made during those years, it is with sadness that I realize there are a number of incidents I had once concealed, believing society was not ready for them, which now seem almost banal in their tragedy and consequence.

For this reason I set about to tell the tale of the Phantom Raiders. I have looked over my notes on the adventure of Tesla's Nightmare as well as those hastily scribbled lines for the Spider Men of Nantucket and these may also find their way to the public eye if breath remains in my failing body to set them down. At first tucked away lest they terrify what I can only refer to as an innocent, unsuspecting world, they can now, sadly, be perused for entertainment today by a populace inured to the grotesque and horrible.

My notes reveal to me that the Adventure of the Phantom Raiders began mid-April in the year 1903 when I chanced to visit my friend Sherlock Holmes with whom I had had no contact for some months. It was early evening and seasonably cool. Holmes had just finished dinner. My friend was much changed since I had seen him last. Although fully recovered from the severe beating he'd suffered at the hands of hired thugs, which has been set down in the Adventure of the Illustrious Client, Holmes seemed almost to be suffering from some form of enfeeblement. Not of the body, but, rather, of the soul. He appeared to have lost weight and his every gesture seemed tinged with a deep fatigue which, at the time, I could not fathom. It was only as the year drew to a close that what lay behind these alterations to my friend were revealed to me.

Holmes greeted me warmly and beckoned me to my habitual chair by the fire. He lit a pipe and proceeded to blow fragrant clouds of smoke into the air. I had brought a fine Havana for the occasion and got it going smartly.

All of London was abuzz with talk of the Phantom Raiders of Portsmouth: a group of ruthless thieves responsible for the loss of thousands of pounds worth of goods which had seemingly vanished from the docks without a trace. The police were baffled and I knew with certainty that Holmes was well informed on the matter as he was with most things of this nature. Of course, one would have to have put wax in one's ears when going about town to avoid hearing talk of it at the time.

I very much wanted to hear his thoughts on the incredible goings on in the southern portion of the country but Holmes simply sat there with his knees drawn up and smoked in silence. I could not tell if he was awaiting some visitor or if his once capacious universe had shrunk down to his pipe and he believed the world outside our windows could go hang. Though long familiar with the great moods my friend was capable of tumbling into, my distance from him over those months made him more of an enigma than was usual ,and I did not quite know how to approach him.

The strained silence was interrupted by the tromp of feet outside on the landing. Mrs. Hudson voice came muffled through the door but she was clearly addressing a gentlemen. A sharp rap on our door signalled the visitor's desire to enter. I cast a glance at Holmes who appeared oblivious to everything that was transpiring.

The door was opened by Mrs. Hudson and she motioned in a tall, lean man with an open red face behind a thick walrus moustache and deep set eyes that missed nothing from behind spectacles. The man was dressed in a suit of the finest blue flannel and the bowler Mrs. Hudson held for the gentlemen was as clean and smooth as a cannonball.

"A Mr. Cornelius E. Rogers to see Mr. Holmes," announced Mrs. Hudson.

As Holmes made no move to greet the man I took it upon myself to welcome him. I shook his hand and offered him a chair.

Rogers glanced at the table still set for dining and dipped his head apologetically.

"I did not mean to intrude on you dinner. Forgive me."

"A Mr. Cornelius E. Rogers to see Mr. Holmes."

"It is no matter," I replied, resuming my seat by the fire.

"The purpose of your visit, if you please."

This last whispered utterance came from Sherlock Holmes nestled in the shadowed depths of his chair. Rogers gave a start, then leaned forward to scrutinize the obscured figure of my friend.

"Ah, Mr. Holmes!" Rogers's countenance brightened. "You are at home, I am glad to see. I am here on a matter of great import."

"Yes, the Portsmouth robberies. Let's dispense with trifles."

Rogers stiffened again at this bit of deduction on the part of Holmes, "But how – "

Holmes sighed. "If you must know. There is a whiff of the sea about you. Your garments, though of the finest quality, are of a southern cut and style and your tongue is tinged with the coast accent. Your hasty voyage to see me rather than telephoning and your subtle state of dishevelment reveal to me that you are a gentleman upon whom calamity has not been a recent visitor. This hasty run up to London to enlist my services either betrays an impulsive nature or that you are merely at your wit's end. I favour the former. All perfectly obvious to those who have eyes to see. I could go on, but shall leave further revelations to you."

Rogers smiled broadly. "Your reputation precedes you, Mr. Holmes. Correct on all counts. I head the Empire Steam Packet Company which does business in Portsmouth where I was born and raised. Remarkable."

Sherlock Holmes gave the briefest of nods. Silence hung about the room as Rogers's countenance became grave once more.

"These accursed raiders will be the ruin of us all!" said he, at last, his frame quivering with the utterance. "Mr. Holmes, I implore you to aid us in ending their reign of terror. You can name your price, sir."

Holmes looked away and I saw the firelight dance in his grey eyes. He set his lips in a hard line as if in the throes of some personal struggle. He closed his eyes for the briefest of moments, then, in one motion, they snapped open and he turned his head to glare at Rogers. When he spoke, his tone was soft and easy with not the slightest hint of strain.

"The facts of the case. If you would be so kind."

Rogers hesitated, then said, "Surely the newspapers have played the thing up. All of England is ringing with it."

"Hearsay and supposition," countered Holmes. "I prefer to hear of the matter directly from someone intimately connected to the crimes."

"Very well." Rogers sprang to his feet and moved about the room with a long stride. "The devils strike without warning, always under cover of darkness, plucking our very best right off the dock. They use smoke to obscure their actions and cover their escape."

Holmes steepled his fingers. "And the police?"

"We have taken every measure to stop these fiends. First we armed our own but that did not produce results. Therefore we demanded the police be brought in. They investigated, patrolled the docks, stationed night watchmen while ships were unloaded – all to no avail!"

"Have they turned up nothing?" asked I, incredulously.

"Not a blessed thing! My associates and I are at a loss!"

Holmes lowered his hands, resting them on his thighs. "Your problem interests me, and I am prepared to look into it. How may I keep in touch with you?"

"I return to Portsmouth in the morning. I can be reached by telegraph, however."

"Excellent. Now, if you will permit me to begin, I shall turn my not inconsiderable resources to the problem."

When our visitor had left us, Holmes sat immobile, lost in deep thought, for some fifteen minutes.

"Well, Watson, what do you make of it?" asked he at last.

"I should think we'll be running down to Portsmouth at first light."

"I agree it may come to that. However, it might be possible to forgo the trip altogether. Shinwell Johnson may shed some light on the matter."

While putting together these memoirs, I have seldom drawn my cases from the latter years of my friend's career. In the early years of the century Shinwell Johnson was a valuable assistant to Sherlock Holmes, though his inauspicious beginnings seemed destined to steer him into the grave prematurely. Johnson began public life as a lethal villain, serving two terms at Parkhurst before seeing the error of his ways. A changed man, Johnson allied himself with Holmes and became his eyes and ears in the huge criminal underworld afflicting London. In this capacity he kept Holmes supplied with information much of which proved invaluable. He was a quick-witted, observant fellow and, with the mark of Cain upon him, was readily accepted into criminal circles. If anyone could shed light on the gang of thieves the papers were calling the Phantom Raiders, Shinwell Johnson was that man.

As it was growing late and I had patients to attend to in the morning, I bid Holmes good night and left him with the telephone in hand while he put in a call to Johnson.

Two days passed, during which time I carried out my professional responsibilities. My only connection to the case came by means of the papers which were playing up the most recent escapades of the Phantom Raiders. They had struck again on the eve of the second night and special editions had been issued covering what little anyone knew about the daring heist. The papers were vague in their facts but hinted that something of great value had been seized and, perhaps, there was some naval involvement. It was only later that I learned that facts were concealed deliberately in the hopes of preventing a scandal.

This got me thinking that I really should check in on my friend and see how he was getting along with the matter. It was while preparing to do so that I received an invitation from Holmes to dine with him and shortly thereafter I found myself seated across from him in Simpson's at our small table in the front window looking down at the roiling stream of humanity on the Strand.

We finished our tea, then Holmes set his cup down, saying, "We must depart for Portsmouth to-morrow."

"I take it Shinwell Johnson has failed."

"Quite the contrary, he succeeded."

"I am afraid your reasoning escapes me."

"Only because you do not have all the facts. Allow me to rectify that with a question: Do the actions of these so-called Phantom Raiders seem to you to be the usual pattern for the typical street thug or deft Johnny?"

"Hardly. The ability of the gang to dodge so large a drag net would render the possibility of them being common thieves impossible."

"While observing anything, dear Watson, once must never jump to conclusions, even when they are correct. As it turns out we are of the same mind with regard to the gang. They are most uncommon. This was my first assumption upon Rogers's visit. However, I had to be certain."

"So you sent Shinwell Johnson into the underworld, where he was unable to root up any connection between the raiders and the criminal element."

"Excellent, Watson! You have hit the nail on the head. Yes, we are dealing with a singular breed of criminal and we must take the hunt to them. Thus we're away to Portsmouth where, by cunning and method, we shall haul them into the light of day. I have sent word to Rogers, asking him to meet up with us when we arrive."

I asked Holmes to send word when he was ready to depart and begged off the rest of our meal in the hopes of getting a head start on the myriad preparations I needed to make before the sun rose. At that time, my practice had grown and was able to sustain both myself and my wife in a manner best described as comfortable. However, in so doing, I had immersed myself in a life that did not allow for one to drop everything and dash off. I had obligations and responsibilities to my patients and my staff. Obligations that kept me occupied well into the night.

When I greeted the sunrise bleary-eyed but ready to set out, it was with a mixture of confusion and vexation that I learned that no communiqué from Sherlock Holmes awaited my attention. I could not make heads nor tails of the matter over breakfast and decided to set it aside until such time as Holmes felt fit to contact me. As I had botched some of my nocturnal scrambling hours before, I dedicated myself to setting them right fully expecting a hasty note from my friend at any moment. None was forthcoming while I ate my lunch. It was while I watched the steward laying out my tea that the message I had waited all day for finally came. Sure enough it was from Holmes and it informed me that we were booked on the 4:00 p.m. train.

I found Holmes waiting for me on the station platform.

"Why have you left our departure so late?" asked I, slightly out of breath from my mad dash to the station.

"I assumed you required time to set your business affairs in order."

Some twenty minutes later we found ourselves nestled in the comfortable splendour of the mahogany-coloured carriages on the South Western Main Line, rattling down to Portsmouth. The dim, cool comfort permitted me the chance to catch up on some of the sleep I'd missed the night before. As I settled in to the plush seat, Holmes was content to stare out the window with that singular look of his I knew so well. It was a look that revealed deep concentration and he was no more aware of the surrounding countryside than I was minutes later when I fell into deep slumber.

When next I opened my eyes it was at the urging of Holmes who was nudging my shoulder insistently.

"What?" I stammered. "What has happened?"

"Calm yourself, Watson. We need to switch lines. That is all."

I shook my head to drive the last remnants of slumber from my clouded brain. Gazing out the window I could see through the billowing steam from the locomotive that we were pulling into Fratton Station, a mere two stops from our destination.

"Switch lines? Whatever for? We're but an hour from Portsmouth Harbour Station."

"We must switch nonetheless."

"Has there been some word of trouble on the line up ahead?"

"None so far as I know."

"Then, why – "

"Watson, pray come! Our connecting train departs in six minutes. There's no time to lose."

No other option remained for me other than to hastily gather my belongings and follow Holmes up the walkway and down the steps to the station platform. There Holmes asked a conductor for the engine bound for Town Station and received a curt reply. Holmes urged me on and we obtained tickets, then fell into our coach seats scant seconds before the train to Town gave a great lurch and ground forward. I set my hat upon a wall peg and stared across at Holmes expectantly.

"All right, Holmes," said I. "What's the meaning behind catching a train which will not reach our destination?"

Holmes sat impassively, as calm and comfortable as though we'd been in these seats since London. He waved a hand casually and said, "Oh, I was merely trying to avoid any further needless delay. The misdirection has gone on long enough." I could glean no further explanation from him.

Town Station was a squat, unassuming little shack on the spur line. However, after we had alighted from the car, Holmes led me to a locked gate flanked by two Royal Marines. As we were in the middle of nowhere, I could think of no possible reason for their presence.

"No farther, sirs," one of the Marines addressed us as Holmes came up to them.

Holmes said, affably, "Forgive me. A word of explanation is in order. We were enlisted by Admiral Edward Rogers to come here. Now, please, if you would be so kind as to open the gate and allow us to pass."

I turned to Holmes, stunned. "Admiral?"

Holmes ignored my query and kept his eyes riveted on the Marines.

"We've no orders concerning anything like that, sirs. Now along with you."

Holmes smiled benignly at the Marine. "May I have your name, sir?"

"It's Cherry. Harold Cherry."

"Ah, very good. Mr. Cherry, if you would kindly call in to your superior and ask him if he has any orders concerning Mr. Sherlock Holmes and Dr. John H. Watson, we would be eternally in your debt."

Cherry, suspicious now, said, "I just might do that if you was thinking of testing my resolve."

"Nothing of the sort, sir. Put the call through. It will clear up the matter in an instant."

Cherry became suddenly nervous and his eyes flicked from Holmes to his partner at the other side of the gate.

"Hamill!" barked Cherry. "Get on the wire and see if there's any word."

The Marine named Hamill disappeared inside a small hut adjacent to the gate. Holmes idly withdrew a cigarette from his case and lit it, puffing stoically in the evening breeze. Hamill returned presently and, not meeting our eyes, inclined his head stiffly to Cherry who was still barring our way. Hamill whispered something to Cherry and the man blanched. Cherry came to stiff attention and stepped to one side. He turned and unlocked the gate from a key on the ring dangling at his waist and opened the door for us.

"Begging your pardons, sirs. A Pullman has been ordered to take you in. It should be here directly."

Holmes tossed his cigarette on to the tracks and turned to Cherry. "Thank you, my good man. I commend you on carrying out your duties."

Holmes glanced slyly over his shoulder at me as he stepped through the gate. "Come along, Watson. We mustn't keep the Admiral waiting."

To say I was stupefied as we passed through the gate and made our way down a short staircase to the covered platform would be an understatement. I felt as though I'd been in a fever for a fortnight and had wakened to find the entire world had changed. A cluster of Marines loitered at the foot of the stairs, but none of them interfered with our progress and I was forced to conclude that once we had passed muster with Sergeant Cherry we were all right as far as they were concerned. They moved off as Holmes and I strode up the platform to a worn wooden bench. Holmes sat and crossed his knees, the very portrait of ease. I, on the other hand, was still trying to wrap my head around what has happened.

"Confound it, Holmes, what the deuce is going on?"

"My good friend, don't tell me you were fooled by the lacklustre disguise Admiral Rogers attempted to hide behind when he first came to see us."

"I was. Utterly."

"Really? Then perhaps the disguise was not so bad as that. At any rate, Admiral Rogers was immediately recognizable to me at Baker Street."

"You've met previously?"

"No. But certain members of the Admiralty had been invited to dine at Buckingham Palace nine days ago and the papers carried a photo commemorating the event. I recognized the man through his disguise from that photo."

"I saw the one you mean. But the photo was of the entire entourage and was poorly reproduced. Do you mean to tell me that you were able to recognize someone from that photo while their features were concealed? Why, I had a time recognizing the King in the photo!"

"You underestimate your abilities. That I was able to pierce Rogers's disguise I can merely put down as a consequence of careful observation. Nothing more."

"And did you know about this closed-off section of track?"

"This is the Admiralty Line and runs directly to the Naval Yards. The track is reserved solely for the use of Naval officers though we shall make use of it today. Perhaps there's a commission in the Royal Navy after this affair is concluded."

"No, thank you very much indeed."

The train rattled in, belching steam. It was a small engine dwarfed by the single Pullman it placed in front of us. We climbed aboard and stepped inside a spacious, though spartan compartment decorated like a club car one might find on a commercial train. There was a bar along one wall and fat leather chairs of a burgundy hue. Holmes took one of these and I sat on the sofa nearby. The train set off immediately.

"But why the masquerade?" asked I, resuming the conversation we'd begun on the platform. "Could not the Admiral have stated the matter plainly?"

"Pride, Watson. That is all. Pride of the fleet. We revere our Navy and its noble officers. If an Admiral of the Fleet was seen skulking into the rooms of a civilian seeking aid on a matter they could not handle themselves, why, it would be scandalous. The disguise Rogers adopted was not solely for our benefit. It was for all of London to see. His deceptions concerning his name and occupation were also a safety measure as he could not be sure of our tongues or our discretion. I trust we have satisfied him on both counts. We took the civilian train down, we transferred with no fanfare other than your bemusement and did not reveal who our employer was until we were face to face with other representatives of the Navy. That should, I trust, clear the air and allow us to conduct our investigation unfettered."

"I half suspected that last theft had an unwarranted air of mystery about it. That is, if it was a simple theft as the papers would have us believe."

"You are exactly right, Watson. The nature of that theft is our reason for coming here unannounced. We have something of a time constraint if I read the signs correctly. This is why I did not want to waste another minute guarding the reputation of the Navy or waiting for a formal invitation from Admiral Rogers. We must investigate the matter straight off."

It was Admiral Rogers himself who met us at the station a scant fifteen minutes later. Sans moustache and spectacles and looking smart in the deep blue of the Royal Navy, I could see more than a passing resemblance to one of the figures in the photograph Holmes had mentioned seeing earlier. I could never have put a name to the vaguely remembered features from the photograph. Then again, I was not Sherlock Holmes.

"Remarkable, Mr. Holmes!" said Rogers as we stepped down from the car. "Truly remarkable!"

He shook our hands stiffly and, aside from the smile on his face, everything in his demeanour bespoke his profession.

"I trust our coming here was not too much of a shock," said Holmes.

"Hardly, considering your reputation. If I might have a moment, please accept my apologies for my earlier clandestine actions. The Navy. You know how it is."

"I do, indeed. Now, let that be the last on the subject. You asked us to look into these thefts and here we are. Let's have at it."

Admiral Rogers motioned us forward and we walked out from under the roofed platform. A pleasant sea breeze emboldened us after the enclosed Pullman. The sun was on the wan and all about us glimmered as though gilded.

"Where do you wish to begin?" asked Rogers. "Perhaps a brief history of the thefts is in order? They began up the coast at the civilian docks. Between the police and ourselves there is too much coastline to cover though we gave it our all. These efforts did produce some results, however: the raiders have taken the fight to us, striking right here in this very yard last night. Don't ask me how. If they've decided to leave civilian shipping alone, well, that's something at least."

"Thank you, Admiral. With your indulgence, I would like to use the last of the light to examine the scene of the theft which occurred today in the wee hours before dawn."

"Certainly. As I expected you at some point today, I ordered the area to be left as it was at the time of the accursed bandits struck. Right this way."

The Admiral had an open touring car awaiting him and we climbed inside. A word to the driver and we rolled along the narrow, cobblestone street towards the docks. Sea gulls cried at the gnawing hunger in their bellies and the dying of the light. Seamen were coming and going brusquely from every doorway set in the low, stone structures on either side of the road and the place fairly bristled with Marines stationed all about, including the rooftops. Every path, road and track led to the sea. Aside from glimpses of the water through the alleys between the structures, the only evidence that we grew near to the water was the very forest of masts stabbing at the sky. These sights were punctuated now and then with the deep bass roar of steamship whistles as the great vessels grumbled amongst themselves.

Presently we came to a courtyard bordered by one-storey wooden storehouses. The ground here sloped gently to the sea which, with our view at last free of obstructions, was laid out before us like an immense bed of embers in the glow of the setting sun.

"Here we are, gentlemen," said Rogers as the breeze stirred the gold epaulets at his shoulders. "My men and the grounds are at your disposal."

"Most kind, Admiral," said Holmes. "I wonder if I might trouble you for a few minutes more of your time."

"For this, of course. However, I remind you I have other duties."

"I will be the soul of brevity, I assure you."

"Proceed."

"All right, then. To begin, let's confirm that it was the Yard payroll which was taken in this last raid."

The Admiral jerked at this extraordinary revelation as though galvanized, shook his head in wonderment and then nodded once in the affirmative.

"Did the theft occur from one of the storerooms or while cargo was being offloaded?"

"We had a barge transferring stores from one of our steamers. The thieves struck while the men were on their way to the storeroom closest to the pier. I'll be damned if I know how they were away so quickly. The chest they stole weighed twenty stone – too much for even two men to carry on the run."

"Your men were attacked from behind?"

"None survived. But that is the look of it."

"Ah, that is curious. Were those guards on the rooftops present as they are now?"

"I have had round the clock watches since the first civilian theft. I see what you are driving at, sir. The men ferrying ship's stores would have their backs to the sea with guards posted in front of them. You are hypothesizing that the raiders struck from the sea."

"The thought had occurred to me."

"If you would both come with me for a moment," said Rogers, rising to his feet. "Barrows, keep the engine running."

And with that Admiral Rogers stepped down. He had a telescope in his fist. We followed him down to the pier. A stone retaining wall bordered the beach and wooden docks lolled out over the smooth sand and the sea.

Admiral Rogers extended the collapsible scope and expertly put it to his eye as he aimed the device out over the water. He guided it with machine-like precision born of long experience until it came to a stop on the right. He snapped the glass down and handed it to Holmes.

"Six degrees to starboard," he instructed my friend. "Off that freighter's stern in the foreground."

Holmes raised the glass and followed instructions, bringing it to the spot Rogers had indicated.

"Does that answer your question?" asked Rogers.

"It does, indeed."

Holmes handed the instrument to me and I put it to my eye. The sea was of a golden hue, then blurred as I sighted. Then the lens came to rest on a nest of odd funnel shapes jutting out of the water. The sight resembled the pipes atop the bridge of a steamship only there was no ship beneath these. My first thought was that a ship had scuttled in the harbour and only the slender funnels remained above the surface. Upon further scrutiny I recognized that what I was looking at were the air tubes of a submersible.

"HMS *A1*," began Rogers. "She's British designed, built by Vickers at Barrow-in-Furness. She's an improvement on the US Plunger Class. The submersible has the very best battery-powered electric motors when submerged and shaft-drive Wolsely petrol engines to move her up top. She'll manage ten knots on the surface and six underwater. With an 18-inch torpedo tube and three reloads, she is 105 feet of British ingenuity. We've had her patrolling the harbour for the last four months when she's not conducting mock attacks. Believe me, Mr. Holmes, there is no way the raiders could get past her if they were staging their attacks from the sea. That's the one line of approach we are certain of."

"Very impressive. If she's been in the harbour since before the attacks began, it's possible her crew might have spotted something. I should like the chance to speak with them, if it can be arranged."

"I suppose something could be arranged. If you don't mind being ferried out to her. We are also conducting a test of human endurance for submersible habitation. The two officers and nine ratings won't set foot on

Holmes handed the instrument to me and I put it to my eye.

land for another three weeks as part of the experiment."

"That is most intriguing, Admiral," said Holmes, clearly impressed. "I shall welcome a run out to them at your earliest convenience."

"I shall see to it at once. Well, Holmes, I shall leave you to it. Quarters have been prepared for you both and I'll have your things brought there. Now I simply cannot spare another moment. Find these fiends, sir. That is all I ask. Until tomorrow, then."

Holmes remained gazing out at the submersible barely discernable by the naked eye. I handed the Admiral his telescope and the man returned to his automobile. A throaty roar of the engine signalled the Admiral's departure. When I turned back to my friend, I noticed a wistful expression on his face as he looked out on the harbour. I followed his gaze and through clouds of steam from docked freighters, I saw what had so captivated him. It appeared to be an old ship of the line. She bobbed at anchor, all of her sails stripped away. The decades had not been kind to her. Algae coated most of her hull and the yellow and black paint typical of the class was all but faded and had been scraped by time and wind down to the bare wood. She was in a dreadful state and I wondered how she could even stay afloat in such poor condition.

"*Victory*," whispered Holmes.

"You are mistaken, Holmes. Surely." I did not believe for a second that the ship we were looking at was HMS *Victory* – that once proud ship from which Lord Nelson had led the fleet, outnumbered and outgunned, to triumph at Trafalgar.

"That is she," said Holmes, his voice barely a whisper. "Watson, it was not quite a century ago, in October of 1805, that *Victory* and the fleet sailed out to meet Napoleon's Franco-Spanish armada. Now she is reduced to this: a buoy for ships better built to navigate around as she rots at her keel, her brave crew and commander all but dust in their graves. Is this what follows greatness? Is this how we reach our end? If so proud a ship and legacy can be left to the ravages of time after such great and lofty service, what awaits us all? Perhaps it is time that I disappear into that little farm of my dreams."

Holmes was seldom so melancholy and I was unsure what to say to lift him out of it.

"I think of those future generations who may come upon your little narratives of our adventures – should they survive down through the years – and wonder what those people will make of us? Will our meagre struggles matter a wit to them? Beyond a source of outdated amusement, I mean. In a world where progress is the only constant, I have my doubts."

Holmes turned about and put his back to the sea. He seemed to shake himself slightly as though settling a thick cloak upon his shoulders.

"Enough of such dreary musings!" said he, at last, and his austere grey eyes flashed. "The raiders! What say you, Watson?"

I would have much preferred to finish our discussion of the inevitable passage of time but acquiesced to the change of subject for my friend's benefit. "It's a queer thing to be sure. With gates and guards on land and that metal beast guarding the sea and shore, it appears that all avenues of approach for the raiders are blocked. And, yet, they come and go as they please, apparently."

"Seemingly. There is an answer to this obscure affair and we shall find it in the details." Holmes gazed up at the setting sun. "There's still some daylight. Let us examine where the crime took place."

We proceeded to the dock from which the ship had been unloaded. Contrary to Admiral Rogers's statements all was not as it had been at the time of the theft because there was no ship moored to the dock. This hardly mattered for Holmes examined the dock, at one point leaning down to stick his head under it. He also scrutinized the surrounding area and the warehouses. An old drainage pipe near the crime scene drew his particular attention and he examined it intently for some minutes before returning to the dock. A patch of sand blown by the wind up onto the planks was of interest to him and I joined him as he bent over it. A series of scattered, broken footprints marred the sand.

"Any views, Watson?"

"From this? Hardly. The pipe seems the most likely clue. All I see here are prints that could have been made by anyone. Aside from one partial set, the long, narrow marks, most likely belonging to a very tall, thin man, there is nothing to captivate me. Do you propose they belong to the raiders?"

"I propose nothing. I simply observe. Let us move on."

As it was almost full dark now and the journey had been wearing on me after so short a sleep the previous evening, my concept of moving on required our settling in at whatever accommodations had been arranged for us and taking some much needed rest. Holmes had other ideas.

"Let us take in a show," said he to my surprise.

"That is a most singular suggestion, I dare say. I can see that you are serious."

"I have never been more so."

"Do you have a particular show in mind?"

A group of sailors was heading towards the main gate. Holmes stared after their broad backs.

"They will show us the way. Pray, let us catch them up."

What followed was one of the most bizarre nights I have ever spent in the company of Sherlock Holmes. We joined the group and Holmes immediately made himself one of them using that peculiar talent he possesses to ingratiate himself into any group. The men were all fresh off the *Fortier* having just crossed the channel from France. With six weeks at sea under their belts, the men were ready for hedonistic pursuits. My army days gave me an inkling of how the night would progress and that the following morning would not be a pleasant one, but Holmes eagerly accepted the sincere invitation from the men and we found ourselves crowded on a bus converted into a makeshift shuttle to and from the Naval Yards and the town centre. The journey was raucous and, I'll admit, great fun as it allowed me to revisit my younger days in Afghanistan.

I was once again amazed at how quickly scuttlebutt can spread through any military organization as the men, straight off, referred to Holmes and I as the 'Admiral's Lads' and many an incredible theory was put forth as to why we were at the base. As for the evening's revelry, the men told us that there was only one place to be and one show to see in all of Portsmouth. They had gotten wind of it from their fellow seamen when they first came ashore and had thought of nothing else as they completed the day's duty.

"All right, lads!" one red-faced sub-lieutenant named Wilson bellowed at us across the bus seat. "Are you with us, then?"

"Most assuredly," agreed Holmes.

"You heard the man, driver! To the Rose and Crown, then!"

And with that we were off. The bus trundled its way along the narrow passages of the town and we shortly found ourselves stopped outside an impressive pub with solid mahogany doors and a warm glow through the arched windows. Next to this was a large theatre lit up like a Roman candle. We were told that the night's true entertainment would be found within its walls.

However, first there was drinking to be done and they herded us out of the bus and into the pub. The group was known to the owner and he welcomed them gladly, which attested to the amount of money that usually changed hands whenever this group made Portsmouth. Ales made the rounds and Holmes and I downed our share. The level of conversations and laughter grew louder with each round and the sailors all soon had that peculiar twinkle in their bleary eyes. This went on for quite some time. I cannot say precisely how long as time had jumped its rails on me as I washed the dust of the road from my throat with mug after mug.

Finally one of the men spied the clock on the wall and slammed his mug down, splashing the contents on his uncomplaining comrades.

"Heck! It's almost time for Sandwina!"

Holmes inquired as to the identity of Sandwina and a soiled handbill was thrust at him. We looked it over together.

The Mighty Sandwina, one Charmion Sandwina, was billed as the most physically powerful person walking the planet Earth. And a ravishing woman to boot! The quick biography went on to say that she was born in Sacramento California, had stood over six feet and weighed 187 pounds while an adolescent and, now having seventeen inch biceps and twenty-six inch thighs, made a habit of breaking horseshoes, routinely juggling 30 pound iron spheres and had, before witnesses, lifted horses, maintained carousels of 14 persons on her shoulders and had carried half a ton of cannons on her back. She had even been the subject of a film by Thomas Edison in 1901. Remarkable to be sure. The men read along with us, some of them aloud, while others roared when certain of the woman's achievements were read out.

"What say ye to that?" one of the men demanded of Holmes.

"I say she is quite a woman. I should very much like to see her perform."

The entire group bellowed at that and Holmes and I exchanged mystified glances as to why his comment should be met with such merriment.

Finally the red-face sub-lieutenant from the bus clapped Holmes on the back, nearly spilling him from his chair and roared, "So be it! What say you, men, shall we show the Admiral's Lads our new girl?"

Mugs were raised and drained at this suggestion and that put an end to the drinking portion of the evening. The group staggered out the rear entrance and round back of the theatre. Fists were pounded against the rusted iron and the door was opened from within. Money changed hands as quick as a wink and the lot of us were hustled through the portal. The theatre was beginning to fill up and was already very close. A smoky haze obscured the feeble light cast down from unsteady chandeliers. The men seemed bent on seats in the third row and when these were filled, promptly moved the occupants along with threats of violence. Seats of honour in the centre of the row were reserved for the Admiral's Lads and Holmes and I settled into the worn maroon velvet. A quick glance over my shoulder at the crowd pouring in revealed it consisted almost entirely of men. I put this down to the womanly charms of Miss Sandwina which had been so amply displayed on the handbill. Before long the hall was full and buzzing with expectation. The lights were dimmed with an accompanying lusty response from the crowd.

"Now you're in for it, lads!" one of the men whispered to us.

The curtain parted to reveal a stage littered with impressive weights of varying dimensions but what caught the eye was a trapeze suspended some fifteen feet off the floor. Then the Mighty Sandwina took the stage. The audience gasped as did I. For before us was a vision of loveliness. With her pert nose, pointed chin and dark eyes she was breathtaking in her beauty. A large, feathered hat perched atop her chestnut hair coiled about her alabaster neck and she was dressed in a scarlet, flowing gown which left her broad, muscled, smooth shoulders to gleam under the muted lights like polished marble.

Moving with feline grace she set about lifting the incredible weights with ease and the crowd spurred her on with much applause. There seemed to be an air of expectation amongst the patrons for which I could find no reason. When the stunning beauty used a springboard to leap gracefully up and seized the trapeze bar, my ears were deafened by the bellows of the crowd. Smiling lasciviously, Sandwina swung herself up to sit on the bar, then proceeded to strip off her gown! This risqué performance ended when the woman's impressive physique was clad solely in a form-fitting leotard. The entire time the performance was taking place, the woman used her sleek, muscular arms to suspend herself, one-handed, from the ropes while removing articles of clothing with her free hand. She waved bawdily to the crowd while swinging upon the trapeze then the curtain fell amidst husky shouts to the contrary.

The handbill claimed that jugglers and a magician were to follow the Mighty Sandwina but Holmes and I never saw these acts. With the curtain having fallen on the female colossus, the seamen hurriedly left the theatre with us in tow. Many of them complained that no attempt was to be made to go back stage and see the incredible example of femininity but already a gaggle of male admirers were clustered about the stage door.

One of the men eyeing the crowd suddenly pointed, shouting, "Hey, there's Dunning at his usual station. And look at that bouquet!"

We all looked at a short, slight weasel-faced man who mopped at his fevered brow as he stood closest to the stage door. That he was known to our companions was obvious but he was a mystery to Holmes and I.

"What of him?" asked Holmes.

"Word has it he's here every night. Like a lovesick pup, he is. Can't say I blame him much as the Lady seems to have a thing for him. He's the only dog to get invited in regular."

"He is in uniform," observed Holmes. "I take it he works at the Yards."

"He's the bleeding Harbour Master," was the reply. "What, did you mistake him for, a Marine?"

The stage door opened and Dunning was quickly admitted. This cooled the ardour of the others and the group headed towards the bus. We piled inside and made our way back to the naval barracks. The trip back was filled with nothing but talk of the vision we'd seen on stage.

At the high, arched entry gate to the Naval Yards we extricated ourselves from the group. Holmes had a rosy glow in his cheeks and I could feel my own face hot with drink. We said our farewells, endured three cheers for the "Admiral's Lads," then we were free to make our way to our rooms. Holmes said nothing during this time but I could see that familiar frown of concentration upon his face. I bid him good night but do not remember how I found my room or my bunk.

I awoke to an insistent rap upon the door that hit my throbbing head like a mallet. I grumbled a reply and a yeoman strode in with a message. I snatched it from his outstretched hand and swayed to the edge of my bed. Reading it snapped me instantly awake and I rose shakily to my feet. It was from Holmes and he had asked me to meet him in a most unusual place. I hurriedly dressed and was on my way.

The day had dawned bright and clear and I had to squint against the sunlight. A steady, bracing sea breeze was a welcome balm to my fevered brow as I had rowing to do. I reached the dock and learned that a skiff had been prepared for my use. I climbed aboard and began rowing out to meet Holmes who for whatever strange reason had chosen to breakfast aboard HMS *Victory*. After some twenty minutes of exertion, I felt much healthier of frame as I drew closer to the dilapidated old ship. The wear of the years upon her was more evident up close, and it was with some trepidation that I moored my boat to the rickety gangway set amidships and climbed up to the starboard side entrance port on the lower gun deck. The ornately carved oak portico over the entrance was badly decayed and worm eaten and I ducked under it quickly lest it chose to come down at that moment.

Stripped of big cannons, the gun deck seemed spacious and I made my way across the sagging floor to the gangway leading up to the Quarter

Deck and found my way to Holmes at the bow of the ship. He was perched on the Marine's Walk – a grilled platform which abutted the bowsprit. With his feet on the bowsprit he had a wrapped egg sandwich perched on his knees which he ate daintily while looking out at the water. He seemed completely unfazed by the heady imbibing the night before. *Victory* moved gently with the tide, creaking and groaning softly. The wind sang in the rigging. Had she sails, I could not help but think the old girl would make a break for open water.

"Thoughts of desertion, Watson?" asked Holmes as I stepped up on the Walk. He was referring to the tradition of stationing Marines here near the bowsprit to discourage deserters thus the name for the platform.

"After last night, I'm considering it."

Holmes chuckled and popped the last bite of the sandwich into his mouth and chewed vigorously.

"What possessed you to come here, Holmes?" asked I. "Surely not a bout of nostalgia."

"I have been charting the movements of the submersible."

"You mean to tell me you can see a craft that is underwater? I think the ale is still playing upon your reason."

"It is not the craft I see. But, rather, its course is revealed through the agitation of the water's surface." He extended a long arm and indicated what appeared to be evidence of a current on the water.

I went to the bulwark of the forecastle, steadied myself on the small signal gun *Victory* used to salute passing warships and cast my gaze out over the sea in search of Holmes's currents. I spied the churning of the water. It appeared to move in a straight line, coming to within two-hundred feet of *Victory* before banking to port and continuing on.

"I see it, Holmes." I rejoined my friend at the Marine's Walk. "But it hardly seems of sufficient interest to pull one from a warm bed after a night of drinking."

"The movements of the HMS *A1* interest me. Admiral Rogers will run us out to the ship in an hour's time so that we might have a word with her Captain. I thought I should see the craft in action in order to determine the extent of harbour she is able to cover. The Admiral was adamant that the raiders could not approach from the sea with *A1* in their path. I preferred to see for myself. *Victory* is the highest point above the harbour while still remaining on the water. She seemed the best place from which to make my observations."

"Of course, once you explain the matter it seems perfectly reasonable for you to be here."

"What do you think of the submersible's ability to patrol the harbour?"

I watched the underwater craft's trail for a minute or two. "She covers a lot of sea and, if I judge correctly, is swift in her movements. I am left to conclude the Admiral's assessment of the *A1's* ability to deter unwanted visitors to the Navy Yards is accurate."

"Then how do you account for the raiders' ability to strike? The land is guarded, the gate barred, effectively securing an approach by land. *A1* is a deterrent for an approach by sea. How did the thieves steal the payroll? Where did they escape to once the deed was done?"

"I can offer no explanation. It is a complete mystery to me."

Holmes said nothing further. He continued to watch the craft for several minutes. I shivered in the stiff breeze. "If you have finished your observations and your breakfast, perhaps we can return to our quarters so that I might take nourishment as well."

Holmes fished into a pocket absently and withdrew a second sandwich which he handed to me. Despite the sloshing in my belly, my mouth could not help but water at the sight of the victuals. Much ale had been consumed the night before but nothing in the way of solid food. I tore into the sandwich hungrily.

"Let us not keep the Admiral waiting," said Holmes.

We latched our boats together, took an oar each and rowed back to the dock. After returning the boats we sought out the Admiral in his office. He greeted us but seemed distracted by the pressures of duty.

"I've made the necessary arrangements to have you taken out to *A1*," said he as he moved papers around on his desk. "I shall not be accompanying you as I've just received word that we are expecting a special guest later today. This comes directly from Second Sea Lord Fisher so there is no putting it off."

"I quite understand," said Holmes. "I wonder if we might have a moment further of your time as I should like to lay a trap for the raiders."

Rogers's mood brightened immediately. "I most certainly have time for that! Word has come down that these raiders are to be apprehended immediately. It reflects badly on the Navy to say nothing of being a general nuisance. What do you have in mind?"

"Are you expecting cargo of any great value soon?"

"The second payroll is due in to-morrow. I'll not see the men suffer at the hands of thieves."

"Would you be able to issue orders to prepare for its arrival tonight?"

Realization dawned on the Admiral's features. "Ah, you wish to bait the villains."

"You have read my thoughts precisely. If they can be made to make an attempt at the payroll, then moving up the timetable will unbalance them as they will have to prepare in haste. In this way we may catch them off guard and they will be most likely to make mistakes."

"That will be their undoing."

"Please forgive my impertinence, but I must emphasize that every command issued about the payroll must be authentic. No one outside this room must know it is false and the same preparations must be made as those for the genuine shipment. Can this be done?"

"You may consider it already done, Mr. Holmes."

"Excellent. Then, if you please, we are ready to visit the submersible."

"Captain Andrews will take you over. He is waiting in the Officer's Mess."

We found Captain Clark Andrews huddled over tea in the Mess Hall. He was a short, solid man of some forty years with the windblown look of the sea typical of the lifelong Navy man.

"You must be the Admiral's Lads," said he, setting his mug down and scrutinizing us. "Come to have a look at our *A1*, then?"

"If you please, Captain," said Holmes.

"Very well. Let's be off, then."

The Captain led us to a long shore runner and we climbed inside. Holmes and I fully expected to row out to the submersible, but the craft had a small motor at the stern which Andrews fired up and the craft sped away from the dock.

"I saw you head out to *Victory*," said Andrews, raising his voice to be heard over the engine noise.

Holmes indicated that we had.

"Loftus will be pleased to hear that. He's the CO of *A1*. Loftus Mansergh is his full name. He's quite the history buff but don't get him started on Lord Nelson, or he'll talk your ear off."

"I shall keep it in mind. Has the crew of *A1* been notified of our wish to rendezvous with them?"

"Yes, she surfaces twice a day to receive messages during this current experiment, once in the morning and once at night. A wireless message was sent to them this morning. There she is."

Andrews pointed to a surge of water bubbling up some two hundred feet in front of us. A pyramidal tower first appeared, glistening wetly, followed by the long, cigar-shaped hull. It looked rather like a ship that had capsized with her keel and sloping under hull visible. The hatch opened and a head with an officer's cap poked out.

"That'll be Lieutenant Mansergh," Andrews explained. "Why, what's he up to?"

The man Andrews called Mansergh was of medium height and build. He was pale of face and had dark hair. He had what at first I thought were bundles of cloth but which turned out to be small flags. He affixed these to the rope running up a pole jutting out from the tower. The breeze unfurled them. The first was a white cutlass against a black background, the second consisted of crossed black cannon barrels on white with a black six-pointed star.

"What is the meaning of those pennants?" asked Holmes.

"It's queer. Mansergh has put up banners for Cloak and Dagger operations and Gun Action respectively. I think the air has made him light-headed. Or maybe he's having us on. Gor! Do you smell that?"

The odour that suddenly assailed our nostrils was pungent and foul, consisting of unwashed humanity, human waste, rotting food and stale cooking. The mix was noxious and horrible and we all had to turn our heads in vain against its assault on our olfactory senses.

"Don't it stink something awful?" asked Andrews, through the collar of his coat, which he had pulled up across his nose. "It's one of the reasons I turned down the duty when it was offered me. How they put up with it is beyond me."

He took up a loud hailer and spoke into it.

"Mansergh, you old dog! How are you getting on!"

The submersible captain raised a hailer of his own and spoke into it. "All right, I suppose! It's a bit tight at the moment! Not even room for a round of Uckers!"

Andrews laughed. I had no clue what they were talking about.

"I'd think you'd be used to that by now! Here! There's a couple of blokes want to have a word!"

Andrews handed the tube to Holmes who put it to his lips. "Halloa! Have you heard or seen anything of the raiders that have plagued the Yard?"

Mansergh paused to remove his cap before replying. "Nay! Not hide nor hair!"

"No sign whatsoever! Clandestine ship movement! Anything of that sort!"

"Nay on all counts!" Mansergh tucked the cap under his arm. His neatly oiled hair had a sheen to it.

The sea air carried a fresh wave of the warm fetid stench towards us.

"That is a snoot full, isn't it?" asked Holmes referring to the odour the crew had to endure for days on end.

"It comes with the territory, I'm afraid!" responded Mansergh.

"Well, England expects every man to do his duty! I commend you all for carrying on under present conditions. Buck up! Your suffering will soon end, I am told! Then shall you have your moment of victory over the travails that assail you!"

"Sorry I could not be of more help to you!" said Mansergh in prelude to ending the interview. "We have our eyes and ears open and stand ready to act!"

Mansergh lowered the banners and disappeared into the tower of the sub. The hatch clanged shut and the water began to churn around the craft. It sank from view in seconds.

Andrews powered up the motor and we went scudding back to shore.

"I'll have to see the Admiral," said Andrews.

"What is the matter?" asked Holmes.

"Sorry, I don't expect a civilian to know. But the air in those subs can get pretty close. So much so that one is like to suffocate and *A1* has been on patrol a long time."

"Elaborate, please," said Holmes.

"Well, you caught a whiff of what they're breathing. Air like that does funny things to a man. Take Mansergh for instance. No room for Uckers? Why, any seaman worth his salt would sooner go without food and water than without a game of Uckers! Not only that, he's the skipper of that boat but was wearing Dudgeon's coat. Bill Dudgeon is the Petty Officer of *A1*. Plus those banners he run out. The Cloak and Dagger and the Gun Action? They are squadron banners. *A1* has experienced neither of these. I understand one of you is a doctor. I'd welcome a professional opinion."

"Yes, that noxious cloud is hardly conducive to proper lung action," said I. "And a lack of oxygen to the brain can create hallucinations due to light-headedness. As I do not know this man Mansergh, I must rely on your assessment of his behaviour, which I take as accurate given your friendship with him. My medical judgment is that the crew be brought ashore and given access to fresh air, good food and clean water after a period of rest."

"I'll let the Admiral know as soon as we reach shore."

"You must not say anything," this from Holmes.

"Begging your pardon, sir?"

"The raiders, Watson. We've found them."

"What the devil do you mean?" asked I.

"You best not be casting aspersions on Mansergh and his crew! Why I've known the man for years. A month of dodgy air wouldn't turn him to a crooked path."

"You are right. But a revolver might force his silence."

I stared openly at my friend. "Holmes, what are you saying?"

"Captain Andrews, I take you for a man of your word. Am I right in this assumption?"

"As rain. Just what are you driving at, sir?"

"Then I must ask for your word that you will say nothing about *A1* or her crew when we reach shore. Do I have your promise?"

Andrews considered for a moment before speaking. "Normally I'd say no, not without a word or two of explanation. But, seeing as the Admiral put his trust in you and he's a good egg in my book, I'll give my word on this."

"Excellent, Andrews. I was certain I had not judged you incorrectly. Gentlemen, the raiders are aboard the *A1*. They have seized control of the ship and are holding the crew hostage. The raiders have been under our noses the whole time."

"However did you reach such an outlandish conclusion?" asked I.

"By simple observation, Watson. The approach to this base from land is impassable. There are guards and locked gates. Marines on the rooftops. Removing land from the puzzle leaves only air and sea. We can rule out the air. That leaves the sea. I concluded that this had to be the approach the raiders are using. Reasoning along these lines, the only obstacle to an approach by sea is the submersible. The submersible reported no unusual activity on any of the nights the thefts took place, or any other night for that matter. However, the raiders had to come by sea, this was the one and only possibility. How to explain the lack of information from the submersible? There were two possibilities. The first was that the crew were in cahoots with the raiders."

"Absolutely not!" bellowed Andrews.

"Thank you, Captain. I am in full agreement with you on the matter. That settles the first possibility. This left only the second hypothesis, namely, that the crew was being made to keep silent about the comings and goings of the raiders. Our communication with Lieutenant Mansergh confirmed this hypothesis."

"How was this achieved?" asked I.

"Where to begin, Watson? The signals: Cloak and Dagger and Gun Action. As Captain Andrews has confirmed that the submersible was engaged in neither of these actions, they hint at hidden hostilities. The cloak, the dagger and the gun. What other reason could Mansergh have for hoisting the banners? You mentioned his uniform, Andrews. Again, a clear signal. Why would a Captain wear a Petty Officer's coat over his uniform? To show us that he was no longer captain of the vessel. Most clever on the part of Mansergh, as a group of thieves would be incapable of discerning one naval jacket from another. The brilliance of the man went further than that. Did you notice that, while shabbily dressed in the wrong coat, he was also clean shaven, his hair neatly groomed? He made a point of removing his cap to show us this in order to convince us that he was not delusional due to the poor oxygen content inside the submersible and that his choice of uniform coat was deliberate. Recall his mention of close quarters. Surely any submariner would be used to such conditions and would not complain of them. Of course, if a ship designed to hold a certain number of men suddenly found itself with more persons aboard that it was fit to handle, then living conditions would be the subject of the captain's complaints. No room for Uckers? Another signal. Yes, gentlemen, the raiders have most definitely secreted themselves aboard *A1*."

"Now see here, sir," said Andrews. "I gave my word but surely we must speak out about this. If you are right, we must re-take the ship!"

"To do so would be to throw away the lives of the brave crew who serve on her. You gave your word and I hold you to it. I have a plan to re-take the ship, and to do it in the best way possible to preserve innocent life. I entrusted you with the conclusions of my mind, Captain Andrews. I ask that you now trust me with the lives of the submersible crew."

I chose this moment to speak up on my friend's behalf. "Captain, if Holmes has thought of a plan to ensure their safety, then you may rest assured that no mind currently extant can think of a better one."

Holmes had given Andrews much to consider and the Captain took his time with it. His struggle played across his features, but when they suddenly hardened with resolve, I knew Holmes had convinced the man.

"All right, sir. I'll hold my tongue. But not for long. I want my comrades off that ship as soon as it is possible to do so. And I'll want in on the action."

"You are a true friend to those men," said Holmes. "We shall put the plan into effect at sunset. Is that early enough for you?"

"It will have to be."

Despite the extraordinary revelations of Sherlock Holmes and the delicate task of freeing the ship's crew from the raiders ahead of us, all thought of the night's dangers momentarily receded when we reached land. For as we stepped ashore we were met with an unforgettable sight. A large dirigible bobbed at its tether in the open courtyard. The tan, cylindrical gas bag, pointed at the ends, arched above our heads, blotting out the sun. The undercarriage dangled from a spider's web of cables and consisted of a flat platform with seating for the pilot. In front a large propeller had been installed to allow the airship the freedom of controlled flight.

A slight, dapper man in a Panama hat oversaw the mooring of the craft by the Navy men. I recognized him at once as Santos Dumont, the inventor and aviator. The self-proclaimed "sportsman of the air" had been all the rage a few years before after having won the coveted *Deutsch de la Meurthe* prize in 1901 for his round trip from Parc Saint Cloud to the Eiffel Tower in under thirty minutes. Revered in his own country as well as in France, he had also generated a great deal of celebrity the world over. With his large ears, pencil-thin moustache and pointed chin, his was a face not unknown to us here in England. Fashionable folk had adopted his Panama and his penchant for high collared shirts as the au courant style of the day.

Holmes dashed up to the man. "Mr. Dumont, a pleasure! Please allow me to introduce myself.

Dumont held up a manicured hand coated with oil. "No introductions are necessary, sir. You are Sherlock Holmes. And this must be Dr. Watson, the chronicler of your adventures."

"Correct, sir. It is a pleasure to meet you. I wonder if you might show me your incredible craft."

"But, of course. It will be my pleasure. You wish to see the future of manned fight, eh? Who can blame you?"

"Ah, not so fast, sir. I predict that the first heavier than air flight will be achieved before the year is out."

"And you are quite right, Mr. Holmes. For I shall achieve it!"

Holmes swung around to address me. "Pray, Watson, you look as if you could use some sun." Then he turned to Dumont. "Would it be all right if my friend were to leave his greatcoat with the dirigible?"

"Feel free, Dr. Watson."

I did as instructed and felt the afternoon sun on my back. It invigorated me as my constitution is best suited for more desert-like conditions and I was grateful for the suggestion.

Holmes gave me a meaningful look. "Excellent! With your indulgence, Watson, I shall meet up with you tonight! May I ask you to go with Captain Andrews and survey the security measures and see that they are satisfactory and then report back to me here at the dirigible?"

Long familiar with my friend and his singular habits, I understood that his meeting with Dumont was not motivated by idle curiosity. What plans moved through the great mind of Holmes I could not hazard a guess. I agreed to meet up with him at the agreed time and went off with Captain Andrews to make the rounds.

The rest of the afternoon passed without incident. Andrews, still reticent about his vow to remain inactive until called upon, showed me the security measures that had been taken to prevent the raiders from striking. Each gate was locked and manned by Royal Marines. And the men on the rooftops were alert, capable and armed. I endured Andrews's grumbling about lost time throughout the afternoon as we toured the Yard but in the end we were both satisfied that the measures taken were more than adequate to give the raiders a hard time of it should they take the bait.

It was near dusk when we returned to the dirigible only to find that the craft had departed only minutes before. We were met by Admiral Rogers who had seen the dirigible off, and he told us that Dumont, his initial discussions on the use of dirigibles by the Navy completed for the moment, had to travel across the bay to Gosport for a meeting there and that the airship would return in the morning. I asked after Holmes and learned that my friend had headed into town on some mysterious errand. The Admiral had my coat over his arm and returned the garment to me as he told us of the recommendation Holmes had made that a squad of Royal Marines be deployed at sunset, on the quiet, amongst the dock pilings. Andrews, determined to be with those Marines made directly for the spot.

After I had said my farewell to the Admiral and was returning to my room to await Holmes, I noticed my coat was markedly lighter. Alarmed I fished in the pocket and learned that my revolver had been taken. My alarm was immediately eased as in place of the pistol was a note scrawled in the hand of Sherlock Holmes. It ran thus:

'*Victory* at twilight. Foc'sle. Tell no one. Await my signal. You will know what to do.'

S.H.

This cryptic missive did not reveal its secrets to me as I stood staring at it. Long resigned to the knowledge that the working of Holmes's mind would forever remain a mystery to me as well, I vowed to follow the directive. It was still half an hour until dark, and as it appeared we were all in for night action, I made my way to the Officer's Mess to restore my energies with something to eat before heading back to the venerable ship.

As night settled over Portsmouth, I found myself once again rowing out to HMS *Victory*. Armed with a telescope, a hooded lantern, several wrapped beef sandwiches and some brandy to ward off the nocturnal chill, I tethered my boat to the gangway and, for the second time that day, climbed aboard the old ship of the line. The ship had a ghostly air about it and every creaking of the ancient timber set me to thinking that some dark evil was creeping towards me. I proceeded with undue haste to the forecastle on the starboard side and set the lantern down. I extended the glass and put it to my eye. All seemed quiet at the dock. The Marines secreted away were invisible to my eye as the fall of night had cast that area in stygian darkness. Well, the trap had been set now there was no alternative but to await the prey. I had not heard from Holmes and this was a cause of some concern. It was not like him to so carefully arrange a snare and then be nowhere around when the time came to spring the trap. I satisfied myself to his absence by using the glass to scan around the warehouses and buildings but of Holmes I found no sign. Thus I set the glass down, had a swallow of the brandy, then took up the night watch aboard *Victory*. The hours passed slowly and a chill seeped into my bones. Despite the cold and, perhaps at the fault of the brandy, I found myself dozing at my station when the calm night finally erupted.

It began with a hiss and gurgle. In my sleepy state I barely discerned the noise which, at that moment, registered to my doped brain as something akin to a great leviathan of the depths gliding along the surface of the water. After it had passed, the sound had lodged in my thoughts and the end result was to bring me awake. Stiffly, I raised myself up by use of the signal gun carriage and brought the icy glass to my chilled face.

As part of the security measures, the lights of all the buildings were burning brightly and together with the small lights on the dock illuminated the courtyard. The glow was cast in yellow streaks over the black water and through one of these bright patches on the sea I clearly saw a large dark shape cut a swath on its way to shore.

HMS *A1*.

The submersible lanced towards the dock using the ship which had moored during my slumber as cover from detection on shore. Men were unloading the ship's cargo. Silent and deadly the *A1* cleaved through the water. As it came into the light I discovered why it chose to approach on the surface. A removable deck gun had been affixed and as I spotted it, the gun flamed with a muted puff and a smoke canister arced out into the night sky on its way to the men unloading the ship. Then the canister hit and thick roiling clouds of smoke obscured my view of the dock. Smoke quickly billowed out encompassing everything. The *A1* disappeared into the cloud and, as she did so, I saw the hatch atop the tower open and dark figures emerge.

With one of my senses deprived, I relied on my hearing to tell me the tale. Great shouts came up from the dock. Rifles cracked and the stamp of many feet upon the boards echoed across the watery gulf between myself and the action. My first instinct was to spring into my boat and return to the dock but my friend's instructions kept me rooted to the spot. It was frustrating to keep the glass trained on the cloud of smoke. All I could see were muzzle flashes, the odd shadowy figure running here and there, several forms pitched off the dock into the water.

The shouted order to retreat reached my ears and figures began hitting the water regularly. They were swimming out to the submersible and I watched in impotent rage as they clambered aboard her sleek hull and made for the hatch.

A sound reached me then to which I could not put a name to the source. It was a high, whining, buzzing keen the likes of which I had never heard before. I threw the glass this way and that but could not find what was causing the noise. At last, I lowered the glass and used the naked eye but to no avail.

Then I saw Dumont's great dirigible descendeing straight down over the *A1* like a judgement from above. It came to float fifty feet above the submersible and a muzzle flash from the airship indicated that Dumont had armed himself. I thrust the glass to my eye and sighted on the dirigible.

It was Sherlock Holmes at the controls, firing down on the fleeing raiders.

I gripped the glass so hard it shook and my view vibrated. If my knowledge of these crafts was accurate, they were filled with hydrogen, a highly explosive gas, and here was Holmes doing battle with armed criminals hell bent on escape! Scattered shots were returned at the dirigible and I expected at any second to see the ship erupt into a fireball. But this did not happen. The men disappeared one by one into the hatch like rats down a sewer drain, rendering the gunfire from above useless. The *A1* reversed direction and started to come about. The Marines continued to fire from the shore, but to no effect.

It appeared Holmes's gambit had prevented the theft but had failed in its attempt to apprehend the raiders once and for all.

The submersible unsteadily came about and it was at that moment that I learned of the part I was to play in the affair. With her stern now to the fire from shore, the *A1* made for *Victory*, gaining speed with each passing second. My first hurried thought was that she meant to ram the old ship, but casting my eyes about I noticed the next phase of the trap Holmes had set. Gun ships were closing in from open water, sandwiching the submersible between themselves and the shore. The only clear avenue was the path to *Victory*. The bulk of the ship made an approach by surface craft impossible and the submersible need only submerge, duck under the keel of the ship and get clean away.

Holmes had placed me here to somehow prevent this from happening. How I alone was to accomplish this I could not fathom a guess. In my confusion I became aware that my left hand was resting on the barrel of *Victory*'s 12-pound signal cannon. The powder was clustered about the carriage and a small mound of shot was heaped to one side. Once while regaling Holmes with my adventures in Afghanistan, I had told him of the singular incident where my field hospital had been overrun by the enemy and I had been forced to use a field cannon similar to this to defend the facility. This thought had no doubt stuck in the vast intellect of my friend and had inspired him to put me "at the guns" to prevent the enemy escaping.

Dusting off my memory of the gun's operation, I quickly snatched up one of the cloth cartridges filled with gunpowder and leaning out from the ship slightly shoved it down and home with the rammer and followed this up with the cloth wad. I rolled the shot down the barrel and followed this up with a second wad. I lacked the strength to run the gun out as the carriage and gun weighed almost one ton so I had to trust that the gun tackles would hold. I fed the breech with priming, stepped back and pulled the lanyard. The gun erupted and the entire carriage reared back taut against the restraining tackles. The sound was deafening and the charge had apparently been mixed with flash powder for ceremonial purposes since the end result of the firing was an immense cloud of coloured smoke.

As I could hardly have sighted the gun or run it out again myself, there was very little chance I had hit the submersible but once I had recovered

The gun erupted and the entire carriage reared back taut against the restraining tackles.

my senses it was revealed to me what Holmes had hoped to achieve by my actions.

Peering through the smoke, I saw the *A1* pitch and roll and, at first, I thought that by some miracle I had hit the ship. I detected no signs of damage but the ship continued to tip and move crazily about on the surface before it righted itself and spun crazily for open water sluicing and swerving about madly.

And such was the effect Holmes had been hoping for. It was clear to me now that the raiders had seen *Victory* as a safe haven and the old ship suddenly firing upon them had startled them with its unexpectedness. Watching the mad floundering of the ship convinced me that the crew, held hostage so long, had taken the reduced number of criminals inside by surprise and were attempting to retake the ship.

I watched helplessly, spurring the crew on in my thoughts as I watched the submersible drunkenly head out into the harbour. The gun ships were moving in to surround the fleeing craft which somehow managed to swerve its way amidst them. It seemed disaster was inevitable and it came with sudden horror. A freighter was steaming into the harbour quickly and struck the *A1* amidships. The submersible capsized and within seconds sank from view. I stared in shocked, silent expectation for someone to make it out of the wreck but I saw no sign. With a heavy heart I left *Victory* and rowed back to shore.

The dirigible was tethered in the courtyard by the time I returned and I cast about in search of Holmes. I found him with the Marines near the ship that had been attacked. They were clustered around the fallen. Two Marines had been shot and killed and third clutched a flesh wound to one arm that leaked scarlet. I came forward at once to render what professional aid I could. As I worked on the injured man, I expected some measure of calm to settle on the group now that the raiders had been stopped, yet the men moved about with purpose. I was at a loss to explain it.

Holmes came up to me as I was bandaging the injured man's shoulder.

"Fine shooting, I dare say, Watson. I expect we'll hear from the gun ships soon that the *A1* has been retaken."

"She is lost," replied I. "You did not see the accident?"

Holmes raised his eyebrows in shock. "We've been busy here and that infernal smoke was a most effective cover. What has happened, man?"

"I fired upon the submersible as you wanted and it had the desired affect. The crew attempted to retake the ship in the resulting confusion but she was struck by a freighter and sunk without a trace."

Holmes blanched. "We must find the Admiral at once."

However when Admiral Rogers stepped amongst us, we could tell that word had already reached him. His countenance was grave and solemn as he spoke with his men to tell them that the undertaking had been both a success and failure. He also confirmed to us afterwards that my fears had been well founded. Not one soul had made it off the submersible before she sank.

The news cast a pall over the scene. Holmes spoke softly to the Admiral.

"Has Charmion Sandwina been taken into custody?"

"She has, the witch. Took six men to restrain her, but they got the job done!"

"What is this?" asked I, looking up from the injured Marine.

Holmes made an offhand gesture. "She was in league with the raiders."

"How could this be?"

"Harbour Master Dunning."

I searched my memory. "The man smitten with her? Lurking about the stage door, he seemed harmless enough. Do you mean to say that he was allied with the raiders as well?"

"Not directly, Watson. While under the spell of the captivating Miss Sandwina's charms, he unwittingly provided her with information about ship movements. Information she passed on to the raiders by way of agents on shore. Surely you knew I had my suspicions about her. Why else do you think I dragged you into that group of sailors?"

"I had no idea what motivated you to do so at the time. What is to become of Dunning?"

"He'll be court-martialled!" railed the Admiral. "The damn fool! He's as responsible for this mess as those filthy raiders at the bottom of the harbour. To think the brave submariners lost their lives because Dunning has his head turned by a lass? Despicable!"

Further discussion of the matter was cut short by a harsh shout from the surf. The Marines had found one of the raiders from the dock action still with life in his body. They hauled him out of the surf and dropped him unceremoniously at our feet. I bent and examined the man. He was shot through the shoulder. The wound was not life threatening.

"What is your name?" asked Holmes.

"Vinegar, sir. Stanley Vinegar."

"Who was your master? Answer quick, man!"

"That would be Mr. Mercury, damn him." The man clutched at my arm. "It was he who hired me on. Yes, I went for a bandit years ago. I don't deny it or anything else I've done in me miserable life. Mercury and that muscled vixen Sandwina was on the look out for men and he paid us well. But not a one of us signed on for that floating hell."

"You refer to the submersible," prompted Holmes.

"Yes! Mercury had us swim out to the boat one night, while the lid was up and it was changing its air. We tumbled inside and took her with our pistols. We've been trapped in her ever since! The foul, fetid iron tomb!"

"Your words are well chosen. For the *A1* now rests at the bottom of the harbour with nothing but corpses aboard. Brave seamen lost their lives for the sake of your greed."

"I'm sorry to hear about them lads. They was good men the lot of 'em. We was twenty of us in that tub. You could not breathe or move without rubbing up against someone. Hiding, desperate, parched with thirst and half dazed by the stench. And we could not say a word lest he sick the woman on us. I watched her bend a man in half once! So we suffered in silence. Mercury didn't mind the muck though. He had plans, he had."

"You'll hang for this, villain!" roared Rogers. "Say your piece and be damned!"

Vinegar raised his hands imploringly. "I was press ganged into it, Captain, sir! Against me will! That poison you salts call air in that tub like to drove Mr. Mercury mad, I tell you! He got it into his head to take the payrolls, then blow up the Harbour with them torpedoes to cover our flight. None of us cottoned to wholesale slaughter. No, sir!"

His body slumped and I thought his consciousness had fled, but he made one last statement. "I'm glad you stopped us. I'm sorry for them Navy lads but I'm glad you broke the hold Mr. Mercury had on us. You have to believe that."

"Enough," said Holmes. "This has gone on long enough."

I looked to him for an explanation, but his eyes bore into the eyes of Vinegar.

"What is this?" demanded Admiral Rogers.

"Gentlemen, I give you Mr. Mercury." He stabbed a finger at Vinegar.

Vinegar's eyes bugged out his head. "Begging your pardon, sir, but you got it all wrong."

"Have I?" Holmes sprang forward and seized the hands of the raider. He jerked them high, palms up for all to see. "Examine his palms. Look beyond the oil and grease he has so carefully worked into them. Do you see? They are as smooth as a solicitor's. Would a man who had lived the hard life this one claims to have endured have such hands?" Holmes released the man's wrists disgustedly. "No, gentlemen, this one made his way with his brain, not his back."

"But, why try to lie his way through?" asked Rogers. "He would have been found out eventually."

"How? With his wretched band dead on the sea floor who would question? By assuming the guise of a misused victim, he hoped for leniency and to be placed under less stringent guard. All so he could make his escape. Hold on to that one. He's as slippery as an eel, the devil."

The man suddenly began thrashing about in the grip of his captors. As I had a free hand I delivered a stout jab that settled him down. I stood and backed away.

"Damn you!" roared the man called Mercury. "I had these clods fooled and would have made my break. If not for you! I swear by all that's holy, Charmion and I will see that you pay for this! Unhand me!"

In response to these threats, Holmes merely turned about and walked away.

On the train back to London the next morning, I kept running the events over and over in my mind and could find only sadness in my breast for the young men who had been so badly wasted aboard HMS *A1*. Holmes, too, was quiet and the nature of his thoughts I could not venture to guess at.

"There is something about the matter that puzzles me, Holmes," said I at last.

My question seemed to revive him. "And what is that?"

"How came you to suspect the woman? Reviewing the matter in my mind, there is nothing I can find that casts the net of suspicion over her."

"Why, it's quite a simple thing. The footprints we observed when we investigated the crime scene."

"Do you mean the partially obscured prints in the sand scattered about the dock?"

"The very same."

"What about them showed you the woman?"

"If you'll recall one partial print was long and narrow. Long enough to have been made by a man, yet lacking the breadth. My conclusion was that, despite its length, it could only have been made by a woman. As this track, clearly female, was made when the payroll was stolen, I determined that a woman had to be involved with the theft in some fashion. But in what capacity? Why bring a woman along on the heist which, you'll recall, the Admiral told us had taken place at breakneck speed? Unless she was integral to the success of the crime. What other conclusion can be drawn from her presence? She was not there for the mere thrill. She could not hope to hide herself amongst a Naval base staffed with men. Thus her presence was necessary in order to carry out the crime. To do so she would have to be an extremely powerful woman.

"Well, I'll admit, this hardly seemed likely and I was prepared to dismiss the notion out of hand, but it occurred to me that a woman of uncommon size and strength would stick out like a sore thumb in normal society and thus the best place for someone of that size to hide would be in plain view. Where else would one find an Amazon of such dimensions but at a show? I determined that a quick tour of the seedier side of Portsmouth's night life would either reveal the women to me or prove that my conclusion was false and I could move on to a new one. The sailors were our best bet for who else would know where to find such bawdy entertainment? When we found Charmion Sandwina, my theory was proved correct. You'll recall that during her act she routinely lifted barrels twice the weight of the payroll chest over her head. With one hand! It's my guess that Mr. Mercury employed her on the theft because she alone could scoop up the chest and dash back to the submersible at full speed."

"If I had not seen the woman with my own eyes, I would not have believed it possible. And your reasoning, of course, strikes me as sound."

The train swayed while we were alone with our thoughts. There was one final aspect to the case that I felt had to be dealt with.

"You took an awful risk attacking the submersible from an airship filled with explosive hydrogen. Whatever possessed you to take such a potentially lethal chance?"

"It was not my intention at first. As your previous artillery experience placed you aboard *Victory*, I thought I would take my place with the Marines hiding amongst the pilings and aid them in driving the raiders to you. However when Mr. Dumont showed up unexpectedly, I could not resist inserting a wrinkle into the plan. As the intent of the plan was to shock and awe the raiders thus giving the crew an opening to strike, I felt that an aerial assault in conjunction with the surprise attack would ensure that this objective would be achieved. I was counting on the raiders not being able to shoot straight in the general chaos that erupted when the Marines struck."

"When *A1* fled she did not handle smartly. I suspect the battle for control of the craft was underway."

"Ah, then my message was received."

"Whatever do you mean?"

"I conveyed something of our intentions to Mansergh during our brief exchange. You'll recall I quoted Nelson's message to the Fleet at Trafalgar: 'England expects every man to do his duty'. As Mansergh was a Nelson buff and the signal became the standard under which the battle was fought, it told him to prepare for action. I next mentioned a coming 'moment of victory' for him and his crew – a play on words to urge him to make his play when *A1* made for *Victory*. I knew the raiders were using the ship to store their booty from my time aboard her."

"I see. You might have at least told me of your plan."

"I could not take the risk that we might be overheard. The raiders had Dunning in the Yard, but who else might be lurking about? For this reason, I kindly asked Dumont to bear my cloak and make for town to arrest Sandwina while I donned his garment, took to the twilight air and concealed myself against the night sky. He is a swashbuckler at heart and embraced the notion readily. I resorted to this impersonation with Dumont to trick the raiders into thinking that we were unaware of their plans."

We rolled on in silence then Holmes gave a great sigh. "This business has caused me to question the work I set my mind to, Watson. I can't help but feel that if we had tried to take the submersible by force early on, some of the crew might have made it through the ordeal. Instead all were lost and it falls upon me to shoulder the blame."

"The plan was sound, Holmes," said I. "You couldn't know a steamer would appear or that the submersible would blunder into it."

"In that you are correct, dear Watson. As for my plan, it was not sound. For it failed utterly and that is what torments me."

"Hardly, Holmes. The crime ring is broken, the ringleaders imprisoned. Tragedy aside, and I do not cast it away lightly, you succeeded in stopping the crime wave. There's something in that."

"Too little, I'm afraid. I'll have a think on this. Perhaps it is time..."

Holmes trailed off and never completed the thought. This exchange brought an end to the affair so my notes tell me. Holmes's retirement from public life some months later completes his train of thought better than I could express in words and is as fitting an end as any to my narrative.

However I trust I will be permitted an addendum to the above chronicle. History has altered the terrible tragedy of how the crew of the HMS *A1* met their end. The official account states that on Friday, March 18th, 1904, whilst on mock attack exercises off the Isle of Wight, the *A1* was in the midst of "torpedoing" HMS *Juno*. As she closed in for the kill, she was struck suddenly on the starboard side, near the conning tower, by the steam ship *Berwick Castle* en route from Southampton to Hamburg. The submersible was breached, flooded and all hands were lost. So reads the official account. Until now, it has been the only one. The brave and terrible tragedy that really befell these men can only be told now after the all too fragile quality of human life has been revealed to all through the horror of the Great War. It is with great honour that I tell the true story of these men. How they fought bravely against raiders bent on large scale destruction and how they paid dearly for it. And how their actions and the shroud of secrecy cast over them protected us, for a short span of years, from the truth about the cruel death and irreversible destruction man occasionally feels compelled to inflict upon his fellow man.

The crew of the HMS *A1* were true pioneers of British submersible development and the first fatalities. I record their names here for posterity:

BALY, Clinton, Engine Room Artificer 4c, 270491
BAKER, George G, Petty Officer 1c, 158859
CHURCHILL, John P, Sub Lieutenant
DUDGEON, William, Petty Officer, 123005
ELLIS, Albert B, Stoker 1c, 149151
FLEMING, Albert B, Chief Stoker, 144822
KING, Charles W, Able Seaman, 184404
MANSERGH, Loftus C O, Lieutenant
PARKINSON, William J, Chief Engine Room Artificer, 268715
ROBERTS, Vivian W L, Petty Officer, 168656
WALLACE, Peter S, Able Seaman, 186888

***

There's No Place Like Holmes

W hile going through the process (and fun) of seeing my very first Sherlock Holmes story get into print and then into stores as part of Volume One of this series, I was introduced to the special place in the hearts of fans held by the characters of Holmes and Watson. The enduring power of these characters is unmatched in fiction except perhaps by such venerable competition as Ebenezer Scrooge or Huckleberry Finn. Promoting Volume One revealed to me an enormous wealth of Holmes clubs and groups all over the world and while helping to spread the news of Airship 27's Holmes anthology to over 20 countries, I was overwhelmed by the sheer number of dedicated Holmes fans and the devotion they hold not only for Arthur Conan Doyle's stories but for the legion of stories that have followed since his death.

And so when the opportunity arose to write a story for Volume Two, it was a bit daunting to say the least. I was now fully aware of an army of potential readers waiting with outstretched hands to dissect any new Holmes and Watson case. But this was a good thing. Because it reminded me that I was only playing in the universe Doyle created and with infinite referees observing my every move, I had better know the rules of the game.

With that in mind I began trolling around in my gray matter for a new case, a new tale to tell. The Internet is invaluable for this. I called up Victorian images, real unsolved mysteries and the like. My first find was a priceless article on the strong women who earned their living in the early years of the last century by the strength of their mighty arms. There were plenty of gallant gals in the early 1900s and I combined two for the mighty Sandwina in my tale. Her peculiar act I borrowed from Laverie Valley's (aka Charmion's) trapeze act which Thomas Edison did indeed film and can be seen on You-Tube today. I took one look at the video and knew a version of Charmion had to appear in my tale.

The next piece of the puzzle was one of those magic moments writers can only dream of. While contemplating the tale, I couldn't get the idea out of my mind to somehow use HMS *Victory*. I had had the privilege of visiting Nelson's flagship on a family vacation to England back in 1975 and was fairly well-versed in Nelson lore courtesy of my older brother, Mark, who is a Nelson buff. Now I had decided my second Holmes tale should be set just prior to the great detective's retirement. My first Holmes tale had been set shortly after he and Watson first met and I wanted to jump ahead to the end of the saga to stir things up creatively. But what was the state of *Victory* in 1903? And how would she factor into my Holmes tale?

And that's when the magic happened.

Hunting up images of the great ship in that time period, I first learned that she had been left to rot at this time – a shadow of her former glory. This fit my tale to perfection as I needed Holmes, with retirement on his mind, to be wondering if his best days were behind him. But I still needed a plot. And then, suddenly, there it was: A photograph of Britain's first submersible, the *A1* cleaving through the waters of Portsmouth in 1903 on harbour patrol while in the background, rotting and forgotten, bobbed *Victory*. Progress and history side by side. The tale just fell into place after that.

With all my set pieces now in place I had to begin the immensely fun task of researching ships and carnival strong women and while researching the *A1*, I learned that the sub had gone down with all hands and these eleven brave officers and men were Britain's first submarine casualties, pioneers in what was then a new venture in human endeavour. Aside from the mention that the ship had sunk with all hands, these men were all but forgotten in history to the extent that I could not even discover their names after endless online searching. In the end I had to contact the British Naval Museum directly and they sent me not only the complete crew listings: names, ranks and so on of all the men who gave their lives, but also all of the technical information they had on the *A1* and I'd like to take this opportunity to thank them for all their help. Now I had the means to honor the brave seamen.

The best way to do this, I felt, was to use the fictional setting of my tale to give their sacrifice more meaning. In reality their sub did collide with a steamer in a tragic accident and that's no way for anyone to meet their end so I decided to have the incident occur as it had actually happened but with a heroic build up. The Naval cover up Watson alludes to helped to tie the real story to the fictional and the names he lists at the end of the tale are the names of the actual crew. It's my hope that listing them in my tale will help to carry their memory forward in some small way. They deserve more than being merely lumped together as "all hands." Also, in my tale, the sub is lost in 1903 while the real sinking occurred in 1904 and the cover up smoothed over this potentially rough spot since in those days people did not have the instant communication we have today. Years between letters amongst family members was not uncommon and thus the fictional sinking in 1903 could be reported as the real life sinking of 1904. For anyone who caught the difference in the dates, I hope this clears things up.

While on the subject of pioneers, I should also mention that Santos Dumont is an actual figure from history and a pioneer in lighter than air flight. As one of the themes of the story is progress and history, I could not resist including this early aviator and inventor.

On a personal note I would like to mention that Admiral Edward Rogers got his name from Ted Rogers, my sister-in-law's father and a veteran of WWII, who passed away while I was writing the tale. He will be missed.

If you've come this far, dear reader, I hope the journey was worth your while and you enjoyed the tale. I've got a lot more Holmes and

Watson in me and I'm just getting started writing of their adventures. Writing Holmes and Watson stories is just too much fun for this writer and I have no intention of stopping any time soon. As for Mr. Mercury and Sandwina? Perhaps they will return some day. But that's up to you. If you enjoyed my tale or any of the others it rubs shoulders with in the book, then let our intrepid editor know by dropping him a line.

Until next time, keep your wits about you. The game is afoot!

***

Ellis Award nominee **Andrew Salmon** lives and writes in Vancouver, BC. His work has appeared in numerous magazines, including *Storyteller, Parsec, TBT* and *Thirteen Stories*. He also writes reviews for *The Comicshopper* and is creating a superhero serial novel currently running in *A Thousand Faces Magazine*.

He has published or appeared in nine books: *The Forty Club* (which Midwest Book Reviews calls "a good solid little tale you will definitely carry with you for the rest of your life"), *The Dark Land*, the first of a series ("a straight out science-fiction thriller that fires on all cylinders" – Pulp Fiction Reviews), *The Light Of Men*, his first work for Airship 27/Cornerstone, which has been called "a book of such immense significance that it is not only meant to be read, but also to be experienced... a work of grim power" – C. Saunders. *Secret Agent X: Volume One* and *Three*, *Ghost Squad: Rise of the Black Legion* (with Ron Fortier), *Jim Anthony Super Detective Volume One* and *Sherlock Holmes Volumes One* and *Two* constitute his pulp fiction work at Airship27/Cornerstone to date.

Andrew's work will also appear in the upcoming *Sherlock Holmes Volume Three* and *Mars McCoy* anthology.

To learn more about his work, check out the Airship27/Cornerstone store (http://stores.lulu.com/airship27) and the following links: www.lulu. com/AndrewSalmon and www.lulu.com/thousand-faces.

Afterword

Don't you ever wish you had a crystal ball? I sure do. That way all of us here at Airship 27 Productions would have been prepared for the overwhelming success of our first book in this series. All of us knew when we produced *SHERLOCK HOLMES – CONSULTING DE-TECTIVE Vol. One.*, that the character had a huge following, we just didn't realize how huge and how eager for new material they were/are.

So before going any further, let me thank you for being a part of Airship 27 Productions' most successful book since the start of our little operation. We sincerely appreciate your support and have been heartened by the fan letters we've received telling us how much you enjoyed those first five Holmes and Watson adventures.

So, here we are with a brand new collection of what we hope you will consider equally terrific tales. By the time you read these words, the new movie, *SHERLOCK HOLMES*, with Robert Downey Jr. and Jude Law will have debuted and hopefully still be playing in movie houses around the globe. If the trailers were an honest peek into the overall film, then this is going to be a big, big blockbuster hit. Believe me, I plan on it seeing it as soon as I can.

And it is no surprise that publishers everywhere have been releasing new and reprinted Sherlock Holmes books to cash in on the movie's popularity. Will this tsunami of renewed interest in the Great Detective begin a lasting revival, with multiple sequels in the future? We certainly hope so. The world is always a better place when Holmes and Watson are active in it.

   Thanks ever, and if you are one of the few Airship 27 readers who has yet to pick up Vol.One, what are you waiting for? It can still be purchased at Amazon, Barnes & Noble online and of course at our own (http://www.gopulp.info/) where you will find all our titles on sale at our regularly discounted prices. We welcome all your comments and stay tuned, we've a volume three in the works.

Ron Fortier
12/12/2009
Somersworth, N.H.
(www.Airship27.com)
(Airship27@comcast.net)

If you enjoyed this book then you will also enjoy:

Sherlock Holmes
CONSULTING DETECTIVE

THE GREAT DETECTIVE IN FIVE NEW ADVENTURES!

Victorian England, a time of historical significance as the world was poised expectantly for the coming wonders and terrors of the new century. Amidst this atmosphere of anticipation and intrigue, one man emerged as a beacon of logic and cold, calculating reason in an unsetting time; Mr.Sherlock Holmes, Consulting Detective. Now he returns in five brand new mysteries by four of today's finest writers.

A famous soccer player is found dead in the club house. An unidentified stowaway is murdered aboard a U.S. Navy warship, while another man is found asphyxiated in an empty, locked room. These are several of the twisted puzzles challenging the Baker Street sleuth as he once again takes up the hunt on the fog ridden streets of London accompanied, as always, by his faithful ally, Dr.Watson.

Writers Aaron Smith, Andrew Salmon, Van Allen Plexico and Ian Watson have set forth exciting new mysteries done in the traditional style of the original Holmes stories by his creator, Sir Arthur Conan Doyle. There are no space aliens or howling werewolves here, simply good, old fashioned whodunits. So arm yourself for danger and all manner of villainy as once again, the game is afoot!

PULP FICTION FOR A NEW GENERATION

FOR AVAILABILITY CHECK AirSHIP27HANGAR.COM

the Light of Men

A STRANGER IN HELL

It is 1945 and the war is beginning to wind down. Allied Forces are pushing toward Berlin with relentless might and the Third Reich is on the verge of collapse. Still, in dozens of hellish concentration camps scattered throughout Germany, thousands of emaciated men and women are kept ignorant of these events. With over fourteen million already murdered in the gas chambers, the Nazis are all too aware that the remaining survivors could become a serious liability, all of them living proof of their barbaric Holocaust.

Into one of these death camps comes a man named Aaron. Unlike the hopeless, starving men around him, he is strangely aloof and detached from the living nightmare that surrounds them. Obeying orders, falling in line with his fellow prisoners, Aaron methodically begins to learn the camp routines in order to fulfill his own mysterious agenda. Is he an allied spy on some desperate mission? Or worse yet, is he a Nazi collaborator sent to foil any last minute rebellion by the inmates? Having heard rumors that the Allied Forces are getting closer every day, many want to revolt and take control of the camp before their merciless captors can silence them forever.

Andrew Salmon delivers a taut, gripping novel set against the background of one of history's most tragic episodes. He adds a unique science-fiction element that weaves its way through this amazing adventure and drives it to a powerful, heart wrenching climax. The Light of Men is a powerful statement on the human condition and the heroism inherent in all men and women with the courage to endure.

New Pulp scribe I.A. Watson brings his own vivid imagination to the Robin Hood saga, setting it against the backdrop of history but maintaining the iconic elements that have endeared the tale of Robin Hood to readers throughout the ages. With beautiful covers by fan-favorite artist Mike Manley and interior illustrations by award-winning artist Rob Davis, this is a fresh and rousing retelling of an old legend, imbuing it with a modern sensibility readers will applaud.

Airship 27 Productions is extremely proud to present –

Robin Hood

King of Sherwood • Arrow of Justice • Freedom's Outlaw

PULP FICTION FOR A NEW GENERATION
FOR AVAILABILITY CHECK: AIRSHIP27HANGAR.COM

PULSE-POUNDING PULP EXCITEMENT from AIRSHIP 27:

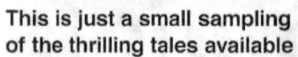

This is just a small sampling of the thrilling tales available from Airship 27 and its award-winning bullpen of the best New Pulp writers and artists. Set in the era in which they were created and in the same non-stop-action style, here are the characters that thrilled a generation in all-new stories alongside new creations cast in the same mold!

"Airship 27...should be remembered for finally closing the gap between pulps and slicks and giving pulp heroes and archetypes the polish they always deserved." –William Maynard ("The Terror of Fu Manchu.")

PULP FICTION FOR A NEW GENERATION!
AT AMAZON.COM & WWW.AIRSHIP27HANGAR.COM

www.ingramcontent.com/pod-product-compliance
Lightning Source LLC
Chambersburg PA
CBHW071238250626
47163CB00001B/236